AUTHOR	CLASS
DWYER - JOYCE, A	F
TITLE	No.
The Glitter-dust	17814571 pp

THE GLITTER-DUST

Glitter-dust is the mysterious ingredient of Alice Dwyer-Joyce's latest novel—the story of an intangible magic and an unconquerable menace.

Out of time, comes Mitchell Allington—celebrated Archaeologist and he meets Elizabeth in a hospital staffroom ... To get caught up with her in relentless enveloping shadows.

There is Anthony Rickady too, expert in criminology, who finds Elizabeth at last, lonely and in danger, in a house that is surely haunted by an uneasy ghost.

The house is owned by Mrs. Agnes Swan—a woman made for murder.

Elizabeth finds herself the white queen in a game of chess, with no hope but of being swept from the board. There is an end game that cannot fail to hold the reader to the last move.

Yet maybe there will be another game, and it will all be played out again, life and love ... and Glitter-dust.

ALICE DWYER-JOYCE

THE GLITTER–DUST

St. Martin's Press
NEW YORK

Robert Hale Limited
LONDON

© *Alice Dwyer-Joyce 1978*
First Published 1978

St. Martin's Press, Inc., 175 Fifth Ave., New York, N.Y. 10010
Library of Congress Catalog Card Number: 77–25771
First Published in the United States of America in 1978

Library of Congress Cataloging in Publication Data

Dwyer-Joyce, Alice.
   The glitter-dust.

   I.   Title.
PZ4. D993G   [PS3554. W9]   813'. 5'4   77–25771
ISBN 0–312–32947–4

Robert Hale Limited
Clerkenwell House
Clerkenwell Green
London EC1

ISBN 0 7091 6736 9

Printed in Great Britain
by Billing & Sons Limited
Guildford, London and Worcester

I dedicate this book to
Professor Patrick Dwyer-Joyce and
his wife, Eve, of Dublin, Ireland

I

THE CRYSTALLISED FORTRESS

I had cleaned my machine and put in a new ribbon. In the bathroom, opposite my study, I managed to get most of the ink off my hands, but maybe I left some on the clover towel, that matched the clover bath, basin, bidet, and lavatory suite. Christine would never approve of that. It was she, who had insisted on the bidet, said no household could be complete without one, but I often thought ours was the only bidet in the neighbourhood. It was quite well known in the village, for our daily woman had spread it around that "her gentleman's new friend" had had a strange contraption put in the bathroom when she made over "the house". I was in the confidence of the country people and I had managed to keep my face straight, when they asked me about it.

"I suppose it would do fine for washing the feet, as you say. I don't think it's a drinking fountain. What would you want a fountain for, with a cold tap on the basin and another in the bath, and water fit for drinking?"

The gentleman was my father, who wrote detective fiction and Christine was his latest golden girl. My mother had been dead longer than I remembered her. I was a strange creature, a hybrid, half Man Friday and half orphaned and mostly so lonely in spirit that I thought I might die of it. My mother had been so long gone. All I had of her were the few photographs and the sentiment in the village that she had been a saint out of heaven. The butcher told me very often she was the finest lady he had ever met and that she had had the heart of a lion.

"You take after her, Miss Grant," he said sometimes, but it was only his kindness, for there was a mouse quality about me and no percentage of lion whatever. One day, I had smiled at the butcher and asked after his wife's backache, just to pretend that I could not overhear the queue conversation at my side along the marble counter. I distinctly recall that there was one fat woman, who "was waiting for her kidneys" and as she was deaf, her whisper was an embarrassment to all of us.

"Grant broke her heart for her then, same way he breaks all their hearts. Isn't it queer the way he's a fly paper for the opposite sex, a rag on every bush and no bush the better of him, but of course, there's plenty of coin, and her new ladyship to change the name of the house to Shangri La. Dead common she is—and Mrs. Grant loved 'The Rowan Tree' ..."

There was a many-splendoured mixed metaphor, I thought to myself, and smiled at the good manners of another woman, who was taken with such a fit a coughing that she was like to choke, and all to save myself from hurt.

"As far as I'm concerned, it's Rowan Tree house now. It's not lucky to change the name of a house ..."

As I left the shop, there would be a huddling together and a closing up of faces and a shutting out of me and I knew the conversation would have grown more interesting, but now I looked at the clover towel and turned the typing ink stains to the wall and thought how like they were to clouds of trouble coming up a setting sun.

There were to be two carbons and a top copy. My hands were fit to perform a surgical operation, for no stain must appear on the "Paper with the Prestige Look". I must take care not to ill-treat the carbon, for carbon paper was expensive stuff in this day and age. In the old times, I imagined, you could have employed three scribes and have a fresh scribe for each page and then choose the best papyrus for the top copy. So here, we were, three sheets with carbon sandwiched between them and all slid under, with a clinking and a bell tinkle, and a slide as smooth as ice, an adjust for the spacing bar and another for the margins and we were ready to go, but I sat at the desk and looked down along the lovely spinney that was the garden, with its statue of Eros in bronze at the far end and the silver birches and the hollies and the clipped edges of box and the path of shaven grass. There was a dove cote, where four white fantailed pigeons lived and the whole thing might have been a setting for Walt Disney. It looked very well for people, who came to interview the famous author too, for not one of them had any idea of the cruelty of the culling of the doves nor the taking of their eggs.

"Sweet, sweet, sweet poison ..." I typed out and the carbons were two scribes, who worked with me.

That was Shakespeare and the end of it was "For the age's tooth," but it was the first part of the quote he wanted for the title. Then I went on to the fly leaf and two other leaves appeared by modern magic.

"A novel by Hamish McFarlane Grant."

Then there were three more sheets of paper to prepare and the top copy the finest quality obtainable. I spun the knobs and pressed the levers and filled in Chapter One, or maybe it was PROLOGUE. Then it was time for the story ... space, space, margin and I was a good secretary by now.

With my mother gone and myself a toddling child, he had had problems. Luckily he was no nine to six worker and his time could be sliced up and allotted in hours and in days and in weeks. There were good honest women only too ready to come into the house and see to the child, leave the rooms tidy and the supper in the oven to heat up. At six in the morning, there would be a motherly person on the front step and the key of the door in her hand and a bottle of milk to heat up and my small self to be lifted and changed and the house set straight and his breakfast brought up. If Hamish McFarlane Grant wanted a few days in London or Paris, I had only to be put in a carry-cot and transported to somebody else's house and I was an adaptable child, though there were those in the village of the opinion that I had not been "brought up proper", only "dragged up". To me, it seemed that I was a child of the whole village. There were so many friends, so many people, who were kind to me, in a form of insurance, that somebody would cherish their children, if they were to die and leave their own little ones.

I recall many a time, when I sat on the door step of very humble establishments and relished a "doorstep" of fresh bread, piled richly with home jam.

It broke my heart when I got old enough for boarding school. It must have co-incided with the first of the resident golden girls, but there was no more room for me in the grey stone house. I can not have been older than seven, when I was delighted with all the clothes, which must be bought me. The village saw to it that my brand-new tuck box was well stocked with food and I was eager for the first day of term. Then came the second great disillusionment of life, worse even than the unmasking of Santa Claus. I knew the sharpness and the misery of home-sickness but after a few years I grew accustomed to it, accustomed to the fact that I had no proper home. True, I went to Shangri La for the holidays and then there was one school after another, and no Shangri La. I had retreated from reality after a while, stopped feeling shame that sometimes, there would be a different "Auntie" at home. Schools were hard masters and school-children cruel. Early on, I learned what mistresses were, when they did not teach classes. I was fourteen the day somebody told me the secret of "common-law wives" and laughed at my shock. There wasn't anything wrong in it. It was a very ordinary state of affairs in Bohemian life and nothing to make a fuss about, but inside in me, there was a toddling child, weeping for her mother and not be to comforted, who could only armour herself against life and seek out a crystallised fortress to hide ... a place where knights were gallant and gentle and true, where they loved one woman and would be faithful to the death and forsaking all other, keep him only unto her, so long as they both should live.

There were several schools and each one of them added a coat to the enamel that protected me. I was a loner. I had a secret world, that came alive at bedtime, where I lived out my dreams between sleep and waking. There was a white knight, who inhabited this land with me and he was a magic being, who changed his individuality. He might be the school music master or a famous star of stage or screen. For quite a while, he was the hero of one of my father's murder thrillers, in a play, that was on at the Haymarket in London. My father must have thought that there was some hope that I would follow in his footsteps and write thrillers because of my interest in this production, but I had no such intent. There were so many schools, for Father moved round the world and sometimes, there was Shangri La for holidays. I went to Paris to French nuns, to perfect my French. Last of all, I went to a Secretarial and Household Management Establishment and there I was to be transformed into the perfect secretary.

Perhaps I was, though a deal I assimilated was of no use to me. I had not to know that it was essential that people must think "sir" was always hard at work and must not be disturbed. I had not to be as careful of "sir's" engagements, as if they were being made for Her Majesty at Buckingham Palace. All I wanted was a good speed in shorthand and typing, especially the latter. I had had my career chosen for me and it would repay some of Father's great kindness to me. I was to become his private and confidential secretary—type his manuscripts from the tape recorder, deal with all his business letters and accounts—file, compile, provide cups of coffee, sweep, clean, entertain and put up with the golden girls and not one of them approved of me. So now, I sat with a virgin manuscript, my fingers clawed over the keys and hating every word I must type.

Here was the start of yet another book and soon it would be on every bookstall in the United Kingdom and then all over the world and the royalties would roll in and the income tax roll out and they never seemed to catch up, one with the other.

"Very well then, Inspector. I murdered her."

I was speaking but it was the voice of a stranger and I could never have uttered such words.

This was the heroine and of course, she hadn't done it. It was only prologue.

"But why?"

Somebody asked the question, but I had no idea who of all the people in the room, had asked it.

"She nagged me all the time. I couldn't do anything right

for her. If that's not enough motive, there was all that money ..."

It was the same old stuff, but it sold. My word! How it sold! The plays were guaranteed to run for ages and I got allergic to being known as "Hamish Grant's daughter." Most of all, I got allergic to the way the people in the village looked at me, pitied me with their eyes and I knew I was ungrateful to them, for they tried to make it up to me, that I lived in a house, where there were "queer goings on".

"It ain't right for a young girl."

Many of the local inhabitants did not care one way or another. You must expect a famous man to live "that sort of life". There were some people, I cared about and I knew they did not quite accept me and that hurt me equal to the pain of any serpent's tooth.

There was a small circle of the elite, the upper middle class. I was allowed an edge and no more, no intimacy and no real friendship, yet probably I imagined the pale of separation. There were the old families, the solicitor and his wife, the doctor and his wife, the lord of the manor. Now and again I might be asked to a tennis party. If there was a golden girl in residence, the house might have been infected with the Black Death, but if Father was between "common law wives" and I between one "aunt" and the next, there might be an afternoon for me at the Rickaby's tennis party. The solicitor, Mr. Rickaby, had a private tennis court in En Tout Cas. He also had a son called Anthony, who was a doctor. Anthony was a dark, shy young man and they said in the village that he was going on to be a "perfesser". He had taken up some branch of medicine that had to do with the police. Now and again, I read his name in the local papers, when he gave evidence in court. More important still, he was the one person in the whole Parish, who never failed to smile at me and pass the time of day, when we met in the High Street. He can have had no idea how important this was to me, for I had many a snub and each one of them worse to bear than a slap in the face. I might tell myself that my father was a famous man, but I knew the local standards and I knew the moral laws. There were plenty of people who pretended not to see me and sometimes, they were pillars of the church or the chapel. One day I would stop and challenge them with visiting the sins of the fathers.

Maybe I had had a score of conversations with Anthony Rickaby in my life. I was shy of him and the talk was always a bit stilted. He was keen on tennis and so was I. I could in no way tell him that I had won the silver cup at tennis at my senior school, but I could talk Wimbledon. Then one day, he put a hand on my shoulder and asked me to come over the next afternoon. They had a tennis party on and he was sure his mother would be delighted to have me. There would be plenty of young people. That froze my courage for a start and I demurred a bit, said he had better ask his mother. She might not want me.

"Why ever not?"

He could not know that his hand on my shoulder was like the touch of a live electric cable, that possessed my whole body with a tingling, thrilling feeling, such as I had never experienced before. I moved away from him a little and then came back along the path and caught his sleeve.

"I'd love to come, but I'm not all that good."

My hand was on fire at the touch of the sleeve of his coat. I remember the coat bound with leather against wear and tear and wondered if he found money matters as difficult as Father did.

"They say you're a very silent, proper, young lady. I'll have Mother drop you an invitation tonight ... and your fame has gone before you. The butcher told me the other day that you could kill a bull with one swipe of your racquet. There's glory for you!"

The next day, there was a note in the letter box, a friendly little note from Mrs. Rickaby, asking me to tea and tennis and from that day on, I often went and sometimes, Anthony was there, but mostly he was away. He worked in hospital and only came home occasionally, but now a strange phenomenon had come about. In my waking-day-night-dreams, he had become my constant companion. He rode a white charger and he was white knight, if ever there was white knight. I was infatuated with him to the last drop of my blood. Willingly I would have died for him, even after that first tennis party, when he broke my heart.

He was polite to me, very polite indeed, but he had no eyes for me. There was a lady doctor, who could not play tennis to save her soul. She patted the ball, as if she were a kitten with a ball of wool. She lost set after set for him as his partner and I annihilated her in a single match, when she won not one single point against my savage attack. I might have been cleverer to have dealt with her gently, but I slammed everything I had got into her. I pinned her against the back line and I do not think she returned one of my services. She packed up half way through and Anthony took her into the house to see if she had strained a ligament. My father had been invited too and he charmed them all with his wit, but I had none. I just bullied every opponent I met with the ferocity of my tennis, till I was quite sure everybody hated me. Then I went home and hammered the keys of the typewriter and knew myself for a creature of no attraction. Yet he came again, night after night, and walked beside me and told me that I was like a honey-coloured fawn ... as if a honey-coloured fawn could play brutal tennis.

So life went on from one day to the next and seemed likely to go on the same way for ever, but life never does. Hamish McFarlane Grant had written so many books. He was well known on the London stage. It was time for him to break into films and that is just what he did. I read the letter from his agents and never thought what it might mean to me. I watched his face as his eyes ran down the page and heard a great shout of triumph, as if he were a huntsman, who had sighted the fox. The golden girl put her head round the study door and came in and he seized her by the waist and swung her round and round, though there was no space for such activity in the small room. A neat pile of typescript went flying to the ceiling and drifted down like leaves in Autumn, covered the floor with typed pages with no order about them. To make it worse, between the two of them, they tramped on the Prestige paper with no respect whatever and I knew there was going to be a great deal of work to be re-done, one way and another. That was my first thought and the second was a jealousy that it had not been myself to be swung round in an intoxication of success. She took no interest in his writing, only in the cheques that rang in. I felt self-pity and knew it to be a loathsome emotion. I pushed it down and listened to the plans being made and after a while it became clear to me that there was no need for me to accompany them to Hollywood. In his eyes, I read the greed at the thought of the world fame the film city had earned for its profusion of golden beauties. I could feel sorrow for her. If he did any writing there and he might not find the time, he would send the tapes home to me and I could convert them to typescript. Goodness only knew how long they would be away, but if it was six months or so, it might be a good idea to let the house furnished. That was not suggested straight out that day. It was produced with a side-long look, after some correspondence between agents and publishers and film producers.

"You could get a bed-sit, in Camford. You'd have my business to see after. Come to that, you could get a secretarial job. You'd make a splendid private secretary. Haven't I been training you for years?"

I was apathetic about the whole affair. I told myself with great firmness that I had no longing to be kitted out in glamour clothes and fly across the Atlantic. The golden girl got enough wardrobe for a real bride and I wondered if the same sort of confidence trick might be played upon her. I remembered the new school clothes and the tuck-box and the loneliness that they were trap to. She would have fierce competition and I was sorry for her, yet I felt that she could look after herself. My father would be like a greedy boy in a sweet shop, if Hollywood were like my idea of it, but my ideas were so often wrong. Still the whole plan went through with no hitch. The cottage was let and I moved into my bed-sit., the same day, they left for the States. They did not suggest that I should see them off at London airport. It would be a lonely journey home and anyway I had to see to getting my stuff moved into Camford.

I concentrated in turning my new home into a home and indeed, it was very pleasant. It looked out on a small park, that had a railing and trees and seats and my room was on the second floor and had a bow window. There was a built-in press, that held all my things easily. There were two arm chairs. The settee made up into a bed by night and was respectable, as a couch by day, with two patchwork cushions. I had borrowed a pair of patchwork curtains from Shangri La—no, I would call it Rowan Tree House now. The curtains were just right for the bow window, especially as it looked down on a footpath with two old Sherlock Holmes lamps, converted to elecricity to light the front door.

As darkness came down, the lamps were a great comfort to me. There were other young people with rooms in the house too, but it seemed that they were intent on keeping themselves to themselves—not in a prim and proper mind-your-own-business way, but modern and casual and with-it and given to playing music loudly at all times.

For the first few days, I worked hard at stuff Father had left me to do and then I sat with folded hands, having answered a solitary business letter. It was no good. I admitted I was lonely again. I decided to get myself a job and one night I went out along the path between the Sherlock Holmes lamps and bought a local paper. Then my luck changed. Perhaps I had always had had good luck. I had had a comfortable house to live in. I had had good schooling. I had fallen into a secretarial position with no effort whatever. Yet I managed to feel a little sorry for myself. I even persuaded myself that the young people in the house in Camford thought only of themselves. I was leafing through the Evening News, when there was a scratch at the door and a girl stuck her head in. She was carrying a transistor set in one hand and a bundle wrapped in newspaper in the other.

"Hope you don't mind me visiting your pad, but I've an idea you're a bit miz. I've got more fish and chips than I can use. Would you like to sit in on them? I got 'plaice and chips' twice in case," she told me.

She sat cross legged on the settee and she divided the fish and chips with great fairness, tore the newspaper wrapping in shares also and advised me to put the *Camford Evening News* under my repast, because the oil came through.

"I must keep the ad. section. I'm looking for a job."

I was like a reservoir that had burst its banks, with the way conversation flowed out of me. Mostly I think we both spoke at the same time and I will never understand how we made any sense, but with the transistor playing as a fortissimo accompaniment, we exchanged life stories. Kit, her name was, and that was short for Kitten of course. She was secretary too but she was not much good at it. She worked at the Hospital. Did I know the Camford General? If you were a proper medical secretary you could get a super job there, but she couldn't spell the stupid words and she couldn't be bothered to slog them up. They were desperate for secretaries at the Hospital. They would take practically anybody, but could I spell crazy words like aorta and anaemia and epilepsy?

"Wait a jiffy. There's a special book and I've got one in my room. The only ones I can manage are pelvis and heart and body and that sort of thing, but I can't even remember whether it is soul or sole."

I sat looking down at the line drawings of little men, that she had filled in, in the margins to pass the boredom It was a dictionary, but a dictionary with a difference. There were some frightningly long complicated words, but there were a great many very easy ones too, even if they were not familiar. I thought I could learn to be a medical secretary, given the time, but it seemed that there was a good chance that I could start off as an ordinary secretary and swim my way up the pool.

Kit ate the last of her chips and screwed up the paper, aimed it with precision at my waste paper basket and wiped her hands down a wool jumper, that was so long it reached her knees. Then she reached for the transistor and turned it off. Her voice was low now and confidential.

"You're hard up for a job since they've left you. Why not come up the Hospital and see the Sec. Queen, see if she'd give you a start?"

Looking back on it, it cannot have been conducted so concisely, all that business, but I never smell fish and chips, but I think of the bed-sit. and the Baker Street lamps and the patchwork curtains. I can never smell that special essence of hospital, without the memory of the long corridors and the room with the tidy desk, where I interviewed the "Sec. Queen".

She was dressed as a nursing sister. I presumed that she was one of the top grade sisters on the practical side, raised to the glory of administration in the foolish way of governmental policy.

"Well now, Elizabeth Grant. What experience have you had and why do you think you'd like to work in the Camford General?"

I concentrated on the starched perfection of the cap, which was like a white butterfly, just paused for a moment on the sweep of her silver hair.

"First perhaps I'd better tell you that I'm after top medical secretaries. They're in short supply, hopelessly short supply."

She knew that I was the daughter of Hamish McFarlane Grant and she was a fan of his. It appeared to me that she knew far more about his books than I did. She discussed them with tremendous interest and not a little humour.

"If you've typed most of that stuff recently, you'll have gone in over the head in medical jargon. Between you, you've done plenty of murders."

I was nervous, gripping my hands in my lap with the hope that she would not notice them trembling, but she was perceptive, determined to put me at my ease and make me relax and thus get my qualities assessed accurately. She smiled at me.

"I'm not implying that we actually do murders in the Camford General, but you must be familiar with forensic stuff and gory details and X marks the body. It's a start."

She laughed at her own idea of what might be help to a medical typist. Then she glanced down at my home address.

"We have a Histington doctor here, Dr. Rickaby. He's assistant pathologist. Do you know him? His father's a solicitor?"

Maybe she took my scarlet cheeks for a reply or maybe she was not interested. I found myself with a shorthand notebook in one hand and a pencil, in the other.

"Letter from one of the consultants to a G.P. Take it down

and I want three carbons please. It's a damn' hard run for somebody without medical sec. training. I'll lend you a special dictionary ..."

It was a newer, cleaner, "Kit's book", but I missed the line drawings in the margins. This copy was pristine and had only been used by clients in the despair of tests. Still, there were three carbons, I thought to myself, so I would have three scribes with no more idea of medical words than my father's typist had. It was an easy letter. There was "appendix" and "cardiac arrest". I wondered if the police came into the latter phrase, but thought it unlikely. I barely managed to keep "pocket of pus" in its right place and not to involve any cats. I have no idea what mistakes I did make, but the sister looked at me with approval.

"We'll lay you off for a week or two and you can swot up the medical dictionary—hang round the departments a bit and get the feel of the place. They call it a 'Complex' and that's right on the button. You'll get lost every half hour the first day. It's all very 'rich and strange', but you'll digest it. You'll probably be able to give your father a great many hints on protocol, when he gets back from Hollywood."

I could hardly believe that they were going to take me on. They must indeed be hard up for medical typists. I spent a glorious time lazing about the hospital, learning which department was which, and where X-ray was and where Casualty was ... and you called that, "Cas" and felt very "with it" indeed. There was a great alphabetic Noah's Ark of letters that all meant different and important things. There was no end to them ... E.C.G. and E.E.G. and U.R.T.I. and P.U.O. There was even a diagnosis called G.K.W. which stood for "God Knows What" and indicated puzzlement on the physician's part. The Complex was a factory for broken bodies ... like a factory to mend broken dolls. Wherever you went, you met slow people, old or young, passengers on trolleys or in wheelchair, stretchers coming in by ambulances and maybe that meant to "Cas" ... cripples who walked on crutches or on a nurse's arm, old grey women, who crept the corridors, like old grey rats, feeling their way along the shining wall, knowing the path by usage. There were nurses and sisters and all sorts of auxiliaries, clad in one uniform or another with name plates pinned to their white coat breasts or with epaulettes on their shoulders. For all the stream of broken bodies, there was a staff of youth that ran the place, with smiles for the most place and with a great sense of youth and health.

I found myself in a typists' pool, a long room with desks at intervals and here was the place that I must force my way upwards, like a salmon on her way up river to spawn.

There was a grape vine of gossip in the typists' pool. News moved with as much speed as the sun might light up the old vine, that covered a cottage wall at dawn on midsummer's day.

"There's Anthony Rickaby coming in now, Miss Grant. He's parked his car and he's on his way in the main entrance. Usually he comes in the Lab. side way and goes down in the lift."

My desk was by a window and I looked at the top of his dark head, recognised the college scarf round his neck and felt a thickness in my throat, that precluded speech.

I had had a letter from Hollywood that morning, forwarded on from Histington. Father had even forgotten to send it to my bed-sit. address. He had forgotten that I did not live at home any more, but it was only an oversight. Yet, it hurt me out of all proportion.

Father was so glad that I enjoyed the job in hospital. The whole thing fitted in with his plans. He liked Hollywood very much and he might not be coming back to England for a longer time than we had planned. I must on no account get rid of my flat. It would oblige him if I could contact the people at the house and angle for a longer let for them too—up to two years perhaps.

I looked again at the top of Anthony Rickaby's head, watched him come up the steps of the entrance two at a time, noticed the leather patch on his coat that was meant for the butt of a shot gun, noticed the leather bound cuffs, that maybe spelt out economy.

Anthony would know that Father preferred his golden girl ... golden girls, preferred the exotic life, and why should

I feel forsaken? I know I felt shame that Anthony should know it. There was nothing exotic about me, nothing any good at all, except my smashing way of playing tennis and now my speed on the keys of a typewriter. The Head of the department was a sour middle-aged spinster and no doubt whatever, this was what I would become with the passage of time.

"Stop chattering, you girls and get on with your work. Miss Grant! Will you come through to my room. I have something to say to you."

I took a last look at Anthony, but it did little to lift my heart. Yet presently, I was raised to the skies, for it seemed that I had proved myself excellent in every way. I was in line for promotion, if I thought I could take it on. There would be an increase in salary, of course, and I would have my own office. I was an example to the modern generation, who did nothing all day except watch the clock and mend the runs in their tights with nail varnish. I took in about half the conditions of the position she was offering me. I accepted it of course, for the bits I picked up sounded too good to be true. I would be one of the special secretaries. It would be my place to hold myself ready for senior staff, when special letters had to be done maybe at short notice ... urgent, important, vital material ...

I wandered along the corridor outside her room and after a long time, it seemed that fate indeed had changed its face from the moment when I had read Father's letter, not more than a few hours before. There was a long window that matched the corridor and the sun dazzled my eyes. There was a man walking towards me against the glare and I did not know him, not till he stopped up short and put his hand out to touch my shoulder.

"Oh, Lord! I heard you were here. I've been meaning to look you up, but we've been very busy. I didn't get round to it. Is your father still away?"

I nodded my head and was glad that my voice did not desert me.

"He's not expected home for a long time. They're filming

another of his books. He's bought a house out there and he loves it."

"But you're left alone."

"I don't think I'm ever alone. I've made so many friends. I like it here."

"You can be loneliest of all in a crowd," he said.

There was no point in telling Anthony Rickaby that there was a new golden girl. She was a starlet, who had not become a star. She had moved in to type the manuscripts, so she had taken my job. She refused to face the English climate. I could look after what business there was here, so I should fall back on the hospital post. There was no point in telling Anthony that the ex-golden girl had been offered a screen test and "had gone to live with a friend ..."

I felt so ashamed of feeling ashamed, but his attention had wandered from my father and his private affairs.

"They say you're getting on very well here ... making quite a reputation for yourself."

He was searching round in his mind for an excuse to get away from me, murmured that he would ask his mother to fix up for me to come to Histington one day.

"You were always very proper about visiting. I'll get her to ring you."

He had left his hand on my shoulder, had not even noticed it was there. Now he took it away and all the pain of ecstasy with it and then he went a step along the corridor and another.

"I must get along. Take care of yourself."

He did not look back at me and I knew that he was far too preoccupied, would forget all about asking his mother to get in touch. I went back slowly to the typists' room and thought that I must be "chap-fallen". It was a grand Shakespearian word, which described my feelings exactly. Anthony did not even know I existed. Yet, perhaps he had a stack of work or perhaps he had one soul-destroying case. Even when he spoke with me, his mind had not been in the long shining corridor. Besides, I should be shot for forgetting all about my good fortune. I was to have a top secretary's position and a room to myself, an electric typewriter, which was so esteemed that for all I knew, it might do the work itself with the help of the carbon scribes. I grinned as I arrived back in the typists' pool, then my antennae picked up that there was some item of vast interest in the community. There was no machine at work and no happy face, only the hidden delight, that accompanies the news of disaster, with a kind of shamed enjoyment.

"That's why he went up the front steps. He must be just coming in to see what's to be done. They say he wasn't there when it happened. One minute, there she was and the next she fell slouched over her desk. Her face had gone all one side. Purple she was and snoring."

There is small beauty in death. I had learned that since I had taken to walking the hospital, but this was different. Miss Bunn was dead, so they said. She had gone from life to death in the twinkle of an eye. The medical details repeated themselves over and over, the intensive care, the oxygen, the thumping of a heart, that was dead. I had just been talking to Anthony Rickaby and it was no wonder that he was preoccupied. Miss Bunn was his private and confidential secretary. I had only to sit silent at my desk and all the details came flooding into my knowledge. Miss Bunn was an old woman, but that might mean anything in this room of youthful aspirants for a profession such as hers. She had been in the Complex since it was built. She had adopted Dr. Rickaby, when he first came as pathologist. She had taught him all he knew. That was easily said.

She had been apprenticed to the old Professor and Rickaby had inherited her. She *was* Forensic Medicine, old Bunn was, had been for fifty years. She had gone round the outside cases with him and she knew more than any doctor.

That was easily said too, but he had stood in the long sunny corridor and talked with me, when he was in dire trouble and put his own troubles aside to show interest in mine. He had not said "Miss Bunn is dead. I have nobody to help me. Think of me."

One girl filled us with all the horrors of forensic medicine.

"Rickaby took old Bunn on all the criminal cases, murder and that. He dictated the findings, as he went along and she took them down, as he spoke them, never turned a hair, just stood there at his left hand, her note-book open and maybe a policeman with his torch, the only light there was."

Then with a swirl, the conversation was gay and cider-fizzing. There were bottles produced like rabbits from a hat.

"Elizabeth's to move up. Congrats! You're to have your own office and work for the senior consultants. I daresay you'll not condescend to put your nose into this department again. Mind your head doesn't get too big to fit out the door. Can't say you haven't earned it. You ain't half worked at it, but what I say is, you've got natural talent."

I sat there and thought of him, of Anthony Rickaby and how he must have been weighed down with a great sorrow, for he must have liked his secretary very much. His work would be piling up—and there was nobody with Miss Bunn's ability to put it straight. Yet it was me, he had remembered, deserted by what he would think was my family, stretching out a hand to put it on my shoulder, to comfort me ... to comfort me, who could be loneliest of all in a crowd.

2

COMMERCIAL TRAVELLER IN BONES

There was no time to spare in the Camford General. Good medical secretaries were in short supply. Empty office cells stood waiting for them and apparently, they thought I was top grade. How I ever came to be so labelled, I shall never understand, though I do admit that Father's stories must have broken me in to disease and death to some extent. I certainly was no stranger to law-courts in print and to doctors, who gave expert evidence, that might hang a villain, if the rope had not been discarded. Father always had it that the abolition of hanging had ruined murder plots and I could see what he meant. There was a dark excitement about hunting down a criminal, but the excitement lost its horror, if a man was just sent down for ten years and not properly hanged by the neck till he was dead ... and may the Lord have mercy on his soul! That was the stuff of good old detective yarns and the same awful thrilling feeling would never be recaptured, or so Father had it. There was the eight o'clock bell and the notice pinned on the prison door, but I have strayed from my subject. The notice was certainly pinned on my door, the day one of the "Queen bee typists" buzzed her way into my proud new office. She was young and pretty, with thick black lashes that fanned her cheeks. There was no guessing the iron capability that existed below the soft swing of her gilded hair.

"I hear that you took dictation from the senior physician himself and came out with your head still on your shoulders," she said and grinned at me and there was something about her that reminded me of Kit and her fish and chips and her illustrated dictionary of medical words.

"Well ..."

She drew the word out ten times its normal length and I knew there was hospital news to follow and indeed it did.

"You know Dr. Rickaby had been slaughtering the typists they've sent him since poor Bunn died, "Where are they getting them these days?" he said to the Governor the other day. "Type! They may be able to type, but they can't spell, nor punctuate nor string words together. They don't know the Queen's English …""

To cut a long story short, he had wandered into the consulting room of the Senior Professor of Physic and had picked up some letter I had just delivered for signature. Without a word of permission, he had taken the top one and read it … read the next line, asked who had done it. It was a wonder that the professor hadn't booted him through the door, but they were in sympathy, or so it seemed.

"Elizabeth Grant? I know her. She's from the village where I live. I'll bleep her and see if she's any different from the othes.""

It wound on in the way hospital gossip does. The conversation had passed from mouth to mouth and not only between the two men. It had descended through the typists' pool.

"He was curious to know if you were tough enough for the path. trade … the criminal side of his business and that." "Times have changed, Rickaby. Women are not gentle creatures in these days." the old Prof. told him.

"It's true, Elizabeth. He said it. Gospel truth! Rickaby said he knew you quite well and that you were gentle and kind. He said you were the most unspoilt girl he'd ever met."

The professor had no interest who did Rickaby's sec. work or who did not.

"Oh, for God's sake, give her a trial, boy. What does it matter, if she goes into cardiac arrest? You've just got to pick up the internal phone and get another cat fish from the famous pool. Typists' pool! It's more like a goose bed. You go in there and you kick them about a bit for their rotten work and a few feathers float in the air and then all settle down again to the status quo and the standards sink too. I tell you, Rickaby. Those girls *don't* know the Queen's English. You said that to the governor, I hear."

So the notice was pinned on my door, for the execution. It was not done by a warder that came through the studded gates with a piece of printed paper fluttering in his hand. There was no silent crowd waiting outside, only a long corridor that reflected the sunshine. The door opened and a nurse put her head in.

"Dr. Rickaby sent me to ask you to go to his room. He wants you to take reports."

My face was either white or red. I never knew which, but she told me not to be frightened.

"He's not as bad as they say. The stuff may be a bit off, but it can be ever so interesting—the court cases and that. If he goes too fast for you, just tell him to ease up on the speed—that you're doing shorthand, not driving a coach and four."

He was half sitting on a tall stool beside a table with a zinc top and well I knew the significance of the table and the antiseptic foreign smell of the room. He glanced at me as I came in and nodded his head at a table desk and I sat behind it with my notebook at the ready.

"It's on tape ... Just listen to it once and see if it's clear. Then take the tape to your room and make a fair copy and six carbons."

I thought of the six scribes now as I bent my head and listened to the words that came out of this wonderful invention of man. He had been careful to get it to come out very clearly. Only once, I had to stop it and listen again and then I had not to ask him for any clarification. Back in my own office, I remembered every detail of Anthony Rickaby. I think I remembered every inflection of his words before they repeated themselves over again. He had not spoken of personal things, had not mentioned any possibility of his mother asking me to come out to Histington to visit, had not asked me if I still liked the hospital. At least, he had asked for my services to type for him. I did not know then how much was to come of that single day's work. How could I? It altered the course of my whole career, of my entire life, though I did not know it then—only knew that I must put every effort into my work and produce such a top copy and six carbons as I had never produced before.

Later on, I put my work on his desk and he looked through it and thanked me, found no mistakes and for that I was glad. There was neither praise nor blame, just that vague smile of his, as if his mind was elsewhere and I was through the door and away, but again, the next day, he asked for me and again in a day or two. Then one glorious morning, he took me along to the Assizes with him, to bring the typescript of some case in order.

"This typescript was made from notes taken at the scene of the crime. There are no additions and no omissions. The second part of my evidence will be of the post-mortem exam. The report of this is typed from my own personal notes, taken at the time of the examination in Camford General Hospital. I would ask your permission, my Lord, to refer to the typed copy, during my evidence."

I was familiar with Her Majesty's courts and I knew a certain amount of procedure. I had gone with Father to get the atmosphere of British justice. Now it was as if one of my father's stories had come to life under the keys of my typewriter and was happening before me in real life, but there was a nightmarish quality, because this was for real. There was no book to be closed and laid aside, no machine to be covered and put away. If a prisoner left the dock to go down to the cells, he might not be a free man for many years. There was terror and a fear of retribution, a knowledge all of a sudden, of crime and punishment, that melted my bones to water. I was glad to get out into the air again and drew in great gulps of it.

The rumour began to trickle through the corridors that I was to be attached permanently to the Path. Department. I was to be groomed for Miss Bunn's position. I was to work more closely with Dr. Rickaby.

Kit listened to all the gossip with much interest. I did not acknowledge my feelings for Anthony. I tossed aside the suggestion that Kit made and we were sharing fish and chips in the bed-sit. again. She had just tossed the remains of the newspaper into the waste basket.

"Perhaps we should get plates heated and eat these things in a civilised fashion," I said.

She sat cross-legged on the floor and shook her head.

"You won't be sharing them with me in this humble fashion much longer, duckie. It's all over the hospital that Anthony Rickaby had a thing going for you. You might be Mrs. Rickaby living in far too exalted circles to eat fish and chips out of a newspaper."

"That's the only way to eat them," I said and then took in what she had just told me.

"Don't talk rubbish, Kit."

"It's not rubbish. God's truth! It's not! Ask anybody and they'll tell you."

"But don't think the food will be all that good in the high-up circles of pathology," she went on and stood on her head like a character in Alice-through-the-Looking Glass, addressing me meanwhile and flapping her feet up and down.

"There'll be formalin in the sandwiches and police canteen tea. You'll stand out under hedges and in ditches and swig cocoa out of some constable's Thermos. Lucky if he doesn't offer it to you in his helmet! He might at that, but I'll tell you one thing, just because I don't want you taken unawares. Anthony Rickaby is trying to find the nerve to ask you to go out with him. I don't mean on cases. I mean to dinner or that. That's what they say, but it's not what I say. I have an idea ..."

I asked her if she was standing on her head to try to get the idea in the correct position to launch at me and she turned herself right way up as gracefully as a ballet dancer.

"All the signs are there. He never stops watching you, unless you catch him at it and then he looks away smartish. He's taken to wearing bright plumage. Didn't you notice that tie the other day, how he's got a new scarf, else that, or had the old one cleaned? The male bird perks up his feathers in the courting season."

She perched on the back of one of the armchairs, till she turned it over on herself and then she laughed till I thought she might go on laughing for ever.

"He's in love with you, but he doesn't know it. You'll have to do something to force his hand."

I assured her that I had no interest in forcing anybody's hand and that she was talking utter nonsense with all that business about birds and plumage and perking feathers. Then the telephone rang, and the call was for me. It was from the Central Police Station. They had Dr. Rickaby in on a criminal case and he had asked them to contact me. He would be very much obliged if I could come down there as soon as I could make it. They would send a Panda for me. I smiled at the word 'obliged' It was a command—an order.

I was in black slacks and a sweater. I had only to put on my sheep's coat and a head scarf, I was proof against the weather. I was proof againsty everything but the terror, I might have to face. I must gather up all control of emotion, all revulsion, not let my imagination go slithering about the possibilities of what the next hour might hold. It might be a stabbing, a mugging, that had gone too far. It might be some young girl ... I had not had much experience of the outside work yet. Certainly I had not attained any of Miss Bunn's calm. As I was taken on a siren scream through the sparse late traffic of Camford, I wondered if Miss Bunn could be somewhere in another world, trying to will good advice to me, but it was a sergeant who was driving the car.

"Keep yourself apart from it, Miss Grant. Don't let your mind fill in details, that have nothing to do with you. It's a case and you're there to record professional facts in an accurate and orderly way. It's not your affair to wonder if they're breaking the news to the parents at that particular moment, or if it's an only child ... or what it felt ... this is your first, isn't it?"

So it was just a case for the most part? I tried to concentrate with all my mind on the words that I was taking down, tried to make sure that I could resurrect them again and turn them into neat copy, to await him next morning on his desk. There were long pauses of course and I then studied the bare police room and went over the details of flat caps and uniform, of shining silver numbers on shoulders, blue shirts, black ties. Then I switched off altogether till there

were more words to claim me. I thought of Kit standing on
her head and twiddling her toes in the air. I remembered
what she had said with a shock. Perhaps she had been joking,
but I did not think so. "There was talk in the hospital," but
when was there not? Kit had her own version and that was
an impossible one. Anthony was not any more aware of me
than he was of the electric typewriter on my desk. He was in
love with his work, totally and completely immersed in it. If I
fell down on my work, he had only to pick up the internal
phone and send for a replacement. I would vanish from his
life and there would be no sense of loss, no watching for me
to come through the door. A gentle nudge from a young
constable at my side returned me to the scene and the fact
that there was more dictation coming my way. Then it was
all over and Anthony was offering me a lift home. He opened
the car door for me and drove quickly and with skill. If I had
expected any conversation, I was disappointed. I had directed
him to the bed sit. and he pulled the car to a halt and leaned
over to click the latch open and let me out.

"Well that's the way of it," he sighed. "All done in one
great volcanic eruption of passion and there's an end to a
possible sixty-seventy years that a woman might have
lived ... a creation that even the most skilled engineer could
never have fashioned—for the human body is such a structure."

Maybe he thought of the perils that might lurk in the
shadow or even in my mind, for he got out of the car and
escorted me to the front door. We went between the Sherlock
Holmes lamps and he admired them. I saw the look of
pleasure in his face, tilted up to catch the muted light.

"Hansom cabs," he murmured to nobody in particular, for
there was nobody there but myself. "Hansom cabs and the
smell of horses and the rustle of straw and the clip-clopping
of hooves."

He took my latch key and opened the door for me and
there was a cut of Cranford about him, as if he were back in
days that were over and done. Then as I stood in the hall and
looked at him, tried to thank him for bringing me home, he
shook his head at me.

"There was mud in the streets though, and crime and ugliness in Holmes's days, just the same as we've seen tonight ... ugliness."

Back at the car, he paused to look at me and still the thoughts were vague-fog, investing his brain.

"But that child tonight, you know, it's a sobering thought."

"All the King's horses and all the King's men couldn't put Humpty Dumpty together again."

He wound his scarf round his throat, his face sombre.

"Goodnight, Liz-Jane," he said and his car was away along the quietness of the street and I stood there, till I could hear it no more. There was one thought in my head that shut out the darkness of the shadows and shut out all thought of the bare police room, shut out all terror and revulsion, closed my mind to his philosophy of man being the most perfect engineering product of the whole world, blacked out the look of the doll-child, done to death. He had called me Liz-Jane. He had called me Liz-Jane. He had called me Liz-Jane.

It was very late by the time I was in bed. I should have slept like a dead woman, but what was left of the night might have been spent flipping over the leaves of an odd scrap book of pictures. I dozed off now and again. Probably I passed a very restful night, because that is usually what expert nurses report about a patient, who thinks she had lain awake for hour after hour, when in truth, she had awakened for a minute and slept again. Now I lived the scene with the police as sentinels. I saw again, the fair hair and the tumbled clothes. Then there was Kit, on her head with her feet in the air, grinning at me.

"There's no need to be a brown Jenny Wren, Miss Elizabeth Grant. Oh, no! I'm well aware that you're a honey blonde, but I'm sure we could improve on that pony tail."

There was a pause and I must have drifted off to sleep, for when I saw her again, she was standing with her hands on her hips and her head on one side and I knew that she had no more substance than a dream.

"I know that navy blue is the right uniform for top sec. ancillaries. You look fine in navy blue and the white collar, never anything but spotless. I've seen you on your way out on cases and you don't give a damn if you look like a rag picker's child, whatever that is ..."

She disappeared and I thought that there was Cheshire cat about her, but she had started thoughts in my mind that kept me restless. It was true, I went out in jeans and an anorak and Wellington boots, if the case warranted that sort of gear. I admitted I wore sensible shoes, but anybody who knows what it is to be on foot for a great part of the day, knows about footwear. Towards morning, I was foolish enough to be planning up film star outfits, that were in no way suitable for a Jenny Wren. I was thinking like a novelette heroine, who has her eye on the boss's son and it would soon be time to get up. I stood in the bath and poured an outsize jug of cold water over myself and hoped that I might come to my senses. At least the shock galvanised me, for I finished my breakfast and was at the hospital half an hour early for work. Also I had thought fit "to perk up my feathers." I was in a black skirt and a white blouse, but the blouse had a special collar. It also sported gold cuff links, that I liked. I saw my reflection in the glass door as I entered my office and thought that indeed I might have stood for the model of the perfect confidential secretary. "With no nonsense about you either," whispered Kit in my imagination. "That's the trouble with you. You're camouflaged. I've thought so for days. The poor bloke doesn't see you."

I shoved Kit and her interruptions into the background and got the typewriter at the ready. It was a long report and I was completely involved in it. The six carbons worked with identical precision and it seemed no time at all, till the whole thing was finished and corrected and ready to put on Anthony Rickaby's desk. I went along to his room and knocked at the door and he looked at me as if he saw me ... looked at me quite a while before he said anything, but then his mind was vague again. There was no "good morning" and no "Liz-Jane." He took the typescript and glanced through the first sheet.

"Have you seen the papers this morning?"

"No, sir."

Now I understood the cause of the preoccupation. I

expected that our case of last night had been making a write-up on the front pages, but it was not that.

"Usually there's nothing of interest in the Press, but you missed something this morning. They've made a sensational find, or so they think. We'll be involved, you and I ..."

He went over to the coat rack and fished a copy of a local paper out of his coat pocket, threw it across to me. I caught it as neatly as I had fielded the ball in the garden cricket matches at his parents' house at Histington.

"Take it back to your office and read it. If what they think is fact, we'll have every archaeologist in the country in Camford."

I sat at my desk and read the article he had indicated, but I could not find much cause for such great enthusiasm.

There was a new building estate going up out by the Castle ruins. The contractors were skimming off the top soil and yesterday, a digger had thrown up some bones. There seemed to be no question of foul play. This was far more likely to be a long-forgotten burial ground, that had been covered over by the centuries forgotten by the generations. Camford had been a Roman settlement. I had always thought it was as full of Roman remains as a dog is full of fleas. It was a commonplace happening to see the archaeologists, that surge of experts, carefully sifting the earth and the soil and the miniscule bits of pottery and tile. Invariably, they were haunted by pretty female students, who hung on their every pronouncement, chipping and brushing and documenting and affixing neat labels. The finds all went into plastic and were carefully packed and one day, they might achieve the British Museum. There was snob value, Royal Society prestige about the activity.

I had no interest in Roman times, but it was almost certainly because of my total ignorance. Give me something to be turned into a good murder fiction, although of recent weeks, I had turned from detective fiction to detective truth, but then truth is always the strange one.

Anyhow, Anthony Rickaby warned me that I might be bleeped to accompany him to the Castle Ruins.

"They want a pathologist's opinion before they make any definite move. I'd like to have you along."

Yet the bleep did not go for me and I acknowledged to myself that I was disappointed. The morning passed and the slow afternoon started. I had plenty of work, so much that I forgot the whole affair. It was pouring rain anyhow, lashing the window, as if somebody had turned a garden hose against the glass. It would be most unpleasant out at the Castle ruins and there would be very little shelter. There would be a tarpaulin cover over the place where the bones lay and that would be it. The uncovered earth would have been transformed into a slithery, sticky, clinging quagmire. It was safe in the office with the rain defeated by the great glass window, that took up the entire area of one wall of the room. I settled for an indoor job, especially when the tea girl came with the trolley and following her, strolled the most junior of the house physicians.

He wanted a letter typed and I was glad to do it for him. He was a pleasant young man and he watched me admiringly as I typed the letter at his dictation, addressed the envelope and stamped it, passed it over to him with its copies. The tea girl poured us both a cup of tea and he made as short work of the biscuits, as if he had been marooned on a desert island for weeks, living on bread fruit and coconuts.

"Don't mind him, miss," said the tea girl. "He's a holy terror for his stomach, if there's biscuits about. I'll bring up some more for yourself, next time I'm on this floor."

"I'll keep them in the safe," I told her and the H.P. lifted an eyebrow at me at that.

"Oh, yes. I forgot to tell you Miss Grant," he said. "There's a man in the Staff Room, level two. He's looking for Dr. Rickaby and he's making quite a fuss about it. I told him that Dr. Rickaby's not in the building, but he's like all the reps. There's no such word as "no". They're specially trained for it and this bloke has a hell of a nerve. I had to promise to get you to see him. Then, when I arrived here, I recalled the letter I wanted typed, thought it might be worth asking you to do it for me. Then there was the tea and I thank you for that. Still, I'll be obliged if you'd see this bloke. He's from

some big London firm, medical "tops". This man sells sets of
bones ... represents a prestige house. They supply hospital
equipment too. This particular chap always sees Dr. Rickaby
and he says he has a firm appointment for today."

Today he was pushing osteology sets and they were in
demand for the students, in lieu of the old skeletons, that had
been used for generations.

"I did my best to get rid of him, told him that Dr. Rickaby
is on the Out board, but he didn't believe me. He's so damned
persistent, that I had to come and find you. He's not half
grotty ... says that he confirmed the appointment this
morning and the bones were first class priority. You'd better
get a move on, for he's waiting to see you."

"You shouldn't have delayed with the dictation of your
letter then, not to mention the tea and biscuits."

I grabbed up my notebook and went through the door at
the double, hearing the Houseman's voice behind me, fading
into silence as I went down the stairs two at a time.

"He's name of Mitchell. For God's sake, get rid of him.
Tell him the Path. department is too busy and that artificial
dead bones won't run away. He can come back again in a
week or two."

At the staff room, I knocked and heard a voice bid me
enter. There had been overmuch of grin on the houseman's
face and a suspicion started in my head, that it was a strange
thing to find the staff room almost empty. I slid round the
door but there was nobody there, except a man, who stood by
the fire, watching the reflection in the glass over the
mantlepiece.

I asked his forgiveness for bursting in upon him, but I was
looking for one of the medical reps. I thought that this could
not possibly be he. He was a tall, well set-up man, with hair
as bright as sunshine. I could catch the clarity and the
greenness of his eyes in the glass and my brain was clicking
over trying how to work out some way to ease myself out of
my puzzlement.

"I'm looking for Mr. Mitchell. A Houseman came to find
me. Mr. Mitchell has an appointment with Dr. Rickaby and

Dr. Rickaby has been called out urgently. You know how it is ..."

If this was Mr. Mitchell, he was like no rep. salesman I had ever seen. I met his eyes in the mirror over the fireplace and thought of my saying that I would take to keeping the biscuits in a safe, against the depradations of young physicians. It was a statement that might have decided an embryo doctor to create a most practical joke at my expense.

Maybe this was Mr. Mitchell, but I thought it most unlikely. The man had a familiar look about him and there was pride and prestige in every part of him. At any rate, I must try it out again.

"One of the doctors came to find me. He told me that there's a Mr. Mitchell here waiting to sell bones to Dr. Rickaby and that he had an appointment."

He was dressed in a tweed suit with a Norfolk jacket. His shoes were hand-made and his tie most honourable.

"He told you that *I* had come to sell bones to Dr. Rickaby!" he said in an astounded voice. "I assure you that's the last thing I'm here for. True, I had an appointment to see him, but my name's not Mr. Mitchell."

He searched about in his pocket and found a tobacco pouch. Then he started to fill a pipe and there was no hurry about it. Slowly, he got it going to his satisfaction, then he rummaged in the pouch to produce some small article.

I knew him. My God! I knew him. His name was Mitchell true enough, but that was only the first part of it. He was famous, world famous, known by millions. I had seen him on television. I should have recognised the leonine head, the crisp wavy hair, the clear bright green luminous eyes and the bristle of brows, the commanding officer cut of his moustache, the wrinkles of laughter at his temples because he smiled so much, got so much life out of life and so much joy.

"Mitchell Allington," I whispered to myself and knew that I must pay a high price for threatening to lock up biscuits against housemen, with strange senses of humour.

"Trying to sell Dr. Anthony Rickaby bones, Madame? I assure you most sincerely that it would be the last object of my seeing him."

He walked across the room and set down on the table the object he had taken from his tobacco pouch. It was some sort of small carved stone, carved in the shape of the serpent, that is the doctor tradesmark.

"Observe that, Madame. It's mine to sell but the Complex could never afford to buy it. It's very old indeed, matched against the 2–4 million years of human man. It's impossible to set a value on it. I had the good fortune to find it, or maybe it found me. It certainly made me such as I am."

"I don't know anything about archaeology," I muttered, my face dyed in shame, knowing that he must think me the greatest dud in the secretarial division. Even my voice betrayed me by turning whisper and I whispered what explanation I could think up, what apology, what excuse and made a worse job of it than ever.

"I recognise you now. You're Mitchell Allington. You must be in Camford to see the Castle site find. I think Dr. Rickaby will be out there now, and I hoped that I was to go too, but the rain was cats and dogs grade and he left me behind."

Well I knew that I sounded like a dog left home from the walk.

He was standing looking at me and taking in every last detail of the dark skirt and the white blouse with the gold cuff links, looking at my cheeks, now as white as the blouse, picking up the loneliness, that I knew lived in the back of my eyes. I wondered what a good secretary would do, for it was quite possible that Anthony had forgotten all about an appointment, that must be of great importance.

"I'm very sorry indeed for making a muddle of who you were. I'm new at the job and not good at it. Would you like me to ring the police and find out if Dr. Rickaby *is* at the site?"

"I'd prefer to stay here and talk to you. Anthony will be back any moment. He's never late and I'm early. We'll go out to the site, if he thinks it's worth it and you can come too. I've heard about you before now, but I never heard any suggestion of you being an incompetent secretary. "Liz-Jane," he calls you and he's very pleased with your work. When he arrives, we'll go out there together and tonight, we'll dine together, the three of us, if you'll accept the invitation. I believe that you're a remarkable young lady, and I am very pleased to have made your acquaintance. The least I can do is to make sure that you learn something about archaeology."

He paused and looked up through the great window towards the heavens.

"A commercial traveller in bones," he said. "Good God!"

He saw I was still uneasy and he came over to put his hands on my shoulders.

"Don't be unhappy. Anthony will be back in his Department by now. He never breaks an appointment, I told you. He'll be here by this and all set for the site again. He'll have gone along there this morning, just to get the edge on me and he'll have all sorts of scientific facts for you to put into neat typescript."

He smiled down at me and I thought that there was magic in the laser beam of his eye.

"I take it that you'll deign to come with us. After we're through the mud and all that learned talk, you'll dine with us. I insist on that as some reparation for the way people have tried to make a fool of you."

He turned the light green eyes on me and I knew that I had never met such a man. He made me feel a different person. I was attractive and full of charm and a splendid secretary and all because that was how he figured it.

"I'll take you both to dine at the Garden House and we'll have food exotic enough for the Pharoahs of Egypt. Maybe I'll talk too much to Anthony about the latest findings and maybe we'll forget all about you, but I don't think we will. I took one look at you and I knew that you weren't a person, that would be forgotten. You'd be discovered again even if it were half a thousand years hence. There's something about you ... and I have no right to be talking in such a manner, when we've just met."

We walked along the level and up the stairs to the door of the Path. Department and there was *Anthony Rickaby's* name in letters.

"He'll be inside waiting for me, yet there'll be no thought

in his mind for thee or for me. He'll be still out on what they call the Castle Site. He'll deplore the mud and the slush and the mechanical monsters, that won't let the dead sleep, but he'll be bound up in the human skeleton and its fate after "a long time in the deep-delved earth." You and I, will be two twentieth century people and if he's a bit absent-minded, don't let it bother you. He's very attracted to you and I'll make sure that he knows you're dining with us. We'll try not to talk shop over dinner but if we bore you too much, just take us to task. It's a mistake for a man to give his soul to the study of a science. There is no other soul in science to reach out to his. It will drag him down till he ends with nothing, like that great fellow pathologist of his ... only his own gas piping and his Bunsen burner and all the hall marks, that proved every classic step he took and he the most famous."

He shook himself mentally and wondered why he was taking to a child like myself in such a serious vein, "took himself to task" for it and turned the knob of the door without a "May I?"

We were in Anthony's office and I had passed some mysterious transformation stage. I was filled with a new confidence, as if magic had actually been performed upon me and I will never believe that it happened any other way. I was all wrapped protectively by the charisma of Mitchell Allington, just as if he put up a shield to shelter me, a dust dazzle of sunshine on motes that besprinkled the air. I found myself smiling at Anthony and telling him what had happened, but there was no mention of medical practical jokes. Mr. Allington had arrived and I had found him. We were all ready to go out to the Castle Hill site and look at the find. I had the sophistication of any of the top secretaries, but it had descended on me in much the same way as the Spirit sat upon the disciples. I went through the day with complete confidence. We drove out to the sea of mud, where the bones were and by then I was fully ready for my part of the expedition. I cannot remember where I appropriated them, but I had protective clothing in the form of a policeman's cape, that covered me well below the long anonymous Wellingtons, that had appeared from a Raspberry Ripple.

My pony tail was safely tucked away under a white water-
proof scarf and I was quite immune to the downpour of rain
and the skid of the mud. There was a tall young sergeant,
who held an umbrella over me and I made notes, even if they
were dry-dampish. At the end of it, there was surprise in
Anthony's eyes, when the dinner invitation was issued. It was
the most fashionable place in Camford and my heart quailed
a little. There was a strange understanding between Mitchell
Allington and myself. I had noticed how he watched me out
on the site, how he smiled when I floundered down the long
slide of a mud bank, when I had joked with my young
sergeant about the umbrella. Professor Allington had been
aware of me and I had been aware of him. Now he knew that
I was fretting about what garment I possessed that might
grace the splendid hotel. We were back at the Complex in the
Pathology Department drinking a cup of something which
was either tea or coffee. I tasted it and wrinkled my nose,
muttered that I would have to get a percolator and make our
own private brew, smiled at Allington.

He was searching about in his pockets for something and
presently he found it and it was just the same procedure as
when he had produced the stone from the tobacco pouch, but
this was a more important thing. He handled it with care. It
was in his breast pocket and it was wrapped in silk. He
unrolled a small bundle and held the contents out to me on
the palm of one hand. At first, I thought they were two long
green stones, carved with skill—jade, perhaps, though I knew
nothing of such things. Then, I saw that they were ear-rings,
most cunningly devised.

"I found these a while back. Maybe they found me. Would
you do me the honour to accept them for all your kindness
today?"

I was aghast at the magnificence of their beauty and could
only shake my head and say that I could not accept such a
present, but Anthony dismissed that and told me to stop
making a fuss.

"Wear them tonight," he said. "They're quite something
and coming from our mutual friend, they're an accolade."

"They're very old," I murmured. "They're almost cer-

tainly far too valuable. I'll take great care of them and let you
have them back tomorrow."

They were warm in my hand and they gave me a strange
feeling that maybe I could always be mistress of any situation
and that was a foreign feeling indeed to me, who had not
possessed the courage of a jack-rabbit ... and he was holding
my hand in his and the ear-rings on the palm of the hand he
held, and his eyes deep and sad for once.

"I found them in Egypt. I've got the strangest idea that
they might have belonged to you from the beginning of
civilisation. I don't want them back. Wear them in the
memory of all the dynasties, that have gone since darkness
ruled the face of the waters ..."

The whole thing was dismissed. Anthony was far more
interested in the bones from the site and in the packaging and
labelling, that had to be done. It was too late to start the
operation, so we just prepared for the morning and then left
the Complex to get ready to meet again for dinner. I arrived
home and spilled out the day's story to Kit and together we
examined the ear-rings. They had been created by some
highly skilled jeweller changed I thought, from pieces of jade,
to become sophisticated ear-rings, that screwed into the lobes
of one's ears. There was certain recent work done on them of
course but they were as old as civilisation. I can find no
words to express the beauty or the grace of the carving. More
than that, they had a power about them. I let Kit fix them in
my ears and again I felt different. My reflection in the glass
was quite changed from the person that watched me every
day. I wanted to dress in my most beautiful gown, but that
was a poor garment. Quite out of control was my brain.
There was no chance that I would put on my modest black
dress with the Peter Pan collar and wear my plain sensible
court shoes with the medium heels. Kit was infected with the
magic too. I might have been a princess of Egypt and she
might have adopted the role of slave. Yet she was slave of
many parts, understanding what I wanted, before I opened
my lips. There was a dream sequence about it and I hardly
remember how we assembled the clothes I wore, yet it was
extraordinary that first I fitted the jade ear-rings in my ears

and my eyes were two emeralds that shone back at me. Dream sequence? It was wizardry. I know the place where I lived had other young girls who lodged there, but it was Kit, who chose the borrowed finery. I found myself in an evening dress of emerald velvet, bare about the shoulders. There was a mink stole from somebody, borrowed plumage too. My hair was brushed till it gleamed and then piled up on my head to fall in ringlets along one shoulder. My evening bag was enamelled metal with a gilt lining, that flashed out a gold lighthouse lamp beam, every time I opened it.

I was some Pharoah's Queen surely, dressed for the ball, but I had no aversion to appear in such borrowed splendour, when I was only a secretary, being taken to supper. I had no fear that my two escorts might not notice me. I had no fear that they would discuss learned topics above my head and that I might sit there and crumble a roll and wish myself back in the bed-sit. with Kit and a paper of fish and chips.

We whipped round for the money for the taxi and presently I was greeted at the door of the exotic hotel by Anthony and Mitchell Allington. I believe that neither of them recognised me. I saw the surprise on Anthony's face, but Mitchell had a different demeanour. There was a great joy about him. There was something intangible that stretched between him and me as real as if a purple carpet had been laid between us. His hands went out and clasped mine and his eyes were as clear as crystal. They seemed to search my face, as if they sought out some most important thing. As for me, I was no mouse, but an attractive woman, dining with two important men and I had a strong conviction that it had all happened before. That was the strange part of it. I possessed the power to attract men and there was a half remembered dream ... gone, as I thought of it. Yet we sat there in the cocktail bar like three ordinary guests and presently went in to dine. Mitchell, put up a finger and touched one of the jade ear-rings and made it swing back and forth. He gave up the whole evening to me and refuted all discussions about the site. Maybe I was Dora Copperfield to him, for he arranged the menu to suit the taste of somebody who had never known crêpes suzettes. I might have ear-rings as old as Egypt dangling to my bare shoulders, but the waiter turned the light low and the flames that licked the pancakes in the copper pan must have flicked shadows about my darkened cheeks. There was something in his eyes, as he watched me that I had never seen in any man's eyes. I tried to include Anthony in the circle of magic, for if ever there was magic, it was here, being spooned gently with grace by a soft-spoken Italian waiter, but it was impossible to gather Anthony. He was away somewhere in his own thoughts, yet he watched us gravely. With hindsight, I know that he saw what was happening and wanted to cry halt. There was no power on earth could stop it. Maybe Mitchell had seen me and I had seen him, away down the years and perhaps we had been washed up on antique shores and there were memories that would not be caught like butterflies in a net. I had not thought it an extraordinary thing to take the ear-rings and wear them and they were some token of pass down the corridor of time. Maybe they had been mine before. It was all happening like water running down a deep silent river. It was as natural as rain falling from the sky and there was no putting it back again. The sweet liqueur of the crêpes was putting dreams into my head, dreams that came from Rider Haggard and She, dreams of the Rameses, Pharoahs of Egypt, dead filigreed in gold.

Tomorrow, I must return the carved green stones, that touched my naked shoulders, but tomorrow never came and the magic stayed. There was no moment when I fell out of love with one man and into love with another. Perhaps it did not happen that way. Anthony was a ghost that faded, faded. Mitchell took substance and sailed like a comet across my skies, through a path of stars. Yet it happened so naturally that there was no surprise about it. I had met him and I was in love with him. I had always been in love with him and I would love him till the end of time. When golden lads and lassies find love, these are common thoughts, that often come to nothing. Yet in love I was and married to Mitchell Allington. One day, I found myself on a plane to Cairo on our honeymoon. It had come about so quickly, that there was a speed about it that did not acknowledge time. So much had happened, yet it seemed so little. It was quite impossible that I was Mrs. Mitchell Allington and that Anthony had kissed me goodbye at the airport. I felt pain at the emptiness in Anthony's eyes and the deep sorrow, wondered if I were the cause of it. I forgot him. God forgive me! I forgot him. He was swept into the past and I turned to face the future. Late that evening, Mitchell stood on the balcony of our suite and watched the sky, his back to the room. My velvet slippers made no noise as I stepped out into a night of stars. The chiffon of my nightgown brushed the sill of the window, as I went to stand with him. His voice was so low that I could hardly hear what he said and he was quite unaware of my presence.

"In such a night

Stood Dido with a willow in her hand

Upon the wild sea banks, and waft her love

To come again to Carthage ..."

"In such a night," I agreed softly and he turned slowly. His eyes were brilliant in the light from the room and he spoke before he thought what he said.

"You came so soon. I've been waiting for you. There were times when I thought it a dream, but it was no dream. You're mine and I'm yours, but I think it all happened before ... a long time ago. This time maybe there will be no tragedy of parting—and I'll stride eternity with your hand in mine."

3

THE GLITTER-DUST

Life is a rare old mixture of happiness and misery, of exhaltation and despair, of sun days and stormy days. Perhaps life is the biggest patchwork of all emotions, stitched into an indescribable pattern. Maybe I learned the unimportance of the individual from Mitchell Allington, for he introduced me to archaeology and made folly of my perspectivce. In my ignorance, I considered we were of some importance. I know I was mouse-humble, but there had been pride about me too, pride about my generation. We were a fine people. We knew it all. We were learning more every day. Had we not gone to the moon and come back again? We had discovered half the wonders of science. We were an ancient civilisation, completely superior to any peoples who had lived before ...

"We're only at the beginning," Mitchell smiled at me. "The human race has existed for a mere one or two million years ... maybe three or four. Civilised, we go back only a few thousand. We're beginners on the earth. Take the dinosaurs. My God above! They lived for one hundred and forty million years and there was no animal to compete with them. They were the successful ones, with brains very small, as reptiles go and with bodies that were enormous, and make what you like of that."

He hypnotised me with archaeology. There had been years past and gone. There had been ages, ages, ages—traces left behind ... ice, stone, bronze ...

My mind could not take in the capacity of his knowledge, but he had infinite patience with me. There might be millions and billions and trillions of years yet to come. Yet he had a strange conviction that love was the strongest power in the universe. Perhaps I comprehended one hundreth part of his vision. I could come to terms with computers and space travel and the proof of examining fossils from animals, that had lived an impossibly long time before the first man, but Mitch had a strange obsession that he and I had lived before, had been lovers, just as we were that first night. It explained the quotation from Shakespeare, "Dido, with a willow in her hand upon the wild sea banks."

We were drunk with love that first night and perhaps I imagined most of the things he said, for surely it could be only a dream that we had loved each other and had lost each other ... that we could have met again and loved again.

"Don't you remember, not even a wisp from an ancient dream, not only from one dynasty to another, but refusing to be lost, because our love was the more powerful?"

I shook my head at him and laughed, told him that it was impossible that I could ever have forgotten him.

"If I had lain in your arms, as I have tonight, how could I ever forget?"

I was unpractised in the arts of love, but he brought me such ecstasy, that I imagined that heaven could produce nothing to match it. On the edge of sleep at last, I believed what he said might have some truth. I was his and he was mine. Life was a gold carpet laid down for us to tread. We would stay together in peace and love. I was not very worried if I had lived before. It was a romantic thought, but I hardly expected myself to have been Cleopatra, who had had the purple sails on her barge. Surely swallows could never have nested in sails? I laughed at that idea till Mitch was quite put out with me and told me that perhaps I had no soul. It seemed quite impossible that I could ever produce a soul from the underworld, time after time, or have hand, act, or part in reincarnation.

Then after a time, I wondered. He was a brilliant man. He was one of the foremost archaelogists in the world. He must understand antiquity. Maybe he was right in the theories he produced.

I got a wraith of what he meant one day when we were on

a dig in Suffolk. It was Roman fort stuff and he had Cambridge University students with him. These particular ones spent their vacation trailing round in his shadow, very honoured, that he was so gracious as to put up with them. They were good too and took care not to damage the precious mosaic he was after. It was very laborious and there was skill and patience and gentleness wanted. I was rather bored with it, but I confess that it was because there was a very pretty girl, who practically threw herself into his arms. She seemed to spend all the time, thinking up intelligent questions to ask Mitch and he was very short with her. I could not bear her hurt in the rebuffing and I wandered off a little. It was a grassy place, smooth sheared by sheep.

"There you see the animal that will endure, ladies and gentlemen," Mitch was saying. "That animal will graze on the site of King's Chapel, Cambridge, when there is not one stone left on another. There will be grass and sheep cropping and maybe Pan with his pipes, playing an ageless melody down by that river you have on the Backs."

I walked off by myself and I think that I agreed with him. In the world today, was such threat to the future. The press of a switch, the push of a button, might send the whole earth, as we know it, swooping down the skies, like the swallows might have swooped round Cleopatra's barge. I walked on in thought. Then, I felt my senses blur, I felt faint memory stir. I remembered ... Yet how could I remember? I had never been here in this place before, yet I knew beyond much doubt that if I walked straight across the grassy turf, presently I would reach a pool of water. It was a fish pool, oblong and surrounded by a low wall of granite stones. The stones should be ivy clad and leaves floating in the water. There must be carp, that swam there, so lazy, so tame, that they could nibble your fingers. The sun was shining the motes into a kind of glitter-dust.

I walked on and there was nothing, only a wall a good way ahead, a wall with an arch, all ruined and used for nothing. It seemed to have no purpose and I could hear Mitch in the ear of my mind.

"And why must everything have a purpose, for God's sake?"

Then I almost fell into the pool. Sure enough, there was water, but the low wall had lowered itself into the edge and the water was shallow and weedy. The carp had gone the way of all living things. It was lucky that I was not seeking to catch fish, but I caught something far more important. There had been fish there long ago. I had remembered them. There had been monks, in brown habits, walking two by two with their hands tucked into their sleeves and their heads bent into humility. Fast days, Lent, Friday every week, these were the lean times. The feast days were for wine from the cellars and for venison and maybe swine from the fen, with crackling from the upturned spit—crackling just as welcome to hunger then as it is today.

The wall with the arch was farther on, fallen on evil days too. I knew it for the side of the cathedral, but it was not mentioned in any guide book. The small portion of wall and the arch ... the same sort of arch I had seen at Ely. I had no idea of history and Mitch would have been very sad about me.

There was still a brightness in the air, a sharpness round the edges of this mind picture. If I walked through the arch, there was a place of graves all set out carefully and tended with love. There should be some marks to the graves and maybe a fine statue, all with Christ's mark. I was through the arch and looking along a field, as smooth as the sheep could make it. There were no mounds and no epitaphs carved on stone, yet I had an unseen diviner's rod and I paced to a place and knew that it was my own grave. If I had a spade, and dug, I might find something to overcome my doubts of being born again and living again. There should be a cross there, but it had rusted away. There had been a stone and it was gone. They had taken it for a mounting block in the Inn Yard, but my man was dead by then. Else they would not have dared to do it. Cromwell had made waste of the place. He had sacked the whole town. There was terror all around me and the smell of burning thatch. There were small motes of soot that floated, from the burning of the roof of the cathedral and the cottages had been afire too and there was such sadness that my heart was heavy with it, and the dazzle dust gone.

The wind whistled across the flat earth and I heard Mitch's voice. There was no doubt about it, for I knew it well, and he was earnest and pleading with me. Before he spoke, almost I heard him speak.

"Don't go away, I'll be with you soon. We're almost finished here but we'll come again."

I was asleep, with my back against the ruined wall. He had thought me gone, till he walked through the arch. I had dreamed a dream or maybe I had seen a vision. He had come to find me and here we were, right in the centre of modern civilisation.

I made him no wiser about what I had experienced. I did not believe it myself. I tucked my arm in his and was alive again and happy again and there had been no terror all about me and the town was not burning. There was no town left to burn and the inhabitants were at rest. Even the monks were gone and fast days mattered no more than feast days, but I knew I had been there, or thought I knew it. I switched my mind off the past and on to the future and took up the present, like a piece of embroidery I had put down, and so we went on living the good life and we knew perfect happiness, him in me and I in him —and should have lived happily ever after.

Nobody married to Mitch could have been anything but happy. I had never known such an existence to be possible. I was the wife of a world famous archaeologist and we travelled down the years together.

Now and again, with a few million others, I watched him on Television and he had as high a rating as any star of film or stage. He was a bright comet. The public loved him. I would watch him on the small screen and think how he loved me and I loved him. Yet we lived alone in a crowded planet and neither of us wanted anybody but the other. "When they go home, we're happy," Mitch would say and that was how it was for us both.

A base was essential. Mitch lost no time about finding one.

The first time we went to the States, we visited Father and with no word to me, Mitch bought the house in Histington. He put the deeds in my hand and told me this was his wedding present to me. This was our home.

"No, your father isn't upset to get rid of it."

I read in his eyes that he understood the relationship between Father and myself ... that Father was just as glad to get rid of me—knew that Father had found his niche in life. Mitch knew what unhappiness I had suffered in Shangri La.

It was he, who changed the name of the house again. It should never have been changed in the first place and Shangri La was an iniquitous name for it. He understood that it would be bad taste to call it Rowan Tree House again. That might sin against my dead mother. There was a lovely rowan tree in the front garden and in Ireland, Rowans were called "quicken trees".

"So now we'll live at 'The Quicken Tree' and we'll set our base there and it will be the centre of the world."

It became a happy place, a refuge from the bright light of public glare. It had deep arm chairs and soft carpets, a fine old four-poster bed and rich velvet curtains. The kitchen was totally reconstructed, yet it was not aggressively chromium and white paint. There were hand-made wall tiles and a dresser with green Wedgewood plates and a wag o' the wall clock and a rocking chair. The whole house was warm against the winters and cool against a too hot summer's day and we both felt happier there than anywhere else, but we spent far too little time there. There was always too much to do. We trekked around the world from lecture to conference, to this dig and that, to open some charitable thing in aid of one society or another. I had no time to collect friends. We never stayed long in one place. Kit, of the bed-sit. days, was the one person I clung to. She still worked at the Camford General Hospital and as often as we returned to Histington, I sought her out. It was the first time we stayed at the Quicken Tree, with all the alterations done and with the builders moved out, that she paid her initial visit.

Mitch had made his excuses early to leave us in peace for our chatter. He was in the study upstairs and he defied us to interrupt him till tea was ready. Kit told me about Anthony Rickaby almost at once, in a conspirator's whisper too.

"Dr. Rickaby's gone to Canada on some super research scholarship. It's quite an achievement. I expect he'll settle there."

"I didn't know. His father didn't say anything about it. He acted as solicitor for us about the house. I'd have thought he'd have told us. Of course, Anthony'll come home."

"He's got a job there with a dozen times more scope that the Camford General. The money for research runs in the gutters out there, not squeezed like tooth paste out of an empty tube, as it is here. You won't see him again. He loved you and he took it hard that he lost you. The whole hospital knew he loved you. Golly! I told you!"

There was a sharp sorrow that I must keep hidden. Had I not seen the look in his eyes at the airport? I had loved him. There was a small part of me that might love him for ever, even if I never saw him again. My love for him was like a flower pressed in a book, found again, after the years had gone. Anthony would meet somebody a thousand times better than I. I wanted the story to end happily for him, because it had ended so happily for me. Kit was looking at me suspiciously and I must make light of the whole affair. I passed it off and we talked about the hospital and after a while Mitch came down from the study and knelt on the hearth rug and toasted muffins for our tea. I can imagine nothing more comfortable and safe and enjoyable, as that room in front of the fire with the smell of toasting muffins lifting to our nostrils. There was some site he was investigating and he told us about it. I hoped that he was not boring Kit by his scientific talk, but when it came to archaeology, it was impossible for him to be boring. He could make any facet of it sparkle and he did it now ... told us all about a group of islands, that he had in mind. They were called the Orcades and they were on the other side of the world.

"They're flat islands, rather like the Orkneys and they're similar to the Orkneys, with chambered cairns and burial mounds and that sort of thing. It's strange that Pliny called the Scots Orkneys, 'the Orcades' ... maybe it's a good omen."

I was thinking about Anthony Rickaby. I missed a deal he told us about the islands and a few hours later, I was hearing Dr. Rickaby's name again.

We had left Kit back at the Hospital, where she lived in now. We drove into Camford and deposited her at the door of the Residence and the porter recognised us.

"The last time you were here, Professor, your friend, Dr. Rickaby was still in Pathology, but he's gone abroad to Canada—won an exhibition, some high-up post. It was soon after you and Miss Grant were married. Of course, you'll know all about it."

Mitch looked at me sharply and I wondered what he was thinking. He watched me closely and I was aware of his watching.

"It was strange his father didn't mention it," he said on the way home and I said that I expected that Mr. Rickaby thought we knew all about it.

"But *you* didn't know?" he pursued and I said that Kit had told me only that afternoon. I passed it all off very lightly or thought I did and as soon as we got back to the Quicken Tree, I asked him about the Orcades. It was as if I had thrust a torch into a pile of dry wood. He blazed with enthusiasm and in no time at all, he had an air map spread out on the table, kept flat at the edges by books.

"There's your first view of the Orcades," he said and bent his head to look at the shadows cast by the burial mounds.

They were a great many islands but one of them was circled by black marker ink.

"That's the one," he said and I saw the green of the island and the blue of the sea, saw the way the sea had made inroads into the land.

"There should be estuaries and coves—good place for swimming."

He called me a Philistine and told me that he was thinking of making me responsible for some of the preparation. He was introducing me to archaeology, like the head of a chain of hotels teaches his only son and heir the business. I was being put on in the ground floor as kitchen boy. I had had several menial posts already.

"I want you to do a bit of research like Rickaby," he smiled.

I looked at the map and wondered what the future held in store for us. Then I wandered off and sat in one of the big chairs and I was sleepy after a long day.

"I was thinkng just now when I toasted the muffins, that prehistoric man cooked his food just so."

He was still joking and I watched him as he took one of the uneaten muffins from the trolley. He wandered off into the garden and came back with a stick and presently he was whittling the stick to a point with his pen-knife, spearing the muffin, squatting on the hearth rug again with the muffin held to the flames.

I was not in a mood for laughter. I was too bound up with the Orcades and my mind was still in the grass green islands, yet I watched him and presently, his outline was blurred. It was an apt impression of the days that were long gone. Almost I saw him, squatted there with an animal hide over his shoulders. Almost I saw him spear the meat and hold it to the fire. Then he was shaking me by the shoulder.

"Wake up, Liz-Jane. Are you all right?"

I told him that I was tired and I had probably gone asleep in the midst of his learned discourse.

"There was no learned discourse. We were just talking about the Orcades, and one of them in particular."

Again, his finger caressed the encircled map island and I looked down at it.

"The island," he said.

I asked him the name of it and he told me "Patanga". It was the first time I had heard it mentioned.

"Patanga," I said and wondered how I had thought his sophisticated self could possibly have resembled pre-historic man. "What does 'Patanga' mean?"

"It's a native word. It means 'the island of death'. There's a jinx about it, a kind of tabu. None of the inhabitants of the Orcades will set foot on it. It's totally uninhabited, but that's good for us, just as long as they give us permission to dig there. That's all we want. They won't go meddling with the work. Of course we'll have to bring labour."

"The island of death," I said. "I don't like it."

He assured me that it meant nothing. I must not be put off by the superstitions of sub-civilisation. Anything could explain the death business. It might have been closed to the other islands initially because it was the main burial place. More likely something quite simple had happened. Say that a ship put in there to water or careen ... centuries ago and maybe it should have had the yellow flag at its mast ... fever. The crew could have broadcast the infection. God above! The sailors might even had something like measles, that had never met a race with no immunity whatever. The islanders could have died, man, woman and child. The ship would be away and to leave a dark island and a darker legend.

"Do you think that any Orcadian would put foot on Patanga again? Along the years, the tabu would have held. The world is full of such places and I'd not start to worry about it tonight. For one thing, it will be a few years before we start on the trip. We have a deal of plans for the future and Patanga must wait."

Yet I thought back to the way he had squatted by the fire and toasted a muffin on a stick, how I had had the same strange blurring of the senses, as I had had at the dig in Suffolk—how almost I had seen him, crouched with an animal skin for warmth, maybe three thousand years ago. I had a misery about me and I wished that he had not picked out a land with such a threat in its name. Granted I was superstitious too, but there was a pricking in my thumbs about the expedition to the Orcades. He noticed it too but he said nothing. The sun was shining into the room and the fears of last night had gone.

He challenged me with worrying about Patanga.

"I assure you there is no cause for concern, but I'd not have you unhappy about it. We'll put if off. There's the rest of the world and we have our whole lives before us."

We wrangled for a while and I refused to allow him to change his plans. It became a joke, and we decided to toss for it. I was accustomed to his habit of carrying various "finds" in his pockets and now he took out a strange copper coin.

"Patanga or no Patanga? You shout!" he laughed. "It's Caesar's head, if you're calling heads."

I called "Heads" and he sent the coin spinning to the ceiling. I picked it up from the carpet and examined the stern face of a Roman emperor. It was strange that it had been left to a Roman emperor to decide whether we went to "the island of death" or not, but I did not know that morning how the single throw influenced my life much more deeply than I could ever imagine. No matter how hard I strained my eyes against the gauze of time, I could see no shadow of Anthony Rickaby, and it was an extraordinary thing that I thought of him then. Surely he had passed into forgetfulness. Anyhow, he would have no interest in what path my feet trod now.

The memory of the dinosaurus flashed for a moment in my thoughts too. It must have seemed to be an everlasting beast, far more important than a Roman emperor. Yet Caesar had just decided to give a thumbs-up to "Patanga". One of these days, I must assemble some books and start research on the Orcades—and the thought of research brought back Anthony Rickaby and I wondered what he was doing in Canada and if he was ever homesick for England, for the Elizabethan House in the High Street of Histington down the road from "The Quicken Tree".

4

PATANGA

Perhaps I had never known happiness till my marriage. I had had a strange childhood with no mother to be Mary, Queen of Heaven, to me. I had never had anybody to love me best in all the world, no gentle loving lady, who knew that I was flesh of her flesh and blood of her blood ... to put it more simply, as Kit would, who suffered more when I had to visit the dentist than I did myself, but then dentists are not supposed to hurt nowadays. I know that the umbilical cord is never sundered ... that mother and child are one flesh till the grave's edge, I consider it a great deprivation, never to have had this union with another mortal. I had grown up like a stray cat. I had learnt to shed my tears in private. I know it to be a sad way to grow up and I pity all orphans. I was number one child for nobody in the world, till I met Mitch and married him and then a whole ocean of tenderness and love burst over me. He was father, mother, brother, sister, family—above all husband, lover, protector and friend. I walked now in a different world. Heaven could have been no happier. Maybe I sometimes thought of Anthony Rickaby, but Mitch was Mitch. He was older than I was. He had not the impatience a young man might have had with my unsophistication. He treated me with kindness and gentleness. He delighted in my youth and enthusiasm and energy. There was a perfection about our life together. I was quite sure that if I were to die and go to heaven, yes, if that came about, I would kneel at the feet of God and pray to return to earth—this earth, that Mitch had created for me and with no thought of the first chapter of Genesis in my mind. That was how it was when we set out for the Orcades and by then some years had passed. I had plenty of time to research the islands and I knew this was to be a sizeable expedition.

It was set up in Camford. From there we planned the journey and assembled the equipment. From there we contacted all the learned institutions. From there went out orders for "ships and shoes and sealing wax and cabbages and kings"—and for best preserved food supplies from Fortnum and Mason's. We ordered geological hammers and many other specialised tools of the trade. We booked tickets and planned river trips. We checked all clothing and replaced anything that was not completely serviceable. We showed budding archaeologists the radio carbon dating device, invented by Libby, Professor of Chicago University in 1949. It could determine the date of organic material by reference to the content of radio active carbon the material had. It had revolutionised Archaeology and it was one of the advantages that "atom power" had,—this by-product of war and peace.

I could go on for a long time with the list of all the preparations, but they would be small interest to anybody. We picked a score of graduates and undergraduates, out of about sixty, keen to take part.

Mitch and I lived in the Quicken Tree during the time of preparation. It was so close to Camford and Camford was Sherlock Holmesian. We preferred it to London. The plans ran so smoothly that it seemed too good to be true. We had been married five years on the eve of setting off and we gave a splendid farewell dinner in the house. There was no doubt that we were setting out with high hearts. I will never forget that evening, with the guests assembled round the table. I will never forget the toasts and the erudition of the humour—never forget the young faces bright with the joy of life—never forget the excitement and the anticipation. There was no thought that anything might go wrong. We were booked into success and success would be ours. Life was a primrose path of sunshine. We were walking down it together and we were not like ordinary mortals. We sought out adventure. We walked tall. We travelled the earth and the earth was ours to explore. The earth was ours ...

It all went so well. There was no hitch in any part of the

journey. There was no baggage lost and no single person late for any part of the trip. All the stores were complete and in the places, where bearers were necessary, bearers were there in plenty. Nobody slacked, no two undergrads fell in love with the same "sweet girl graduette". Nobody got heat stroke or chickenpox or malaria. Not one person complained about a sore arm after inoculations. This expedition was impossibly perfect. We were twenty two people, maybe a little tired perhaps, but so content with our own capabilities for efficiency, that Mitch muttered under his breath to me, that it was too good to last.

I knew it myself, but if I did not say it, nothing would go wrong. I had been on many expeditions by this. I was a seasoned campaigner and I had never known a trip, where there had been no disasters. Natives would refuse to take us up river, because of some superstition. When we opened a tomb, our local workmen would go missing. There would be one tabu or another. If one opened the tomb, a great curse would fall on the people. Some government official would turn up at the last moment and the whole thing be cancelled, and we would strike camp and go home.

Yet our expeditions had been very successful. I was a good luck piece, Mitch said, but never so powerfully had my good luck quality worked till now. This was what archaeology should always be, with the islanders of the Orcades only too delighted that we go where we wanted and dig where we pleased. Anything we wished to take away with us was ours. There was nothing on Patanga that anybody wanted. It if pleased us to find it, it was ours, whatever we sought, yet no man, woman or child of the islands could set foot on Patanga. For them, the island was bad. It had been cast out of the family. It was a place for the dead only and this was the rule of them all.

I had been married over five years when I stood on the ship, that had brought us there and looked across the thrown down green counters of the Orcades. Some of the others had gone with Mitch to pay respects to the chief and bring the gifts from over the seas. It was all so much common politeness and there was great ceremony about it. I should have liked to go with them, but a woman was not allowed "in the council seats". There was no such thing as "woman's lib." In politeness, I might have had to squat in the full sun outside the Council Hall on the main island and it was losing face for the expedition if "the woman of the white professor" appeared in such lèse majesté, Mitch assured us.

The craft we travelled was like a ferry across the Humber, a ferry that was well past service and had not been repaired or painted for twenty years. I stood and leaned against the rail and wondered how Britain ever had the cruelty to sell her old ships to foreign bondage. There should be some place for old tired ships. Better if they had sunk them in Scapa Flow and let the money go hang. Why lower them to peoples, who had no idea of the glory of ships? I stood at the rail therefore and sulked a little and gazed over the Orcades and was cheered with them. I had seen Lismore in the Hebrides—the island of no mountains and no trees. Here before me, I had gathered a flotilla of Lismores, the same well-grazed flattish islands with no trees, but there were low hills, that must be the burial mounds and a great number of these on Patanga. Patanga was different from the other islands and I had a good view of them all. The sea had run inlets into Patanga as if it searched for something that was not to be found. There were coves and fiords and the estuaries, all alive with sea birds. There were sandy beaches, silver against the green grass. The mounds were silent. Anyhow I could hear no sound with the wash of the sea, but I knew that the grave mounds were silent. I knew that they had been silent so long a time, that they had lost the sense of sound. They were too calm and the grass was billiard-table-smooth. The birds on Patanga were unafraid of man. I might not be standing near one of the holy places, but I knew that my ear would not hear sound, nor know unrest. Here were the places of the dead, unvisited, deserted, unexplained, but of tremendous anti-quity—almost beyond the understanding of man—unless we were successful.

There was a retired doctor in the complement of the expedition. His wife had died and he had been due to retire from his general practice. He had left England very willingly

and he was one of the most philosophical men and I had ever
met. I had picked him out for special friendship for I knew
how he missed his wife and he was odd man out in all that
youth and enthusiasm. On the trip out, we had had long
conversations or had sat silently and we had learned how to
talk to each other in silence. I had experienced how kind a
stranger can be. By now, we were confidantes and old
friends. He had time to spare for me, when Mitch was busy.
He came now to stand beside me at the rail. It was a pleasant
day, not too hot and not cold. His eyes were moody as he
looked at Patanga and we started to talk the eternal topic of
us all that had been discussed from start to finish of our
journey.

"It's a bonny place. They said the other night that mebbe
it were left empty because of reverence for the dead, but the
dead are soon forgotten by them that are nae their ain kin. I'd
say there was disaster here. There's no possible chance of a
Pompeii, but it was something like that ... a wrath from the
Gods, like a mist that came up one night out of the sea. Here
was an island that was destroyed. That's my bet. There was a
sickness, and you can take any guess you like at what it
was ... maybe something that had never been in civilisation
yet. It left the land empty and left enough fear to the rest of
the isles, so that no other man, woman nor bairn ever would
turn the bow of a boat in on yon bonny shore ... and from
one mouth to another it passed, down a lang while, a
thousand years or two, and the fear growing in the breast ...
not fading away."

I was tired of the subject of the isolation of Patanga. I was
glad to see Mitch's boat pulling back to the ship and soon he
had come on board.

"There's no objection to our starting tomorrow. We'll get
the stuff off smartish. We'll open up the burial mound we
agreed on and we'll go in along the side first, as we
planned ... a shallow trench. Then we'll strike down
through the top of the mound itself and come into the burial
chamber, right in the centre gold of the target. If we don't
make history on this dig, at least history to match the Scots
Orkneys, then I'm way off."

That night over supper, he dipped his finger in his glass of wine and drew a circle on the white table cloth ... dipped it again and blobbed in a spot in the circle. It only took a third time to dip his finger and then he was marking in the radius running from circumference to centre.

"You all know how they did it in the Orkneys. We take a trench of top soil along that line and we examine the strata. We want to know who's been there before. We take out the stuff carefully and we're looking to see if we really are the first and I truly believe we are. When we have the trench out we go to the heart."

He looked round our faces and his eyes came to rest on my face, no less enthusiastic it was than any other there. His arm rested on my shoulders and then the index finger of his left hand lit on the spot in the circle's centre, hit the cloth with a sharp impact.

"We strike down plumb centre and we'll go slowly and carefully, for here's where we find what we're after. Here was the burial chamber. I've told you how they made the walls. There were no arches, just horizontal stones, piled into what we'll call dry walls nowadays in Welsh Wales. If an arch was necessary, it was a trestle that held the dry wall on its shoulders ..."

He demonstrated what he meant by putting a straight arm on my shoulder.

"There's the top strata of your dry wall and there's your horizontal. It would hold up the whole world."

His elbows were on the table now, supporting his chin.

"It's been a long time and our radio carbon dating miracle will tell us how long. I tell you that the splitting of the atom will save the earth and not destroy it. Atomic gadgetry tells us how many years a man's lain dead, be it four thousand, it will not hold the secret from us. God only knows what we'll find there. If you're after treasure, there may be graven images beyond price. Think of Egypt. There may be things not yet dreamed of waiting here."

He was filled with excitement and he carried us with him. He was sparkling with confidence and fulfilment. Had not the hour come?

Dr. Brown sat on the other side of me and his head inclined to mine. His whisper barely reached my understanding.

"He knows well that there's another side to it. You can find ither things in places like this. The puir wee rabbits were innocent enough. They played about the grassy banks and hedges. They delighted a child's heart in picture books. Walt Disney put an innocence upon them, made them the perfect cuddly toy. The farmers did na think much of them, but a creature has to live. What harm a few grains of wheat? Yet Satan stole myxomatosis from the Lord and laid it on them, like one of the plagues of Egypt. He banished them from the earth, with a wee microbe, that was as powerful as Mitch's dinosaurus ... virtually. There's nothing to say we'll find something in the bottom of the pit and that is a good name for it. It might banish man from the earth, the way it banished Orcadians from Patanga. It's not impossible. We'd best pick our way with care down yon shaft."

He shook his head as if he were impatient with himself and begged me to take no notice of him.

"This ship's well provisioned. Who'd have thought they'd feed us so well in this God-forsaken spot, but we'll rough it once we go ashore. I've had too much Highland Dew tonight for my ain good. It's the best medicine in the world if you've got memories to drown, but when they've drowned, there's a way they have of springing up like dragon's teeth and tearing the heart out of your breast."

I reached for his hand and took it into mine and hoped I comforted him and never knew that in a short while, it would be my hand reaching for his, to comfort me.

In the morning early, the operation of disembarkation started. The sun came up from below the world and the day with it and there was a patch that ran across the water, that was gleaming and golden and looked so solid that we might walk upon it. A mile off, in a flotilla in the sea, were the native canoes, primitive craft, made of tree bark, such as Robin Crusoe might have made. There were perhaps twenty of them, all held silently and motionlessly and one more ornate than the others. They sat there and watched us and

made no sign of any kind. They had tried to dissuade the
white man, but it was of great importance to him, if he dug
on Patanga and he had no fear. White men were not afraid of
the old gods. He had brought rich gifts to the islands, things
such as they had never seen. There was wisdom in the head
of the white chief. He had proved it. They had a thing called
a wheel and now they had not to draw a loaded sled on two
sticks. He had shown them something he called a ladder
too ... It was without number the wisdoms he held in his
head. It was a great sorrow that he had not the wisdom to
keep his foot from Patanga.

Always they sat and watched what we were doing, but
never once did they interfere with us and at last, we came to
forget they were there. Now and again, we recalled their
presence and sometimes, some of us would row over to them
and bring them some of the miracles of our century. They
were solemn and awed, yet delighted like children at so many
simple things ... tinned food, fruit preserved in bottles, a
knife sharpener, that was just a wheel that turned ...
mirrors, fishing tackle, a mask to cover the face so that
swimming under the sea was child's play, fish flippers, that
fastened on the feet made a man swim like a fish.

On shore, we set up camp. It was not the hot season. We
planned the settlement near the mound we were to open. We
brought all the mechanical equipment in from the ship. We
seemed to have usual British Army camp-style. As for dress,
we wore denim shorts and shirts. Perhaps we looked like an
army unit in matured faded blue and in white and in khaki
drill. The climate was temperate and the season smiled on us.
I can see Mitch in khaki shorts, his rope-soled shoes
immaculate, his open throated shirt fresh from the iron, his
face as well shaven as if he was due for an investiture at
Buckingham Palace, and always the hair making brightness
round his head, always the light green sea eyes, as deep as
seas always are and luminous, with fish too that swam in
them, of sheer joy in life and humour, with love for me.
Perhaps there was a trace of Montgomery in him, for there
was spit and polish and no sign of slacking. There was a
standard and that must be held.

What use is it to go on? I can see it, if I shut my eyes, the camp near the smooth green mound—the mound maybe fifty yards across. The khaki canvas of the tents gave it all a camouflaged atmosphere. Inside, were the stretcher beds, the tables, the mosquito netting, the electric lamps, that worked from our own dynamo, the water jar, that somehow kept the water cool, the shower to wash, the sleeping bags, the black box with the first aid kit ...

There were two sleeping tents and a mess tent, a special oblong laboratory place lit brightly, where specimens were to be taken for scrutiny and package, where the log was written and notes made, where all the important business of the expedition to be carried on. It was all so like all the other digs I had been on. This one I only wish I could blot out of my brain, but it will never be blotted out, till God in his mercy blots everything out for me.

Picture it then, with its army atmosphere and its youth and enthusiasm and its cheerfulness, yet seriousness too. See Mitch, the day we started the digging, agile and young, at the slicing of the first sod of the first section of the radial trench. Above all I look at the flap, flap, flapping of the empty tents.

"Let's see if anybody's been here before us. I'd guess not ... not for a great many hundreds of years. May good luck go with us!"

So we opened up a deepish trench along the radius of the mound. Slowly and laboriously and with incredible care, we opened it and we sieved every ounce of the soil we took out. We peeled off the grass in a layer and rolled it and put it aside to replace it. In the earth we found nothing, just good fertile soil and a stone or a pebble, but nothing of note, just part of the side of a little hill, that had lain undisturbed for a long time. It might have grown vines. It might have been a place where sheep grazed and gave their wool and so gave clothing. Almost certainly there had been sheep and lambs and fleece and milk, but we found no clue.

All the time, the canoes stood off shore and watched us and the men were impassive. Not once did they approach the island. Not once did they attempt to communicate with us. I said to Mitch that perhaps they thought we would find treasure. If we came up with gold, it was like we would have our throats slit and our treasure stolen and our bodies sunk in the sea.

Mitch was quite shocked at that.

"It's not gold we're after. Surely you understand that? Gold's nothing. It's knowledge we're seeking ... knowledge of what the world was like thousands of years ago. You disappoint me, Liz-Jane. They're curious out there and they intend no harm to come to Patanga. It's a holy place. They seem to think that we're some sort of supernatural people with all our paltry modern magicians' tricks. They allowed us to dig, because of that. They trust us and they implored us that we do not go ahead with the dig, for our own safety. They wish good to us, not harm ... They're simple people, and there's no evil in them. This place has got a sameness to the garden of Eden before the serpent. We'll not change that. They are waiting to see us go our way in peace and in friendship."

We struck down through the centre of the mound on the thirteenth day. We had found nothing so far, at least not any great find. Now we hoped to hit the actual burial chamber and excitement was frothing the camp. We must go carefully now, layer by slow layer and every ounce of earth searched and sieved, every solid piece of stone put in a plastic container and labelled, packed away with as much care as if the Crown jewels were involved.

I have no wish to describe what we found, but it must have been an archaeologist's dream. Perhaps the mound was thirty feet tall in the centre, sloping down gradually to the perimeter. It is soon told and I am sure, over the years to come, there will be many accounts of it. Perhaps these sheets of written paper are all that will ever be seen by future archaeologists but maybe mine has no importance over those the experts will write. I only remember Mitch's excitement, hardly controlled as we reached the top of the stone chamber, maybe four feet down. It was roofed by slabs of solid rock, cut about nine inches thick and so placed that they held up the earthen roof. The chamber was walled with what I call dry stone, of cut rock, like planks, and upheld by horizontal rock sections, that, as Mitch had said would uphold the whole world.

"No light has ever shone here, no light as we understand it today."

He had taken a reading and he knew that we counted in thousands not hundreds. We were back to the beginnings of man. There might have been the light of the sun or of fire, sheep's tallow burning on shell perhaps, but down here at the bottom of the mound, when we had removed the slab roofing, light did not readily percolate. Our dynamo driven electric light was one of the modern wonders and the electric torches were not to be understood, yet we lit that deep underground with a bright radiance, stronger than the sun in the sky. I felt like Prometheus who had stolen fire from the gods.

There was a smell of dust and decay, air, long forgotten, an indescribable smell, but with no unpleasantness about it, a smell, that had been put away and forgotten, like a flower in a book, I thought, and in a flash remembered Anthony and wondered what he would think of the place, and where he was.

There was other chambers that lay off the main one, but these were narrow and far lower in height, like passages might be. Perhaps they led from outside in, for as they ran towards the edge of the mound, they got lower till they reached earth level.

We stood there in silence for a long time and looked at the contents of the mound, as if we would write down each detail in our minds and never forget it and that is just what I did. Anthony might have been taken up with the study of jurisprudence. Mitch must have been involved in bones and here were bones, if that was what you sought. There was debris of course, from so many dead years. It had to be brushed away gently in parts, but there was not so much as one might expect. The stone walls had kept the dead inviolate to any debris but their own. There were a great many bones and they lay different ways ... some in an orderly manner, with arm bones along the sides and with foot bones stretched out, what remained of them. Then there were disordered heaps of odd bones, maybe, as if a body had been left standing and had shrunk down and down, till it disintegrated to a thing with no order whatever. There were bones, that seemed not to belong to anything but themselves, a foot perhaps, with something, that might be leather moulded around about it. There was a skull and long bones with it and ribs as if they had been flung down on top ...

I just stood there as still as marble and looked. Mitch had been at great care to test the air inside the mound and proclaim it safe to breathe, before he had let us go down. Now he went first into one passage after another and there was silence that fell on us all, for we realised that we must be the first people to stand where we stood now, since thousands of years before Christ had been born. It was the find of the century, I thought, but I knew very little about archaeology. I could only stand and wonder and after a time Mitch came looking for me. There was a triangular shaped stone at his foot and he squatted and almost touched it but not quite.

"Do you remember the eoliths, the 'dawn stones' from the plateau gravel of Kent, or the crag implements of East Anglia? They're not accepted as of human origin nowadays, or mostly not, only yourself would accept 'the dawn stones,' because you said it was a super name for a flint instrument. You insisted in being in a minority of one and to hell with archaeology, you said. It's a super name. Your father would have jumped on it for a book, you told me."

I knelt beside him and looked closely at the stone, knew better than to touch it or move it in any way.

"Here's an implement then, or is it just a natural formation of rock, one of your 'dawn stones'?"

I knew so little about what it might be, but there was a great triumph about him.

"Pick it up and look at it. Is it a weapon or a tool for work? Was it used to cut meat for food, or meat for sacrifice? Was it used for human sacrifice? Was it red with sacrifice? Is it a stone of sorrow?"

I was more interested in the bones. After a more learned session with somebody, who knew something about what we were doing, he came back to me.

"They buried man in an upright position, in a horizontal

position. They even buried him as if he lay again in his mother's womb. You know all this and you're supposed to be over there with Alex Brown documenting the finds, not standing and staring at a piece of stone, as if you had seen a toad hatch out of a cobble, in Regency London. I used it just to tease you."

He lifted it into a hand too carelessly and threw it towards the roof slab, caught it again as it came down past him. Again, it mesmerised me, I watched his hand as he caught it, was startled to hear him draw in his breath.

"Damn sharp!" he said and sucked at his thumb. "I ought to have had more respect for the stone-age idea of what's sharp."

He passed it to me and told me to be careful of the blasted thing. Perhaps it was a very holy relic, that should not have been treated with such irreverence. There was a bead of blood in the web between his thumb and his index finger and he sucked at it, cursed his own clumsiness, was put out with me too, because I made a fuss about it and went away and fetched a dressing and a bandage. Then I made him wince with anti-septic.

"For God's sake!" he said, going against all his own teaching. "It's nothing to worry about. Here we are surrounded by the most amazing finds and all you can think of is a jab in my thumb. Don't you realise that we've likely hit treasure trove? There are weapons and personal possessions, lying there just for the taking. There are bodies buried in the side passages, and I guess that they had their slaves thrown down nearby to guard them in the under-world. There are skeletons, just dragged in and left. There are remnants of skeletons and we don't know yet what despoiled the missing bones, or what happened. We have a jig saw puzzle here to last us."

I felt the ice of a great foreboding coming over me. Perhaps tomorrow "the Lord might require my soul of me", I thought, as the Bible said. Nobody else seemed affected by it and there was excitement on every side. We planned a magnificent supper and there was no doubt that we would open a bottle or two, but that night, Mitch was not hungry.

He made no fuss about it, and mentioned the fact to nobody in the camp, but Alex Brown watched him anxiously and asked him about the cut on his hand. Mitch laughed it off and when Alex persisted, got angry about it. It was foreign to him to get angry about something so ordinary. We often cut our hands on these digs and we certainly treated wounds with respect, but we did not get angry because somebody showed concern.

The supper was "camp best". Fortnum's tins were opened long before they had any right to be. We ate exotic dishes but Mitch pushed his food round the plate and ate nothing, just drank too much, but only water and I wondered why he was so thirsty for water and not for best Dom Perignon champagne.

The talk was ebullient. Looking back, it seemed to me that everybody spoke at once and that only some sense came out. There was mention of so many things and all to do with Geology and flint arrow heads ... archaeology and stone age man and bronze man and this and that, back to our old faithful disnosaurus.

It was hot in the mess tent and we moved out after we had finished supper and tidied up. I went a little bit away and looked out to sea and they were still there, the natives in their flotilla of canoes, still as silent as as quiet, and as watchful.

From somewhere behind, where I stood, I could hear Mitch arguing with Alex Brown, that he did not require a shot of antibiotic. Its value was like gold in these long-dead places and he was not going to throw it away on a scratch. I turned and walked back to them. Mitch's face was flushed and I hoped that the flush was from the fire, for we had lit one to keep the insects at bay. Yet we were well away from the fire. A small qualm of worry took me in the pit of the stomach, that Mitch could have fever. I recalled the bead of blood again, between thumb and index finger and remembered from days at school, when I had been very small. There had been a theory in my class one time that a wound in the web of the thumb was lethal. The poison got in some way and up into the wrist into the big veins and your days were numbered. Again, I saw the spot of red, where the flint had drawn blood. "I ought to have more respect for the stone age idea of what's sharp," he had said.

Now he lifted his eyes and saw me standing there in the shadow of darkness. He said something to me in a loud harsh voice but it was nothing I could understand. It was in a foreign tongue and I was convinced out of all reason that nobody in the camp would have understood what he had said. It was illogical, but I was convinced of it and a great terror blew through my heart like a biting wind. He gestured with a hand towards the tents and it was clear that he was telling me to go to my bed. I might have been a dog, with the tone he used to me and Alex put his arm through mine and made light of the whole thing. Yet Alex was just as uneasy as I was and went off to the tent where the first-aid kit was stored. Mitch looked at him doubtfully and then back at me and after a time, he followed after us. He shrank from Alex's hand and watched him, as he got out the needle and syringe, the pledget of cotton wool, the swab of spirit. There was no doubt that he had fever. There was puzzlement on his face. The lamp shone as bright as steel against the steel of the needle and against the forceps that held the swab and I was astonished to see fear in Mitch's eyes, see that he drew back, as a small child, might have done. I did not understand what was happening, just knew my own fear and that was one that I would in no way accept. Then it was all over, this moment, when Mitch knew me, but did not know me. He shook his head and seemed to come out of some extraordinary nightmare. He was the familiar Mitch, who rarely spoke a cross word to me. His hand was rolling up his sleeve and he knew well that an injection was nothing to fear. His arm came out and there was no flinching now.

"You'll be able to lie easy in your bed," he laughed at Alex. "Isn't it a dreadful thing when an experienced physician mistakes the effect of Dom Perignon for a touch of fever?"

He decided to turn in early all the same. It seemed to me that he was asleep, as soon as he lay down. I went back to listen to the talk over the camp fire and again there was amusement about the effects of champagne on a tired man. I could have told them that Mitch's glass was still full. It had held champagne, but the wine had been fed into the sand and it had been replaced by water. There was no point in putting the thoughts into their heads, that had already crept into mine. I knew that Alex Brown was uneasy. I knew that perhaps his imagination did not possess the dreadful power to walk the territories, that mine did, but he had seen the blood drawn. He had seen he stranger, that had appeared for maybe three minutes, to look at the camp as if it was foreign to him, to look at the men about the fire, and lastly to find me with his eye and signal to me to go and to go quickly.

There was no doubt whatever that Alex Brown knew there was danger. He had seen delirium before. He came into our tent a few times during the night and I thought it likely that he slept not at all, yet in the morning, it all seemed to have dissolved with the darkness, all the doubts and fears and suppositions, all the possibilities of what might occur in this strange land.

He broke the edge of the news to us over breakfast, with Mitch still confined to his bed.

"The Professor's off colour today. It may be that there's some noxious thing down yon pit. I'd prefer if you'd do as himself says for a day or so. Put the diggings out of bounds for a wee while. See how the master goes on."

It had not dissolved in the darkness. The fears came rushing in and overwhelmed me and that was the first of the awful days. I went back into the tent, where we had had supper the night before, looking at the canvas and thinking how empty the place was. There was no sign of life and no sound of jubilation. There was no writing on the wall and no memory of the feast of Nebuchadnezzar, King of Babylon.

Through the flap of the tent, I could see the ocean, where the flotilla of canoes stood well off shore, silent, watchful, patient.

"THY FOOL, THIS NIGHT THY SOUL SHALL BE REQUIRED OF THEE."

We had shone bright light, been down the corridors of the years. Probably we had gone far past the feast of Nebuchadnezzar, King of Babylon.

I wondered if history went in rings, concentric down eternity.

5

THE AWFUL DAYS

They dragged away one by one, the awful days. Mostly one was worse than the day before, but there were cruel times, when whatever evil thing it was, retreated a little, like a cat looses a mouse and lets it think to run free. Looking back it is a strange jumbled nightmare and no matter how I try, I can get little order in what happened. Mitch was very ill. There was no doubt of that. Alex brown tried to speak comforting words to me. Tropical diseases were "kittle cattle". No English doctor knew anything about them, but many a black man had been given up for dead the night before, only to be found ploughing his corn patch the next day, walking round and round his ox-drawn primitive piece of machinery, and the patient look on his face matching the beast's.

Then, would come a lucid time, with an improvement for Mitch and he would be up and dressed with no permission from his medical staff. he would sit at the supper table and laugh at our anxious faces. He even opened more of the Dom Perignon to raise a glass in a toast to his physician and also to his nurse and that meant me. Could he produce any alteration in our decision to proceed with the dig? He agreed that observation of strange fevers was a necessity, but look at him now! Surely it was past the wasting of time. Soon we must go back to our scholastic endeavours at Camford. Under our feet lay treasure trove for the whole world ... and Alexander and myself had been seeing too many T.V. films, where men turned into vegetables and grew branches instead of limbs, because of some virus. He was better. He agreed that he had been slightly ill, but the danger was past and if we kept the canoes on station out in the bay much longer, it was worse than slavery. Let them cast off and go home.

Then the next day, would come the cat again with the mouse under her paw and the temperature soaring ... the rambling mind, that was the worst part to bear, the turning away from food, the yellowing tinge of the skin, the falling of flesh and the fading of health, the loss of that wonderful brightness and energy. God help me!. The encroachment of the end.

I am muddled in what happened. There were so many things. There were so many promises of reprieve and so many bitter disappointments. Then there was so much involvement with different sources of help. We were an international expedition. When our first finds hit the press, we were in the eye of the world. We were top line news. Soon reporters might begin to arrive on Patanga, television crews, other archaeologists, but Alex Brown took charge of that. It was one of the small things that stay in my mind, the message that went out on the radio. I could imagine it as it went round the world like Ariel, saying so much and so little. No landings were to be permitted on Patanga. There was illness, that might be serious, that might be connected with the opening of the burial mound. Patanga was in quaratine, but would be released as soon as safety was assured.

That message seethed interest, as if a hive of wasps had been overturned and Mitch was worse. He began to have more of moments, when he left us for some other plane, when he spoke in an unknown language and glared at us as if we were savage strangers, at all but myself. Me he knew. Me he addressed, though I understood no word of what he said. I looked at him and thought how changed he was, his features sharpened and his eyes enormous, so that there was a terrible beauty about him.

Then the radio messages began to pour in and the discussions spin back and forth. It is so confused that I have no hope of making sense of it. The British Navy put transport at our disposal.

"It was imperative that Professor Allington should be

moved quickly to a base hospital. Stand by for further suggestions."

There followed days and times and names of eminent medical men, who also wore the uniform of Her Majesty's Navy. There was a list of the bases and the lab. facilities available. I listened to them all, or read the signals. The R.A.F. was quick off the mark with speed in its wings. The Tropical School of Medicine could make personnel available. It had gone on a long time by this and we could only wait. We had sat round idle for days, hoping whatever it was would go away. Mostly I stayed with Mitch and did what nursing there was, talking to him or silent, praying in the night, as he got worse and worse. Now and again, would come the really frightening hours, when he became a stranger and spoke a stranger's tongue. It was then I knew that there was no hope for him, for death sat in his eyes and in the fingers that fidgeted the blankets. He came out of one of these spells one night and found my hand in his, looked at it for five minutes without a word and I dared not speak to him in case of driving him back into whatever place he frequented, when the strangeness was on him.

He turned my hand this way and that and I sat there and waited and at last he spoke, but though it was in his own voice and with his own words, he still made very little sense.

"It's not going to work this time, my darling. I see it again and we've missed it. 'Only a little while.' That's our destiny. Listen to me and remember what I say. For God's sake watch out for me. I'll come back for you. Haven't I always come back for you? Nothing will ever shake our love. We're not 'time's fools'."

The pages of my memory flip over, one after another, but there is no order to them and sometimes, a day is happy and Mitch is better. Then comes a long reaching into eternity, when he lies past consciousness, with all the preparation for air flight at the ready to take him to hospital. I am never far away from him and looking back now, I can see every detail of the tent and the bed and the small stretcher where I sit or lie. I see the night moths against the light and all the minutiae of medical equipment. Once again, I dip the gauze swab into iced water and lay it on his forehead, hear the sigh, just that tiny sop of relief to a headache, that is a vice on his brain.

All the time, there is activity, but there is very little near our tent and people step quietly past or come in for a moment, to put a hand on my shoulder.

I hear what is happening in the world, but it cannot be happening to me. Sometimes something dramatic comes about, like the day the canoes drew in to the land, but stopped short of the sandy shore and the small rocky cove.

There was a parley at sea. Alex Brown went out and two of the boys from the University. I watched them from the tent, for Mitch was asleep. A kiss on his cheek and a hand to straighten the covers and I was over by the flap looking down at the age-old design of the canoes against the modern rubber dinghy and its noisy outboard motor. There was great ceremony of greeting. I have no exact notion of how they made conversation, but maybe they were like children from our own world, who do not require words to pass on knowledge. It is no good staying back in that corner of my mind, I shun it, as I shun many memories.

Alex Brown had studied humanity for a great many years and he had deep wisdom of his fellows. He managed to pick up the crumbs of what might be information, almost certainly was near enough true. It was true the leader was sick. He had cut himself on a grey stone. No, they would not come ashore to the camp. Nobody went on Patanga. There was bad god on Patanga. Even with no grey stone, man died. It was a place for the dead and not for the living.

That was how it might have run. Perhaps it meant nothing even remotely near that, but I think it did ... and there was more to come and maybe Alex Brown made it all up and if he did, there was no blame to him, for there were young lives at sacrifice. We must leave Patanga, but we must close the mound and put a powerful seal on it. They themselves would never land on the island. It was tabu. We must seal up the opening with a mighty seal and we must go and there was no welcome for any man again ...

I remember the past in short clips and one of them is the

sealing of the mound. I asked to be present. Indeed we were all there and our faces set in sorrow. It was one of Mitch's lost days. There was a devil in the island and his name was death ... I thought, as I stood in the sun. The birds were singing, and there was no hint of evil. Yet evil there was. Alex had told us that there was no hope of finding out what was wrong with Mitch, till we got to a hospital.

"There's nothing wrong with him. What tests I can do or send come back negative. I'll have to wait for the Tropical men, and viruses are tricky. Thank God he's strong. This thing is so virulent that it could wipe out a continent. There's no crying halt to it ..."

They lowered the slabs and put the mound back as it had been, removed no single item from it and laid the grass back in neatness. In a little time, there would be no trace that anybody had been there, only the great seal and that was a simple thing. It was Alex Brown who made it, from two strips of chromium. He fashioned without grandeur, just two inch strips of chromium, joined into a cross with a chromium screw, but it was simplicity. He had engraved something across the horizontal of the cross and I bent my head to look at it.

Noli me Tangere

He knelt down, when the mound had been restored to its former state and he set the cross on the central place and it caught the sun in its hand and threw a dart of brightness back at the sky, and the men were speaking in low voices about the inscription.

"It's what Henry Tudor wrote on a band of gold about the neck of Anne Boleyn." We had a divinity student with us, a lad that would soon be a shepherd of sheep and was fulfilling the reputation some of the divinity students had, and the medicals too of sowing their wild oats, while there was still time. He was a happy chap usually, but there was no joy in him today.

"Touch me not," he translated, "Christ used the words to Mary Magdalene after his resurrection. 'Noli me Tangere ... I am not yet ascended'."

Mostly it did not seem possible that it was really happening. There was the arrival of the Fleet Air Arm ... the loading by skilled gentle hands, the leaning out to wave goodbye, the queer sound the doors of the craft had, the take off from the flight deck. There was so much kindness, that I know if I lived out eternity, I could never hope to repay it. The morale was so high with the Navy that my hope ignited from theirs. Then there was the landing for refuelling and taking off again and a journey that would never be over. The people had kissed my cheek as I quitted Patanga, every member of the expedition and I could feel my cheek still and know the good will they bore for us, queueing up like little children at the end of a school party.

My life became divided up into sections of time. We came in to some enormous ship in Plymouth and from there we went to London. There was a helicopter flight or perhaps there was. There was the sprawl of London and a roof and a lift and a side ward, with nurses in soft soled shoes and masked faces and gowns, that they took off when they left the room and put on again when they came back. Alex Brown had managed to cling to his patient and he went into a huddle of learned consultation and the charts, that were kept in isolation turned from the first sheet of all, into a clip board of progress. There was no conclusion to be made. One virus after another and the anti-body titres no help. It was blank. Blood normal, all the dozens of things in blood that could be accounted for. They were all there and correct, but the blood wasted away. There was no noxious finding and Mitch should have been a normal healthy man, with great success his by right, but as it was, he was dying.

The very distinguished gentleman who told me the truth wrapped it up in such a learned manner, that I could in no way make any sense out of what he said. He took my hand and started again at the beginning.

"There is no doubt about it, but we'll never prove it. There was some extraordinary virus in that pit that had lain for thousands of years. He broke his flesh and he got it into his blood. Man had never been exposed to it in this world as we know it. He had never had a chance to find a defence against it. We'll go on with the cultures, of course. We've proved that it seems safe enough. I don't mean to say that. What I want to tell you is that this infernal position is not transmittable by contact. Do you understand? It must go in the blood stream. It attacks the patient's blood and it destroys his cells. There's no replacing them, for you know we've been pushing in packed cells. That means concentrated soldiers, sent up the line in great batallions. They're there and then they're destroyed, but we can't find out why or how, only that by God's grace, the thing is not transmittable just by contact."

Alex Brown gripped my hand in his and his face was far sadder than mine. I had lost all power of emotion.

"You could take him to the Quicken Tree. You've had an awful time. It would be quiet there and ..."

"He'd like to die there," I finished, for he saw that he had implied that there was no hope left and was appalled that he should have done such a thing.

"We won't stop trying. We'll keep hammering away at this thing, but he's tired out and his resistance is low. It would be nice to lie in bed at home and listen to the rooks in the morning."

I looked at them both and my mind was trying to grasp the fact that hope had been given up. I could not grasp it. Surely there was something could be done? They had taken tests and then had done X-rays. They had taken bone marrow out of his breast bone. They had exhausted him with all the interference, I thought with anger, and then knew what a fool I was. The world had given him the best possible chance of life and he was going out on a sea as yet uncharted ... or was he like a rabbit with that dread sudden disease, a disease that was as cruel as Atilla, the Hun, as cruel as the atom bomb?

We talked for a long time and we made arrangements. I have no idea what they were. I have no idea how we travelled only that humanity was much kinder than ever I had thought it to be. Mitch went on his varying course, sometimnes recovering till I thought it all a gigantic mistake and then falling back into a flare up of the disease that swept all before it like a flamegun. He was the same delightful husband that I had always known and there was no doubt that he had his eyes open to most of what was happening. He wanted to go home. Alex Brown might like to come with us. The three of us would plan the next expedition and it was time that we went to central Europe again—and he loved me very much. He would never stop loving me and I would never stop loving him, "till a' the seas gang dry and the rocks melt i' the sun ..."

He smiled at me and his smile was a ghost. His features had thinned down and there was a sharpness to his nose ... a classical look like a saint in a stained glass window. His eyes were brilliant and clear and all-seeing, as if he could look back down the years to the beginning of the universe ... look forward to the last syllable of time ...

Then we were back in the stone house and we had reached the next stage of the journey. The sand-glass seemed to be running more and more quickly and I prayed for death for myself, offered myself as a sacrifice to God, as a price for his life ... and had my offer refused.

"How long?" I had asked the Professor of Tropical Medicine and he had looked at me with gravity, over the lower glass crescents of his spectacles. I had wondered idly for no reason in the world, if he saw the truth more clearly over the tops, that were unglazed with lenses and if he sought the truth about me and what more suffering I could bear in watching the last grains.

"Not long. Three months, a few weeks more or less. He's begged me to let him go home to his house ... the Quicken Tree, isn't it?, Brown would stay with you and there's nothing much in the way of nursing, just tender loving care. He'll not be short of that. He never says much, but I'm quite sure that his eyes are fully open to the truth. He accepts it and he's courageous. He recognises that there will be pain ... hard, physical pain, but there's modern medical skill to ease that. He can go to Camford by ambulance for his transfusions and of course, my colleagues will only be too happy to visit him at home. We've heard great praise about the Quicken Tree."

It was the rowan tree that was the first thing to greet us as we turned in by the front gate in the ambulance. Its berries

were like sealing wax in the sun. The door stood open and
there was Kit on the step with her face so happy and
welcoming that I wondered if it had all been a bad dream.
Then there was the fuss of the unloading of the patient and
Alex Brown getting down from the seat next the driver to
supervise operations. There was a flurry to get Mitch to the
four poster bed, but he defeated the idea of that and settled
into his own armchair. The happiness on his face, the
exhaustion after the journey, the weakness, the brightness of
eye, the pallor, the strain were all there and Alex Brown
telling us that the patient had stood the trip well. Then Kit
was involving me in serving tea to the party. God bless her,
she had a pile of muffins before the fire and the toasting fork
at the ready and she made the miracle of a happy home-
coming, by slandering the way Mitch toasted muffins. Oh,
no, he wouldn't be allowed near them. That was her own
task, if the ambulance men didn't want to be eating char-
coal ...

I can see her now in her washed out blue jeans, that were
short in the leg over knitted socks and tennis shoes. After a
glance at my face, she stood on her head and waggled her feet
in the air, just to cheer me up. Little did she know how
nearly she broke my heart with the memories she called up.

The fire was already lit and the coal glowing for the
toasting ceremony. We all knew that by right we should have
insisted on the four-poster bed, maybe with the red velvet
curtains drawn for the dusk of rest and quietness. Yet there
was eternity for darkness and quietness. I thought what a
strangely merry party we were, with the two ambulance men
sitting on the carpet, and Alex in my armchair and Kit
toasting muffins and myself making the tea and pouring it
out and the old medical jokes being produced and enjoyed, for
all their age.

Then suddenly it was over and the men would help the
patient to bed before they went back to London and soon that
was done and they were gone, with Kit and I waving as they
drove down the village street past the Rickaby's house. It was
lucky that I had so much to do. Mitch was to rest and I
tucked him in, pulled the curtains, kissed him, promised to

call him in a few hours. We had come home, he and I, and
was that not a great triumph? Home was where we wanted
to be and here things would get better, I promised him, and
left him asleep. Then I ran down the stairs to the kitchen, to
hand-made tiles and the green Wedgewood plates on the
dresser. I sat in the rocking chair and rocked myself back and
forth and Kit came and sat at my feet.

"I'll come out here every hour I can, Liz-Jane. I'll help
you. Don't worry about the housework. If necessary, I'll
chuck in my job at the typing pool. I was never much cop
anyway. I'll never leave you, nor desert you."

It was like Ruth and Naomi all over again and my unshed
tears choked me. I just clutched at her hand and there was no
necessity for conversation between us. Then we started in to
work like slaves. I am sure she had cleaned the whole place
from top to bottom, but if she had, we did it again and had no
thought for the fact than it might not be necessary. She was a
great one for fish and chips, was Kit. Towards seven o'clock,
she went trotting off down the village and came back with the
newspaper-wrapped fish and chips under her arm. There
was five minutes, while I made an omelette, small and dainty
enough for any invalid. Mitch complained about having to
eat it, while Alex and Kit and I sat round the fourposter bed
and ate fish and chips. It was wonderful. I felt so happy. It
was not going to happen after all. The learned men had been
wrong. This happy house would work the miracle for us and
everything would end well. I slept at Mitch's side that night
and felt the brightness of hope. My dreams were happy.
Then the next day, the mask of happiness was turned to the
mask of tragedy. It was as if I sat in a theatre and looked up
at the plaster faces above the stage and the lines on the face
were down drawn, the eye and the mouth lines. The face
with laughter at the temples was gone and with it the gaiety.
The suffering came creeping back like a devil from which we
had thought ourselves free. There was the Brompton cocktail
to have, the injections ... and they must not be rationed
meanly.

"The splenic pain is severe," they had said. "The muscular spasms are agonal, but we have drugs. You must not hold back. There's no point."

Alex Brown took blood up into a syringe in a day or so, shot it into a bottle, that might have been made of crystal so clear it was. I drove to Camford General to Haemotology with it and avoided meeting anybody I knew. The telephone rang presently and Alex talked for a long time to one of the most famous haemotologists in the world. Later on they brought out a van from Blood Transfusion and there was activity about the four-poster bed. The room turned to a clinical place and not the warm soft haven it had been the night we came home, but Mitch was better and the drugs had eased the pain. The eminent haemotologist took tea with me the next day, sat in front of the wide rough stone mantlepiece and shook his head.

"I'm very sorry, Mrs. Allington. We've not done trying yet and there's no question of our giving up. The case will have been explained to you. It's some unknown virus, we presume and it's untraceable. It has a capacity for blood destruction that we rarely see. It's progressive and it's insatiable. We think it's fatal and it might be better for you to face up to the fact that it's unstoppable. It's a science fiction character, that could clear the whole earth of life. Yet we must never abandon hope."

"Perhaps it's harder on you to be tossed back and forth between hope and despair. It's crueller than a single blow that blots out life between one moment and the next ..."

I had abandoned hope, yet somehow in the joy of coming home to the Quicken Tree, I had found it again. Now I put it firmly away from me and tried to resign myself that I must lose this person I loved so much. I would have seen the world well lost as long as I had him, but there was nothing I could do only wait and pray. It was Kit, that kept me able to survive the torment ... mine and his, but Kit was not there on the worst day of all. Alex Brown was not there either. They had had to go away for twenty four hours. I am misted in my mind that I forget the reason. I know Kit's mother was ill, gravely ill. I am selfish to have grudged her time away from me. Alex Brown had gone up to town in the car to fetch some new chemical they were going to try. There was delay ... a rail strike, a pea-souper fog. It's all clouded in my head, as if the fog had invested my brains too. It was a month after our home coming and there was no hope now. There was death in Mitch's face and he had stopped eating or virtually so. He could not come downstairs and the games of chess had been abandoned. He lay there and slept most of the time, talked in a whisper. The night I was alone with him, we communicated sometimes but only in little runs and then in long silences. When he slept, I sat by the bed and wanted to pray that his breathing would stop. The pain had become brutal and the drugs could not bring him full peace, only a dulling. I wished Kit had not had to go and I wanted some other person with me, but there was nobody I could think of. the room was dim and there was a fire in the grate. Now and again a log sneezed out a shower of sparks and sometimes an ember dropped into the hearth and sent a spiral of grey smoke up the throat of the chimney. The clock on the mantlepiece ticked in its frenzied way, but it moved very slowly. It was only five minutes past two in the morning and I should lie down and sleep, but in the small hours, sleep and I were strangers.

I could ring a doctor, but what could any doctor do? They had all tried so gallantly and they deserved to sleep, not to be called out by some hysterical woman, who had lost her courage.

It had gone on so long and there was no kindness in prolonging Mitch's life. This was one of the crazy thoughts, that visited me and must be put out like a snuffed candle. Yet they came alight again. If I could find the will to pick up one of the pillows from my side of the bed and lay it gently on his face, for how long, one minute, three? Yesterday they had told me there was no hope whatever. I must prepare myself for the end and very soon. There was no point now in prolonging life. It had struck me cruelly that sentence, so very final. "There is no point now in prolonging life ..."

He opened his eyes and took my hand in his and his voice was almost inaudible.

"Do you believe that a soul can pass ... from one life to

the next ... that a person can come back again and again ... maybe improving over centuries ... and centuries?"

It was his old topic that he had lived before and so had I and I nodded my head to humour him and said that of course, I believed it.

"Nothing's going to happen to you. We're getting you well."

There was a sadness about him, that tore my heart. His hand clutched at mine as if he struggled to hold me and never let me go.

"We'll meet again ...' he said and I bent to kiss his cheek.

"Of course, we'll meet again." I said and my voice was an aged crone's voice, the voice of a witch. "Close your eyes and go to sleep."

His lashes were long on the planes of his face and the hollowed cheeks were dark shadows.

I thought he slept and I got up softly and went round the bed and picked up the jar of his sleeping capsules. If I did not get sleep, I must lose my reason. The panic rose in my breast as it had taken to doing twenty times a day.

"Let it be me, God, not him. I cannot watch him die. I cannot live without him."

He lay on his pillow and there was sweat on his brow. I sprinkled Cologne on a handkerchief and brushed it on his face, put some on my hands and stroked his hands between mine. Then I picked one of the big white capsules out of the jar and then another, put them into my mouth and ran water at the basin, swallowed the capsules down and knew that soon I would sleep. I stood on the height of a precipice, where I asked if I should go on taking one after another of the capsules. The pain of being without him was too great to bear, but these were the thoughts that always haunted me in the silence of the night and he was asleep. I was numb and unreal, floating about the ceiling, looking down at the fair-haired woman, who must watch her husband die. I lay down beside him and took his hand in mine. His mouth was slack and he was soft-breathing in his throat and I was drowsy and drowsier. The drug was floating me out and away into a blackness, where no dreams came and the clock had hardly moved past the quarter after two.

There was somebody knocking at the door then. I was too sleepy to move for a while. I waited till it came again. If I stayed here quietly, they might go away and I could fall down into sleep again. It was too late to open the door. It was far too late. I opened my eyes and it was broad daylight. The clock in the hall struck. One, two, three, four ... Mitch's hand was still in mine. I became conscious of it slowly, cold, stiff, marble. I jerked myself upright in the bed and looked at him and my heart stopped, thumped, raced. His eyes had turned to opaque glass. His mouth was open a little way, his skin waxen. I touched his cheek with a finger and it was cold. His arm would not lift. It was stiff and cold and dead. I became conscious of it slowly, stiff, cold, dead marble. All the time, the knocking at the door went on, more and more insistent, louder and louder. A voice called up to me from the drive below.

The hands of the clock stood at four, but it was four in the afternoon. The night was past. I had slept nigh fourteen hours. I still wore my blue housecoat. I was just as I had been, when I had lain down last night, but the night was gone. I jumped out of bed and the room swam round me. Then I was on the landing and down the stairs and there was a tall shadow against the glass. Then the front door was open, but I had no recollection that I opened it. There was a policeman standing on the step.

"Beg your pardon, ma'am. The milk hasn't been taken in, nor yet the papers. I had a peek through your letter box and the letters were on the mat."

He stooped and picked them up, put them on the hall table.

"We know the professor is ill. We keep an eye on the house. I thought you might be in trouble."

He glanced down at my bare feet. My mouth was so dry that I could hardly get the words out of it.

"I went asleep just after two ... two last night. I hadn't slept. That's no excuse. I slept till you knocked just now."

I sat down on the chairs, my head in my hands.

"I think he's dead. I didn't wake up. Oh, God! Suppose he wanted something and I didn't hear? I went asleep."

He put a hand under my arm and guided me into the kitchen.

"Put the kettle on, ma'am. Make some tea. I'll have a look upstairs, see if there's anything to be done. If he's gone, from what I hear, it will be a release. There's no cause for you to be blaming yourself. I'll fetch your slippers, time I come down again, don't want you to catch cold."

"But I went asleep," I said.

"The kettle, ma'am," he prompted me. "We'll make a pot of tea. You'll soon feel better."

I held the kettle under the tap, filled it, put it on the gas jet. I was a mechanical doll and somebody had pushed a key into my back and wound me up. I watched the mauve flame against the aluminium of the kettle. There were clicking sounds in my head and a shower of sparks rocketing across my brain and all the time a voice that said "A watched pot never boils." Then he was back again, the policeman, his face shock white against his black hair.

"He's gone, ma'am."

He glanced at my face and away again.

"He went very peaceful in his sleep. There was nothing you could have done if you had been awake. It's all over, the suffering and that. There was nothing that would have saved him, they said. You should be glad it's done."

"Of course, I'm glad. It's gone on month after month and no hope at the end of it. Last night ... I think it was last night, I thought if I could put the pillow over his face and let him go free, I'd have done it. Then I saw it was because of my own pain I'd have finished it."

"Don't talk like that. You're upset and you don't know what you're saying. Don't worry about anything. I'll get the doctor on the phone and he'll come over, the undertaker too, if you say who it's to be. We'll have the deceased moved to the Chapel of Rest."

"I don't want him moved. This is his home. It's dark and cold in those places and he hated them. He'd want to lie in his own bed until ..."

I stopped up short and found the kettle in my hand and did not know how it had got there. It was automatic the making of a pot of tea, the letting it draw, the pouring it out. Then I was sitting on a chair and the cup was empty, the doctor was there and had been upstairs and come down again. He stood by the table with all the tablet bottles in his hand and the two bottles of mixture, the white and the clear.

"It's over and he's better off than any of us at this moment. You must cling to that fact."

"Did the constable tell you I went asleep? I took two of the white capsules. I went asleep and I didn't wake up. I blame myself."

"What nonsense! You've got nothing to blame yourself for. You've done everything humanly possible. You've been wonderful. Don't start thinking foolishness. He slept it out—didn't even move. Nobody could have helped him, as you've done."

He turned my attention to the drugs he carried in his hands, in his pockets too, the syringes, the ampoules, the capsules and the mixtures, the trappings of terminal illness.

"I must destroy these. Some of them are dangerous and they mustn't be left about."

He uncorked the pain cocktail that Mitch had taken with gin and the thick syrup gurgled out of the bottle and swirled round the waste in the sink. The white mixture washed the last of it away and the tablets jinked against the stainless steel in a maelstrom of dissolution. Then the telephone rang and the policeman was away to answer it and back again, for the doctor was wanted urgently at his surgery. It was an accident case, a child with his foot caught in the back wheel of his mum's bike.

"He's bleeding badly. Janet says to come quick as you can."

Dr. Jones was gone within two minutes. He promised to return later. He shoved the jar of white capsules into my hands.

"I've got rid of the other things. See to these for me. Pull the celluloid covers apart and throw the powder down the drain. Better still, put them all on the fire."

The constable went to see the doctor on his way. I stood there and clicked the capsules round in their brown container. Causer was the policeman's name, Peter Causer. They called him "Tin-Leg" in the village, because he had had a fractured leg once and had been in a long awkward plaster cast for months. The sergeant had had to help him to the lavatory and everybody had been amused by this, but there was no fun left in the world now—no fun then for poor Causer, and I was still walking in my sleep. I might wake up presently and find I had had a nightmare, but there was the container with the capsules and I must pull them apart. The boiler fire was out. The bedroom fire was out. I was too tired, but I must make an effort to pull them apart and flush the powder down the sink, yet I could not make the effort. I put them on the shelf by the tea caddy and turned back to wash up the cups.

Then the great gaps began to come in time. I did not remember his arrival but he was there, the undertaker. There were decisions to be made. I set myself like a tired old horse at a series of jumps, hesitating a long time before every answer. There would be no post-mortem exam. I was quite certain about that. Had they not done enough tests on him? The coffin would be oak with a brass breast plate and it was for burial. Just the name and his birth and death. I wrote it in blocks. Mitchell Summerfield Allington. I gave detail of a burial plot in the Histington church yard. The undertaker's registered nurse was on her way and she would see to putting things in order. No, I didn't want him moved. He was to lie in his bed, till the time came for the funeral.

It all went on for a very long time and I knew it could not be Mitch, we discussed. The nurse brought the truth back to me with the force of an atomic bomb. His signet ring lay beside his watch on the table at my side.

"You'd better take charge of these, Mrs. Allington."

She was very kind. I pitied her that she spent her life at such tasks. The undertaker kept her fully occupied with a tumbled queue of deceased. It was awful to think of a young pretty girl doing such work, but she shrugged it away.

"Somebody's got to do it."

Causer took her to the door after he had made us cups of

tea and I heard her laugh, when she thought they were out of earshot.

"My patients don't complain any. It's not every nurse can say the same."

"She'll hear you."

Then the constable had popped up again like a jack-in-the-box. He had known my father well before his American days. If I gave him the number, he'd try to get a cable off. He loved my father's books, never missed one of them. Things were all getting out of sequence. the doctor was back and I had a glass of sherry and a white tablet. Then they all came one by one, the vicar, my solicitor, Mr. Rickaby and that was Anthony's father. The vicar knelt down and prayed and my faithful constable knelt down too, his face getting red with embarrassment. Then Kit was there, and I flung myself into her arms and she hugged me and wept, but I had no tears to shed. There was so much to be done. It was all scrambling my mind. There were days that followed and I made no proper sequence of any of them. The nights were dark, but the days were dark too and it was a mad world, with no reality.

"We've fixed the traffic arrangements for the internment, ma'am. There'll be people up from London, representatives from the Royal Society and the Archaeological Society and the British Legion and the Government, the Salvation Army. The road at the church is narrow and there's that blind corner. It's not so easy outside the house for that matter, but perhaps there won't be such congestion here."

Then one day, there was a reporter on the phone and he wanted to check for obituary notices. He wanted a list of the publications Mitch had done and I turned my head and read the titles from the books on the shelf at my side, my voice as flat and dead as an Egyptian tomb. It was a great tragedy that Professor Allington was dead. It was a blow for Archaeology. No, we had no children.

"It was a pity," he said. "A son might have carried the torch."

Then there was my father, on the transatlantic line and I could hear him far more clearly than if he had rung in from a call box in the village. There was no chance of his getting away. There was a picture on release in a kind of American "Command Performance". Some day, he would fly over and visit with me, but just for now, I would know how grieved he was. He would send a floral tribute and I could understand his deep sorrow. One day, he'd tell me personally and in the meantime, I was to take care of myself and not grieve too much. I had all his love ...

Kit was my saviour. She and I worked at all the things that must be done, but she did the bulk of the polishing and shining and entertained the callers, prepared the funeral meats, let me stay in the room with Mitch for hours at a time, with my hand on his.

One day, she whispered more bad news in my ear and I knew the strength of love she bore for me.

"My mum's very bad. I got away for these few days, but she's going fast. I have to go home. Dad can't manage. I'm going to have to live up there permently, to look after him. I promised her. She'd not die happy else. It's a long way away, Honey."

"Not your mother dying, not her too! Oh, Kit. How can there be so much loneliness?"

I'd be alone. My only close friend was Alex Brown and he had his son and grandchildren. He had hastened back with the chemical still in its lead container, the modern produce of atomic energy, that was as powerless as all the other miracles the physicians had tried ... and I owed them so much, that I could never repay them, and somebody had said Alex's son was ill.

I sat in the pew in the church, between Alex Brown and Kit and knew that without them, I could not endure the agony. Mitch's coffin stood on the trestles in the nave with my red and white carnations, clove-scented and sweet, against the dank smell of the church. Kit's touch alerted me to stand up and I got to my feet and gripped the front of the pew and willed myself not to sob aloud. The church was packed with people and the banner of the British Legion was a glory. There were extra chairs in the aisles and still there were mourners, who waited in the back porch and out among the graves. Not so long ago, I had come up an aisle to be given to

Mitch in marriage, no it had been a long time, five years perhaps. I could not remember. His hand had stretched out to take mine. I thought of the brightness of his hair as he lay in the coffin and how strangely dark his eyelashes, over the waxen cheeks.

Then as if a slide had shot forward, we were at the open grave. they were getting ready to lower the coffin into the darkness and I could not bear it. I concentrated on watching every last detail of the skill of the undertaker's men. Somebody was putting a posy of flowers into my hand ... a small circular bunch of lillies of the valley.

"Take the flowers, madam. They're for the top of the coffin."

She did not seem to grasp what to do, this woman at the coffin. I looked down and saw the brass plate and the inscription. The flowers were frilled with blue. They were a cool fragrance against my cheek.

"I am the rose of Sharon and the lily of the valleys." I remembered. "As the lily among thorns, so is my love among the daughters. As the apple trees of the wood, so is my beloved among the sons. I sat down under his shadow with delight and his fruit was sweet to my taste ... He brought me to the banqueting hall and his banner over me was love ..." a balcony that had been a hotel in Cairo ...

"Throw it into the grave, honey."

They fell more softly than a sigh, more lightly than the handful of earth would.

"Earth to earth, ashes to ashes, dust to dust ... "

I was not to hear the clods that fell on the coffin. Alex Brown had his arm about me and was leading me away and Kit was at my other side, but there were strangers that came to talk to me. I spoke to them with the animation a puppet might have had, but they seemed content.

"I met your husband in Egypt once. It wasn't history to him. Archaeology was living and breathing and of tremendous concern. He was the greatest ... no replacing him."

It was a short way back to the house and P.C. Causer was there to wave the traffic to a halt or summon it on its way. He held up a line of cars to let ours through and gave me a special salute and his uniform was parade spotless, his buttons like little suns, his boots very polished.

The sitting room was a throng of people and all about me there were kind words, that opened wounds. There were black dresses and white starched aprons and butterfly caps that sat on the waitresses' heads. There were plates of sandwiches and sherry on trays, small dry biscuits and bridge rolls filled with lobster. There were paté and petit fours. There were spiced delicacies of every sort. I was the taffy-haired girl in the black dress, who held a glass in a white-gloved hand, who made polite replies, who was not to be moved to weeping ... and it went on for ever. I did not notice the way they all trickled away, by ones and by twos and by threes. Quite suddenly they were all gone and maybe it was the next day. I do not know, only that they were all gone, except Mr. Rickaby, the father of Anthony, who had come to read the last will and testament. It could not be the next day, for Kit was still there and she had to leave as soon as may be, and Alex had to go too. It was true that his son was ill ... gravely ill. I had thought I had imagined it.

The evening was coming down and Kit had been busy in the kitchen. There were four of us, who sat round the dining room table, Mr. Rickaby, Alex Brown, Kit and myself, but I did not know if they had left and come back again, or what time it was. I knew that Kit's mother was so ill that Kit must be off in the morning. Alex's son was worse too. Yes, it was true. Again I had hoped it was nightmare. He intended to go north by train. He was explaining to Mr. Rickaby that "the boy" had a very virulent form of pneumonia and Alex's face had aged since the glad days when we first arrived on Patanga. The island had brought none of us any luck. Kit was the only person, who kept up any pretence of courage. She gave me good warning too to gird myself against more ill fortune.

I can see her now, in the kitchen, with the supper ready to serve and she had arranged who was to be present and what we should eat, for I was incapable of stringing two thoughts together. I had offered to go with her to help out at her home, but she had refused, told me that there was enough for me to deal with in Histington.

"You've got to make your own way and it's not going to be easy. The will's not good. Old Rickaby is worried sick about it. Besides, our house up north is one up and one down. There's no room to swing a cat, even if we had one to swing."

Her smile was nailed to her face like a flag nailed to the mast. There was going to be no surrender, just that calm efficient production of supper for the four of us, with a tin of soup opened and fried croutons to bring it to life, with fish fetched post haste from the village chippie, and disguised in parsley and tartare sauce, till nobody could have guessed its source, with ice cream and hot chocoate sauce and walnuts flaked on the top ...

Then it was all cleared away and she and I washed up and presently, she sat us round the table with great formality for the reading of the will, sat next to me and my hand gripped in hers.

Mr. Rickaby gestured to her to stay by me. Then he broke the seal on the will and cleared his throat to begin.

"This is the last will and testament of the late Mitchell Summerfield Allington ..."

It went on for a long time. Things had got a way of doing that in the last week. Mr. Rickaby finished it at last and laid it on the shining mahogany and looked at me across the table, glanced sideways at Alex and Kit. He could not know that I had understood not a word of what he had said, but perhaps he did, for he started again, more gently.

"I urged your husband to take out a substantial life insurance. Given time, he would have done so, but he had no thought of death. I'm afraid, dear Liz-Jane, that for all his achievements and honours, you may find yourself in extremely reduced circumstances, and I do mean extremely reduced circumstances."

If it was disaster again, I could not grasp it. It could not be possible that he was bringing me bad news, not the destruction of a way of life, the further destruction, the annihilation of the golden days I had lived for the last years. Anyhow they were gone with Mitch's going. There was more talk, but I could pay little attention. Was I not back at the edge of the grave and soon the men would have shovelled earth down to cover the brightness of the name plate.

Mitchell Summerfield Allington.

The posy of lilies of the valley would be quite buried by now, and darkness had indeed come down.

6

MILTON MANOR

It was the next day or the day after then or the day after that again and I was alone in the Quicken Tree. Kit had gone and Alex Brown, but there were plans for us to see each other and a pretended brightness, that was a lie. Mr. Rickaby had called once more and he and I were in the sitting room and I asked him to go over it again. He sighed and looked at me sadly, for he had told me so many things and told them over again. It is no good remembering them now. It was just that I was almost without means. There had been no insurance and Inland Revenue had robbed Mitch of all the treasure he had brought in. He had not made provision for an early death. He had even told Mr. Rickaby that he was not given to early death and that there was plenty of time left, for the dull stuff of insurance and wills.

" 'This night thy soul shall be required of thee'," I thought and cared not at all, that I had no money left.

"You can always go back to your position in the hospital," Mr. Rickaby had said and I had smiled at him and reminded him that Anthony, his son, had gone away.

"I know that you don't want to be reminded of any of the past," he said. "They'd be glad to take you in the Camford General, but you've set your heart against it. You're looking for a place to hide out from your happy times, though they'll come again, I promise you. I think I've found something for you ... near to home too."

I could not afford to live in the Quicken Tree.

I must consider what to do with the house. There were so many possibilities. I could let it furnished, or unfurnished. I could sell it and sell the furniture, but the rent would be income.

He had given the matter great thought and he had searched round in his mind for a living-in position. I could get one easily enough in the Camford General Hospital, but he knew I was against familiar places and maybe I was right. I should make a clean break of it. By chance, he had another client, name of Mrs. Amelia Swan. Doubtless I knew Mrs. Swan of Milton Manor? Milton was more or less on our doorstep, six miles away, big old house in its own spacious grounds. There was a housekeeper and an elderly couple called Casey. The staff had all been there for years, even since before the late Mr. Swan's demise. They had kept maids at one time and more recently a lady companion, but lady companions were a thing of the past. Now Mrs. Swan had decided that she wanted a resident secretary. She had a certain interest in the family business, but really it was probably a substitute name for lady companion. I might have very little to do in the way of secretarial work in the world of commerce ...

He smiled at me over the rims of his glasses.

"Oh, come now, Liz-Jane. You're looking for somewhere to hide, if ever a person was. This is the perfect place. Pack up your possessions here and lock the front door. Let it stay for a while, just as it is. I have a feeling that you might come back again and find that happiness had come back too."

I left it to him to speak to Mrs. Swan about it. She asked me to come to tea with her, the next week. The money seemed right, if you thought of the fact that there would be free board and lodgings and as old Rickaby said, "the table was good." I might be expected to help with a little light nursing, but I was adept at that and I was a wonderful companion.

"And incidentally, about your little friend, Kit. It came to me that you might be wondering what to do with your husband's personal effects." Mr. Rickaby said. "It's such a painful decision and I know that there are charities by the score that would gladly accept the things that can be of no use to him now. Kit has a father and the family are very poor.

Her father is a pensioner and the way pensioners are placed in this day and age, they have no possibility of buying new clothes ..."

Kit was coming down one day soon.

"I'll pack some of Mitch's clothes up and send them off. He'd be more than welcome, Kit's father."

When he had gone, I went upstairs and shut the door, stood with my back to it and knew blood in my mouth from a bitten lip. There is no good recalling the shoes from the low shelf, the brown brogues, the red leather slippers, the dressing gown against my cheek? In his wallet I found the photograph of myself and had not to turn it over to know what he had written on it.

"I am a rose of Sharon and the lily of the valleys."

Then Kit was there on a flying visit and I was embarrassed in asking her to accept Mitch's belongings. I had sent them on by Road Transport. She burst into tears.

"If you knew how hard it is to make ends meet! I'll take good care of them—never stop thanking you in my heart."

Then she was gone and the house was silent again and I was dressing to go to Milton Manor for my interview. I looked at myself in the mirror, chalk face, carbon smudges under the eyes, black suit, straight taffy hair in a pony tail. Then Mr. Rickaby was at the door in his car.

"I see you're ready on time. That's a good thing. Mrs. Swan's a stickler for punctuality."

I hurried out through the rain to the Rover and he opened the door for me to get in and the rain pattered on the windscreen. He started the wipers again and peered rather helplessly at the dashboard, as if it had as much complexity as an aeroplane. The car started with a jerk, for his mind was not on his driving, but rather searching for some topic of conversation.

"My son, Anthony, asked to be remembered to you in his last letter home. You know he's in Canada, a doctor, a pathologist."

He took his eyes off the road and we were in peril from a lorry for a second or two. Then we were in the clear again.

"He's coming home soon, some new exchange scheme, I

think. His mother's delighted, of course and so am I. Dear me! These roads are a death trap nowadays. The young men drive like charioteers. A person's not safe."

I was glad when the gates of Milton Manor came in sight, but Mr. Rickaby grumbled that they had not been left open for us. He fumbled with the latch of the door, but I was out of the car and had the gates open, had waved him safely through and shut them again and was back in the car, mumbling that there was probably a dog in the house, that might get out if the gates were not secure.

"That's true, my dear. No doubt that explains it. There's a small black terrier, very old now. He's Mrs. Swan's constant companion. Still, she could have sent Casey down to open the gates for us."

There were trees everywhere with bushy undergrowth out of control. The drive wound through a dripping tunnel and water coursed in the runnels down the sides. Grass grew in the middle and there were trees fallen everywhere, tangled in brambles and elders. Here and there were big neglected patches of rhododendrons. We wound on and around and about and finally came on a full circle, where the drive curled, before it took itself back to the front gates.

The house was very grand, a Victorian Manor of two stories, with steps up to the door and two pillars flanking them, five windows across the top and four below, weeds between the stones of the steps, gravel grassy, lawn a meadow. It was a rambling old house with an air of decrepitude about its grandeur and the rain was dripping off the eaves to a terrace below, to form pools that reflected the greyness and the shabbiness. We went up the steps and Mr. Rickaby pulled the bell. A dog barked from inside but far away.

"I hope they put that animal in the kitchen. He's a cross little chap and if he's there, he'll nip your ankles, if you don't watch out."

Nothing happened for a time and we knocked again, yet still there was no sign of us ever gaining entry. Mr. Rickaby fretted vaguely about the delay and had his hand raised to the knocker again, when the door opened silently to show a big heavy woman, who stood on the mat and looked out at us without a smile, then she stepped back and let us in, took Mr. Rickaby's hat and coat, and put them on the hall stand.

"This is Miss Mannion. She runs the whole place, has done so for years. I don't know what Mrs. Swan would do without her."

She made no move of any kind except to walk along to the door on the left and open it. She had soft flat shoes, like slippers and for all her weight, she moved without a sound. There was stealth about her, a watchfulness. I went into the room and saw Mrs. Swan for the first time. She had a high-backed blue Windsor chair by the fire and lifted a lorgnette from a table at her side and watched me as I traversed what seemed to be an acre of carpet, till I stood before her. There was a musty smell about the room as if no freshness had ever blown through it, as if it was part of a scene, past and forgotten. The furniture was heavy Victorian. In the mirror over the red velvet mantlepiece was a doll's house picture of the scene, with myself standing before this aged lady, begging sanctuary.

"We're in good time, Mrs. Swan. Here's Elizabeth Allington. I think you'll find her all I've said of her."

I held out my hand but she did not seem to see it.

"How do you do?"

She said nothing and there was no sound in the room. except the spit of the rain down the chimney into the fire. She sat, still as a statue, looking at me through her glasses, from my shoes to my legs, to my body, to my hair and back down again.

"She's pleasant anyhow. I'll say that for her."

She threw the lorgnette with a clatter on the table and looked up at me.

"Well then, Elizabeth, I must first say how sorry I am for your bereavement. I lost my husband ten years ago and I know how it is. Of course, he left me well provided for, not a pauper, but I've never recovered from the blow and never will."

The wind threw a handful of tears against the window panes and she fluttered her hand against her breast.

"I was never strong as a girl. His death put paid to me. I suffer with my heart, as Mr. Rickaby will have told you."

She looked at me more sharply and asked me if I were strong and I told her I had never been ill in my life. Then her hand was out imperiously and she asked me for my letters of recommendation ...

Mr. Rickaby was ill at ease. He had taken a stance with his back to the fire.

"I've explained all that, Mrs. Swan. I can vouch for her. The Vicar can speak for her. The hospital can give her a reference if you insist on it, but surely you have gathered that? She's Mitchell Allington's widow."

"That doesn't supply her with nursing diplomas," she said and there was anger in her that I was young and she was old, that I had known what it was to be married to a famous man. There was vinegar instead of blood in her veins and if I had any sense, I would have taken myself away, but I wanted to hide out and where better than this old house? Here was Miss Havisham's Satis House and Great Expectations all over again and nobody would ever come here and I could hide like a hare in a form in the grass and never face life any more, and one day, Mitch would come back. Had he not promised it? We would be together again.

"I nursed my husband, I'm not afraid of hard work. I'd be glad of it."

"Then you're very different from any girl of your generation that I've ever met. With no letters of recommendation, I couldn't pay you the wages I offered our mutual solicitor."

The drip from the leaves made a pattering on the veranda and splashed against the window to intensify the rain. There was a patch in the corner of the ceiling that ran down the wall-paper in a grey line. I fixed my attention on the tartan rug in the dog's basket by her chair.

"I promise you I'll do my best. If you'd explain what you want. I'd like a trial. If you don't like me, I'll go away."

I waited a bit but nobody spoke and I went on with it.

"A living-in would suit me nicely. I've been left badly off. I'd be most grateful."

Mr. Rickaby was angry at her attitude to me. He pointed
out in no uncertain terms that he was my solicitor as well as
hers. It had all been explained to her and the arrangement
almost made. If she was going to go back on her word and
start higgling like a pig jobber, it was time for us to take our
leave ... and goodday to her. There were plenty of other
posts available and there were institutions, who would be
honoured to engage me, knowing the debt that civilisation
owed to my husband. Besides, it's a secretary she advertised
for, not a nurse-companion.

She capitulated without loss of face. I could move in as
soon as I wished and it was a simple job of course. She
wanted a secretary. She was still on the Board of her
husband's chain of stores and there would be secretarial work
to do, but not too much. I would eat with her and if she had
guests, Miss Mannion would serve my meals in my rooms.
There were odd jobs that I could do, change the books at the
library, do the messages, keep an eye on the staff.

"You'll take Finn for his walks too. Casey had him out just
now. He's let him get wet. That's why he's in the kitchen,
drying out. Otherwise you'd have been introduced. He's my
dog."

"Does Finn shake hands, Mrs. Swann?" I asked and she
gave me a look as piercing as a dart and old Rickaby smiled
at me, as if he said "a hit, a palpable hit."

We had tea served by Miss Mannion, exquisite cucumber
sandwiches and rolled bread and butter. Miss Swan ruled
that I must pour out and she did it, just to spite Miss
Mannion, who took herself off sulkily on silent feet. Afterwards she was recalled to show me my apartments. Mr.
Rickaby accompanied us on the tour, whispered in my ear
that he wasn't too satisfied with the afternoon's work.

"I think that I've made an error of judgement, my dear.
She's a strange character and you've never learned how to
speak up for yourself. I'd forgotten what Anthony used to say
about you, when you were still in a gym dress with plaits
down your back. He called you 'a kind gentleness,' yet when
you worked for him, he was very taken with you. Mind you,
'a kind gentleness' is not right for Mrs. Swan's resident

secretary. You'll have to stand up for yourself and that's a tall
order after what you've just been through."

He sighed and Miss Mannion turned round to see where
we had got to our journey up the front stairs.

"Cling to your humour, my dear. 'Does Finn shake
hands?' I liked that. I really did. She saw it too, saw you had
the measure of her. I've been a fool. My wife and I would
have put you up, but she's been away ... flew out to Canada
to Anthony to come home with him ... took long enough
about it too ... it was just an excuse for a holiday ... and to
make sure Anthony's plane didn't crash, if you please."

I glanced into the rooms that had been allocated to me and
then we went back downstairs and Mrs. Swan and I made
our pact. I was glad to be out in the rain, sliding down the
wet snake of the avenue. In the Quicken Tree, Mr. Rickaby
watched me in the glass over the mantlepiece and the fire still
burned brightly and glad I was of it, for a cold had come into
my bones.

"Mrs. Swan's a wealthy woman. Her husband left her
very well off. She told you that. She'll say he was in
commerce. So he was. He was in hardware, started off selling
kettles in his mother's front parlour. By the time he died, he
had three hardware shops, all corner positions and every one
of them a gold mine. They had no children. There's a
nephew, a child of her sister. You'll meet him one day for he
visits there—name's Roger Hawkins. He's a peculiar
individual-sea-faring man, black beard. He's got a gold ring
in one ear, though I daresay that's not so eccentric as it might
have been twenty years ago. He hires out yachts on the
Mediterranean."

We had had a cup of tea and a biscuit. Now there was
business to attend to and my stomach turned to water at the
thought of it.

There were papers to sign and I must decide about the
Quicken Tree. His advice was for me to let it stand as it
was ... furniture and carpets and curtains—just to cover
everything in dust sheets and visit the place from time to
time. If I decided to sell up and let the house go to the highest

bidder, it could be arranged, but it was a final step to take and there would be no finding again what I had lost.

I wondered how he thought I could ever find that, but I took his point. Mitch's car I should keep. Mrs. Swan had a barn that would hold a dozen cars and she had made no objection. If I was careful, I could afford to keep the long white Alvis. How could I afford to see somebody else drive about in it?

"There'll be very little left, when the estate's settled. The Inland Revenue produces these situations with iniquitous repetition. Mitch just counted on having many years to come and then suddenly, there were none left. 'We know not the day nor the hour', Liz-Jane. Thank God my wife is hale and hearty. You don't know how I'm looking forward to her return with Anthony. He'll take up his old position at the Camford General, but there's talk of a Professorial Chair at the University."

He smiled gently.

"I'm quite sure that your old job as his amanuensis at the Camford General would be open still. He was very impressed with your work."

He stood on the step as I saw him off.

"When you get to the Manor, Liz-Jane, I would implore you to stop your ears to all the talk that goes on in the village and in the house and elsewhere maybe. They say it's haunted, but that's nonsense. I imagine you may hear 'bumps in the night', but that's usual in old houses. Don't be frightened at anything you see or hear. There's always a logical explanation. Above all, don't forget there's still laughter in the world. Laughter will get you by. Remember how long I've known you, back to the days when you knocked us like skittles around our own tennis court ... turned Anthony quite against that charming undergraduate from Girton College, by beating her six love, six love, six love. He always held that it was because she arrived at a village tennis party in frilly drawers, if you'll excuse me mentioning unmentionables, but I believe that it was your own ferocity that attracted him. I can see you now. You were wearing your school gym kit, with a blazer badge like a Knight's

emblem—a kind of a standard that you were determined to
defend against all comers. It's strange how a scene comes back
as sharp at the edges as if it happened only yesterday. You
had plaits down your shoulders with red bows to match the
blazer and a fringe on your brow and you glared out from
under the fringe as if you hated the whole world. You
maneouvred her into a singles and you slammed her against
the back line like a human canon ball and you won ... God
bless you. You won."

"Six love, six love, six love," I smiled and he bent and
kissed my cheek and wished my happiness to come again ...

I watched his car drive away and felt the loneliness of the
house like a desolation, but now the Quicken Tree must be
left. There was work to be done, and I might be tired enough
to sleep. I had lost track of the time but it came round very
soon. The day of Exodus.

The Wedgwood plates were arrayed on the dresser and the
wall tiles gleamed. The knives and the forks and the spoons
were ranked in the cantecn. The kitchen jars were lined like
soldiers along the shelves and then suddenly I came upon
them, the white capsules in the brown glass jar. They clicked
softly in my hand as I spun the container slowly round. I had
forgotten all about them. "Caps. Dorminal", I read. "Two to
be taken at bed-time."

I was supposed to have destroyed them, but the fires were
out now too. It was time for me to leave. I shoved the jar into
the pocket of my camel coat and knew that there would be
fires at the Manor House in Milton, which would eat them
up as quickly as any fire. The woman, who had seen them
during the last few days had laughed about them. She had
come in to help with the rough cleaning and she had been a
jolly creature. She had remarked at them and at her doubts
about the possibility, that I "would last long beyond at the
Manor."

"I should hang on to them capstules, ma'am. You can use a
handful to put paid to the old duck, if she were to get too
broody. There'd be no doubt they'd settle her hash and keep
her clacker quiet. They say in the village that she's a right old
trout. She's so mean that she'd skin a flea for the hide and

tallow. I wouldn't fancy a job up there. That house is haunted. They never manage to keep staff there, but Casey and his missis and that Miss Mannion."

"Mrs. Swan's been very good to give me a roof over my head."

"That's as may be, ma'am, but there's never smoke without fire."

I put my hands to my ears and she laughed at me.

"Put some of them bombs in her soup, if she gets past bearing. Still and all, she's worth a packet. She might leave you something in her will, for she'll be trying to make up to you, and you being a perfesser's widow and him a famous man who wouldn't look the side of the road she's on. You could have got a job on the telly to give talks and that, if you'd wanted."

I saw her through the front door with the salvage she had gathered from my wreck. Then I was ready to go. I went into the bedroom and looked at the four poster bed, that stood much as it had always stood, with the heavy embroidered quilt covering it and the curtains of red velvet folded back just so. This was the end of it all, the ends of the nights when we had lain in each others arms and known what heaven was like, where we had laughed and loved and thought that happiness was for ever. It was time to go, long past, long past.

I had packed my clothes and put them into the white car in the drive. I had only to walk down the stairs and turn off the water and the main switch of electricity, do all the final things. There was nobody to see me off and I thanked God that I had kept the house, that I had not sold Mitch's car. There was nobody to wave me goodbye and I was glad of that too.

I slammed the front door. The Alvis started like a bird. I had to get out to shut the front gate and now the house was empty, but P.C. Causer "had his eye on it". The road went by far too quickly. I was at the Manor gates almost before I had left the Quicken Tree and really I could have done with more time, to get myself orientated to the change that was taking place. The Manor gates were shut, but Casey was there, leaning over the top of them like a country man, but he was too sophisticated for a farmer in his blue uniform and the cap with the shiny peak. He was any rich woman's chauffeur handyman, a legacy from a deceased husband, used to the customs of a world, forgotten. His hand went to the peak of the cap and then he was opening the gate to let me through, shutting it again, coming to the car window.

"Good-afternoon to you, Mrs. Allington. I thought I'd see you in. You'll be lonesome the first day and be glad of a welcome, no matter how humble."

His voice was soft and there was the lilt of an Irish brogue in it.

"The name's Casey. I live with my missis in the side wing of the house up above. God! That's a powerful car you've got there. I daresay the mistress will be put out by your possessing such a vehicle. We have a Rolls in the garage, but it won't beat this. For God's sake, don't park the Alvis where she'll see it every time she comes out to the yard. It might be better to shove it into the old coach house so Herself doesn't often clap an eye on it, and have a fit."

I knew that the gloss on the old Rolls would match the polish on Casey's boots. The car and Casey would be the one vintage. The coachwork and his leggings must be a miracle of polishing. I was surprised that he thought I should try to conceal the Alvis and looked over my shoulder, as if I wanted to escape.

"Don't go looking back. Face the front, like the good soldier you are. Sure, you never know what lies round the next corner. Maybe there's fame and fortune again."

"And happiness?" I asked him bitterly and was astonished at the ease with which we could communicate.

"Aye, and happiness too. It's all darkness today. You're a wee ant on a fragment of cloth and in the cloth there's embroidered bits, gold and purple and black and the yellow of the sunshine. The whole world is black because the poor ant has got herself on a black bit. Who's to say there's not gold all about, waiting for the tread of them meek little feet?"

"It's very kind of you, Mr. Casey ..." I began and put a hand on his.

"Casey, just plain Casey. A man in my position is a servant. Nobody calls me anything but Casey, unless it's Pat. Perhaps you'd like to call me 'Pat'? I'm 'Pat' to my friends."

I thanked him, but he was not finished with his philosophy.

"It's not all dust and ashes, Acushla. There's no fire in it at present, but 'tis not all dust and ashes, though you're thinking it is. There's a lost look about you and you're in need of a friend. If anything was to go wrong up above at the house, call out for me or my missus. We'll not be far away."

He gave a deep sigh for he did not relish saying what he said next. He had come walking down the avenue to meet me and to start me off the way I was to go on.

"Watch out for Miss Mannion. It's a snake she is, and maybe I'm a Judas to come tattling round behind a person's back, but you've got to know. I'll get in beside you, if I may, and you'll take the car up the drive and round to the back. It got into my head that you might drive up to the front steps, the way you did the other day, and it wouldn't do, at all, at all."

He guided me round the back to a cobbled yard and a big old harness room, that made a wonderful garage. We parked the car and he toted the luggage for me, to the back door, and through it to a back hall, that was almost as big as the hall in front ... flagged too and with the same indefinable smell of damp about it. Miss Mannion appeared and looked at me and there was disappointment in her face that I had not knocked at the front door and been rebuffed. The servants' stairs was a narrow corkscrew of bare boards, which deposited us on a landing. The front staircase was a glory of architecture, which went up to a half landing and on to the top hall. Had I not climbed it and admired it, but it was not for me. I was "servants' hall" and what did it matter when the servants were the lords of creation compared with their mistress, for Mrs. Casey had come out of a door at the side of the top hall and put her arm about me, kissed me and hugged me against her side and asked God to pity me in my great sorrow and might the soul of the one that was gone from me, rest in everlasting light.

The front stairs came up to the landing and there was a door to the right and a door to the left. Miss Mannion was with us, listening to every word that was said and she nodded at the door on the right and almost stood guard over it.

"That's Mrs. Swan's room. Your apartments are opposite. You'll be near at hand, if she rings in the night."

Casey had already opened the door on the left and I saw that my "apartments" had been made ready for me. The brass bedstead had a white counterpane with bobbles on the edges and the sheets were old Irish linen. There was a basin with hot and cold, a heavy wardrobe, ugly Victorian, a chest of drawers, a dressing table, but I had seen them before. My sitting room was a pleasant place, that overlooked the gardens in front. It was all chintz curtains and chintz chairs and furniture, that had outlived its usefulness downstairs and had been relegated to the servants' quarters, but who was I to find fault? I could never expect the luxury, the glory, the richness of velvet ... the perfection of a Tudor four-poster bed. It was all finished. I offended Miss Mannion for a start by turning on the hot water at the basin for she thought I was trying her out on the temperature of the water system.

"I don't need an overseer. The water's hot," she said huffily.

Casey held out his hands to her in entreaty.

"Isn't there enough unpleasantness in this house, without you declaring war on the new lady? You always get it in your head that the mistress puts these lady companions above you and you take it out on them. It's terrible foolish for you to be thinking they leave because of you. They go because of Madame's tongue, that and the noises, that creep about the house."

Miss Mannion had gone with a hunch to her shoulders and Casey was following her, but he turned back to speak to me again.

"Watch the terrier too for he's a holy awful man for a bite. Mind yourself, when you go in the sitting room door, for he'll be lying in wait to have a go."

I went down the front staircase half an hour later when I had unpacked some of my things. There was a marble statue of a nude lady on the newel post, a lamp held above her head. Somebody had thought fit to drape her loins and breasts in white linen and I mourned that there was nobody to share the small jokes now. Mitch and I would have laughed before the fire in the Quicken Tree sitting room and talked about the narrowness and the propriety of minds, but there was nobody now to carry the jokes home to, as a dog might carry a bone. I walked across the hall and went through the door. There was a loud barking as I turned the handle and then I was inside in the same acre of carpet. I was greeted with fury as an old Manchester terrier hurled himself out of the basket. The furniture was not antique enough to have beauty, I thought, but for all its fustiness it was a lovely room, with two windows that reached out to the lawns and collected a superb Tree of Heaven and weeping willows and stout oaks and a yew hedge at the side. Then my time had run out for observation. I had my ankles to think of and I squatted down and held out a hand, palm up in surrender, smiled at the way the hair stood along his back like nap on velvet.

"Poor old chap, come and make friends," I said and knew better than to show fear. "I'm not going to hurt your missus."

He was in bad shape. He was very old and he had some skin trouble, that must have been hell, for he had scratched and left bald patches in his coat. His eyes had the milky look of cataract and he shook his head, as if he had ear trouble to add to all his other discomforts.

I turned his collar and read his name, put out a tentative hand, palm still up to grant him the victory. Mrs. Swan, over in the blue chair by the fire, as if she had not quit it since my visit, watched every move I made.

"He won't make friends, Mrs. Allington. You're wasting your time. You're lucky he didn't bite you. He bites everybody."

"He's got a bad ear."

I found a tissue in my pocket and rubbed it inside the ear he held low. He lifted his head and scratched his appreciation, put his front paws up on my knee. He took a great interest in the stuff I coaxed from his ear and wagged his tail, followed me across the room to the fire, where I dumped the tissue.

Then I held out my hand again and was moved to find his paw come to rest in it. He made a sizzling little noise, as if it was a trick he had learnt a long time ago and had almost forgotten.

"There's a thing then," said Mrs. Swan from above my bent head. "I never saw him behave like that, with a person come new to the house."

"He's got canker in his ear and it's bothering him. I'll take him to the Vet's if you like, and iodine oil might cure those bare places in his coat. We had a dog like that once …"

The dog had been my companion in my childhood loneliness and I remembered him now, recalled the warmth of his velvet coat and the faith in his heart, then pushed all thought of him out of my mind and begged him to forgive me and to understand, thanked providence that his grave was still at the Quicken Tree, with the chieftain's stone at his head, knew that the chieftain's stone was just a square block of lime that I had stolen from the rockery and chisel-inscribed with RODDY.

"So you're a veterinarian as well as a nurse, Mrs. Allington? I'll decide when it's necessary for my dog to have veterinary attention. Go away and wash your hands."

She was angry when Finn followed me to the cloakroom and back again. He jumped into his basket as soon as I sat down in the drawing room.

"He's very old … twelve, thirteen," she said.

"That only make's him more valuable, doesn't it?"

"Off with you then and ring the Vet. Tell him it's Mrs. Swan of Milton Manor. Tell him I want him here to see the dog. I'm not having Finn sitting in the dispensary of his. It's nothing more than a stable."

I did as she asked me and then we had tea. Miss Mannion served it gracefully. I was sent back to my place, when I tried to help.

"You're not a waitress. It's Mannion's job."

I read bits from the papers, and bits from woman's magazines, then a passage from a novel she had from the library. After what seemed a long time, we dined and Mannion served clear soup with croutons, steamed fish, tiny pancakes with lemon slivers, coffee done in a Cona, all perfection and no praise for the chef, only a snap at me.

"Don't sit down and get up again as if you were on springs. Mannion waits on table. You see to my stomach powders." Miss Mannion came in with a shining silver tray, a glass, a jug of milk, a spoon, a white cardboard box. Mrs. Swann opened the box and took out the folded papers, showed them to me. Each paper contained exactly the right amount. I was to tilt the contents of one into the glass, add the milk and stir it. Then she drank it down with great importance, as if there was to be more ceremony to it than there was to the dinner and tea put together.

"It's a very special prescription, that Dr. Jones insists on. Each powder is wrapped in a separate paper. It'll be your task to see that we don't run out of powders. I get twenty four at a time, sometimes forty eight. They're difficult to dispense so ring the chemist well in advance."

I listened to a full record of all her illnesses over the years.

"I'm a martyr to my stomach, always have been. I can't eat anything and when I do, I get this frightful pain. Of course, the doctor knows nothing about what it is, but at least these powders help me."

She looked at me irritably after a while and said she went to bed now. It was my task to help her. Tomorrow I must help her get up and bathed and dressed. Then there would be the messages to be done and maybe some letters for typing. Mannion would give me the shopping list and I must keep a strict account of what I spent. It was best to start as I meant to go on.

I helped her to bed and she found fault with me, most of the time, but I was past heeding her. I was away in the privacy of my own mind, remembering the bitter-sweetness of settling Mitch down at night, the creeping in beside him, the losing of myself in the safety of his arms, a safety that was going and going and gone. This was the start of another life. The next day would give me the first complete example of twenty-four hours. Just now, I wanted to sleep and forget, but all too soon the night was gone and it was time to help Mrs. Swan up again, when she had had her morning cup of tea and Miss Mannion had brought her breakfast up to her room.

There was a pile of letters for me to read to her, but she scrutinised each envelope and kept some of them confidential. I helped her get up and we "did the letters" in the sitting room. They were from different businesses, three of them, all ironmongers' shops, each one from a different part of the country, but trading under the name of SWAN OF LEEDS. She kept her confidential letters close and gave me no hint of what they were. Then she dictated some answering correspondence, waited till I typed them, signed them and made great business out of very little. She produced the stamp box out of a locked drawer in her desk and passed it to me, as if she presented me with the Bank of England, took it away from me again and locked it back where it belonged.

Casey was a great comfort to me in an interval break over a cup of tea in the kitchen.

"Don't take any notice of the way she lets you know she puts no trust in you. I've seen plenty of girls tread the path you're treading upon now and their hearts scalded with her goings-on. She's a right old rap, may heaven forgive me for saying so, but she was never any different, even when the master was alive. He was worse than she was, God rest him, but it wasn't the sorrow of his death, that turned her blood to gall."

After lunch, I helped her to bed for a rest and then helped her up again, did not get her hair done to her liking and she took the brush from my hand and threw it across the room and Finn had the kindness to retrieve it for me and bring it back to my feet. She leaned on my arm down the stairs and walked on a black ebony stick. Then on the half landing, she saw the priest arriving at the front door and stopped up short.

"That's Father Gillson."

He came across the hall and waited for us beside the naked lady with the linen drapes and she took her hand from my elbow, positively ran down the last flight and seized his hands in hers.

"Dear Father! How good of you to call. I hope you'll stay to tea."

Miss Mannion had opened the front door and now she stood silently waiting. She could not fail to miss hearing what Mrs. Swan said to me.

"Go along to the kitchen, Elizabeth. See that Mannion doesn't make a mess of it. She's ham-handed with dainty things."

I stood with my back to the kitchen door and looked at Miss Mannion wearily. I did not care what became of me, but I hated the hurt in the old house-keeper's eyes. I loathed the spite that was directed like a sword between the two of us, the way Mrs. Swan deliberately caused pain and unhappiness.

"Don't take any notice of a silly remark like that," I said. "You know it's not true. It's just general bloody-mindedness and old age. I have no intention of ever overseeing your work. What's more, I haven't the ability to do it and I never will."

She turned her back on me and her shoulders hunched.

"Set the trolly if you like. I don't care for her or for you or for Monseigneur Gillson. He can think what he wants to think and he can go and say to the nuns what she said about me."

I sat at the table and put my head in my hands and a bell jangled on the wall. I whispered to Casey, who was cleaning silver, if he thought I ought to go.

"You'd better go as quick as your feet will carry you," Miss Mannion snapped at me. "She's going to introduce you to the Monseigneur, more than she ever did me, but she'll know who stands by her in the end."

Casey was trying to keep out of women's quarrels. He laughed.

"It's time Master Roger paid us a visit. She's like a spitting cat because he hasn't been and she thinks he's neglecting her. Just wait till he comes on a visit, Mrs. Allington. You'll see a new woman, as soon as he puts his foot over the threshold."

The bell rang again and I ran through the baize door, along the hall and into the drawing room. Monseigneur Gillson made me a little bow, as Mrs. Swan told him who I was. I knew him by sight from seeing him walking through the villages in his black cassock, and round flat hat. He always carried his breviary in front of him and his lips muttered silently, as he prayed. He would have been more at home in France. There was a dark-jowled, dark-eyed look to him, that was unenglish.

"I must offer you my sympathy," he said in a soft voice. "I will pray to God to bring you comfort."

Finn had come rushing out of his basket to mock-protect me from our visitor and was making determined attacks at the heels of his shoes.

"Take him out. Take him out. Take him out," Mrs. Swan shrieked at me and I gathered the little dog into my arms and moved to the door, and the priest's teeth were white against the sallowness of his face, as he told me that Finn was a poor judge of character. He only made friends with the gypsies."

Mrs. Swan remarked that I would not thank him for his opinion, that Finn had made a friend of me from the first day he met me.

"And with Roger," said the Monseigneur. "I suppose he's still captaining some yacht in the Mediterranean. I'll hope we'll have him in Milton soon."

I put my fingers round Finn's greying muzzle and scolded him as he made another attempt at attack.

"You're a bad fellow," I said. "It's not done to bark at an eminent and holy man."

"I'm sure the father will excuse you, if you take Finn into the garden."

Father Gillson opened the door for me to go and bent his head down to mine, as I passed him.

"God is good," he said in a low tone, "Have faith in Him and He'll bring you peace in your heart. That's all that's necessary ... faith and patience and time."

I felt the tears in my eyes, for I found sympathy hard to bear. Finn was trotting off on the grass, looking back at me, barking in a high, sharp, asking-for-something voice. He searched the unkempt clumps of grass and presently, came back and put an old grey ball at my feet. I threw it for him and he was after it at once, very excited. I imagined it had been a favourite game and that he had had nobody to play with for a long time, but he got very breathless over it. Miss Mannion materialised beside me with her measured slow tread and startled me.

"He's not allowed play with the ball ... not for years. His heart is bad."

I sat down on the circular wood bench under the Tree of Heaven and invited her to sit with me, but she had no time, for there was work to be done. My offer to help her was turned down abruptly. I promised that I would be careful with Finn and just roll the ball a little way and she took herself off as silently as she had come. It was quiet and melancholy and lonely below the enormous branching tree. Miss Mannion might have been a ghost for all the effect she made on the Manor grounds. Surely there should have been bird-song, but the spinney nearby was silent. The only living creature was Finn at my feet, very happy to play ball again. He waged an imaginary war with it, rolling it over between his paws, growling with ferocity. He retrieved it from a yard's throw with an importance, that made me smile. He took it away to the safety of the spinney and pretended to kill it, sat down to rest for a while and then brought it back again. It should have been pleasant sitting out there in this gracious estate, but there was a "sleeping-beauty" quality there. The princess had been bewitched and was sleeping for a hundred years. Thorns had grown up about her lands, but here was nothing tangible. yet there was a spell on the place, so that no bird called, no children laughed in the garden. Only Finn and I were alive and all the others had gone. There was no happiness here. Mitch had gone and there was a foreboding of misery that lay before me, greater than any I had yet known. I tried to shake off the night, that had come down upon my soul, walked a piece down to a pool, that was oblong and weedy and ugly. In summer, it might be carpeted with water-lilies. Perhaps in summer, things would be bearable, but I knew things would never be bearable again. The fault was not in the Manor. It was within myself. I could always go, but I knew that a hard employer was the right choice to make. With kindness and indulgence, I would go to pieces. I turned back up the grassy slope towards the house and saw the Manor from a new angle. There was a wing that jutted back on the right hand side. It was hidden by a tall hedge of yew, with an arch cut in it. A path ran along the side of the house, through the arch. It must lead to the cobbled yard at the rear. I walked through, with Finn pattering at my heels. This was a sizable wing with three windows up, three down. There were bars to all the lower windows and to the far one at the top. That would have been the nursery in the old days. No child could ever escape that nursery and no burglar could break and enter below. The window at the far end of the lower storey had pebbled glass. Maybe it was some sort of office. It might even have been a school room with the pebbles put in to stop small eyes straying from lessons.

The shrubbery was neglected. A brick wall separated this section of the ground from the cobbled yard, where the Alvis was. I tried to get a plan of the whole Manor lay-out in my mind. This wing was inhabited for I could hear a peevish voice protesting from inside. Yes, the wing ran behind the kitchen. On the top floor, it would be a corridor that stretched from my rooms to the back of the house. I had not seen a corridor, but there was a closed door beside my bedroom door, that probably opened on a passage ...

The door to the wing from the garden was at the back. I heard Pat Casey's laugh and the scrape of the back door and Mrs. Casey came out. She must have seen me and come to ask me in. She came round the corner to find me, smiling at me and putting her arm through mine. Finn knew her, but he attacked her with his usual ferocity, wagging his tail all the time to show that it was just a game. She told him to stop his nonsense, that she was not in the least terrified of him. She was wearing a blue nylon overall and her iron grey hair was satin smooth about her head. I expected her to bring me into the house, for this must be the Caseys' quarters, but instead, she led me back under the archway and on down the lawn to the Tree of Heaven.

"I hope you'll settle down, Mrs. Allington. The others are always up and away like the wild geese, after a few weeks of Herself. Small blame to them!"

She drew me to sit by her on the seat under the tree and then she saw that I had been rolling the ball for Finn. She made great laughter out of the fact that he would in no way retrieve it for her.

"Och, you're an obstinate devil, just like the one inside, but I don't mind you and I don't mind Herself. Show her you don't care and she'll soon stop, like Finn does the barking."

Casey and she lived in the wing, quite independent of the main part of the house. They had their own kitchen, living room and bedroom and they lived quite separate from the Manor and that was how Mrs. Swan wanted it to be. They could go and come as they pleased and they had worked for the Swans for a long, long time.

"The place has gone down. You should have seen it in the old days. The garden was a picture. Casey does his best with it and I help him an odd time, but 'twould take two men, whole time. Casey only just manages to keep it down. There's a deal to be done, inside and out. We used to have girls from the village for the housework, but they don't want domestic nowadays ... want the evenings free and who's to blame them, with the factories sending buses out to collect them and week ends off and money to be spending on discs and perms and stick-lips and that? Times is changed ..."

Times were indeed changed. I stood up and put my hand against the trunk of the great tree. Mitch had it that a spirit lives on, no matter how things changed. I got a sudden feeling that his spirit was all about me ... wondered if it had infiltrated the tree and if he breathed the murmur, that whispered through the grace of the softly moving branches. It was as if Mrs. Casey could read my thoughts, for she looked at me with her face sharply upturned.

"Don't be frightened if they tell you the Manor's haunted. I know the village is always on about it and nobody will come here and stay long. Don't listen to it, just shut your ears. It's pub talk. There's nothing men won't get up to for conversation when they have a few pints. I'm Irish and so's Casey. We'd not be the ones to deny, if there were to be a ghost walking the old house. Now I'll tell you no lie. Down in the Barley Mow, that say that a "grey lady" treads the top

corridor. That's the one that runs from the back of our wing
to the top landing. If you ever heard the like, they say she has
a child in her arms and it crying! I give you my oath, I never
heard or saw the like in the top corridor and it going past my
bedroom door. Sure, there's always noises in an old house in
the dark. I've lived in that part of the Manor for a long time
and I never saw anything in the way of a ghost."

I looked down at her with sad eyes and told her that I had
no fear of ghosts ... only a longing for one particular spirit. I
asked her in a whisper if she thought I would have fear if my
man came walking down the corridor to find me. I began to
tell her about some of the things he believed and the sorrow
in her eyes matched the sorrow in mine. She told me that, of
course, he would stay near me and even from heaven he
would watch over me and almost I wept in her arms, but
Finn was barking and Miss Mannion had come in her
soft-footed silent way and all thought of the supernatural had
been put to flight like the mist before the sun.

"Mrs. Swan will soon be ringing the bell for you and she'll
not like you gossiping on the lawn ..."

Mrs. Casey made some joke to cover the awkwardness and
was away, but Miss Mannion was walking me like a
prisoner across to the front steps.

"You needn't be hoping to make a bosom friend of Casey's
wife. the Mistress won't have you making free with the
Caseys. They keep themselves to themselves. Mrs. Swan will
come down on you like a thunderclap if she finds that you're
in the side wing. Mrs. Casey knows better than to ask you
there even for a cup of tea. There was a girl lost her job over
it. You'll get no invitation from the Caseys, much as they'd
like to be entertaining visitors."

That was the way it was to be and there was no
explanation. The Caseys were friendly. They made my stay
in the Manor bearable, but their friendship stopped off short
at the door to their part of the house. I never penetrated into
the wing in any way. The curtains were thick webbed with
net, the walls too solid for sound. The windows were always
shut and the door closed. It was a mysterious forbidding
place.

Every day was a replica of the day before. I got up at six thirty and bathed and dressed. did out my room. Then there was Mrs. Swan to attend and Finn to be taken for his walk on the lawn. It was so much routine and waiting on Mrs. Swan was the important part of my work. The secretarial side was nothing, just an excuse to cage a lady companion in a job, which no modern girl would accept. I wanted a place to hide and I had found it, with this hag-witch, who nagged me endlessly. I would stick it out, but the situation was getting me jittery. In the small hours, I heard the noises of the old house, whispers that murmured outside my door, steps along the landing down the wing corridor. There seemed to be a weeping that percolated the walls, as if the grey lady did indeed walk with her baby. I had taken to imagining things. One night my bedroom handle was turned and I thought the door clicked against the latch and clicked back again. I was glad I had shot the lock, but surely there were voices, that argued on the landing, though I knew there should be nobody there? Sometimes, Mrs. Swan's bell would set my heart racing ... summoning me from my wakefulness to get her a warm drink from downstairs. I came to dread the walk past the white-shrouded statue with the light upheld in her hand. There was always the feeling that somebody had been on the stairs a moment before, that somebody had just come into the kitchen and was somewhere in the shadows.

I stood three months of it and then I knew I could take no more. With Mrs. Swan's cheque in my hand, I gave her my notice. I remember that I picked Finn up under one arm and held him close just for comfort, while the white rimmed irises surveyed me with fury through the lorgnette. There was no doubt of it. Her words poured down on me, how she had just begun to get some use out of me. She had trained me and she had paid me far more than I was worth. She would not be put upon. She just would not accept notice and if I did insist on leaving, I would go with no reference from her.

"Where are you to get a job with the character I'll give you? Any prospective employer will ring me up and I'll paint you in your true colours."

I held the cheque out to her and she was all conciliation suddenly.

"Settle back and stop all this nonsense. This place had been a haven for you and you'll not want to get out in the world again. I don't think that marriage held all that attraction for you. Maybe your husband's death was a release for you? I've heard you laughing and joking with Father Gillson. 'It's not done to bark at an eminent and holy man', indeed, and you in the house a few hours and your professor in his grave as many days. It would sound nice in a reference, wouldn't it?"

She laughed and made a joke of it, but I knew she was serious.

"I'll stay on, but Mitch's death was no release for me. If you knew what it was to camp on Patanga and look to sea at the canoes lying offshore! If you knew what it was to see that grave mound opened up and know that no man had looked down the shaft to an archaeologist's dream for thousands of years ... that no light had shone there ever, since the slabs of rock had been laid down thousands of years before ... and the perfection of that last expedition, the camp near the smooth green grass of the dig, the khaki canvas of the tents, the mosquito netting, the trestle tables, the lamps from our own dynamos, the water jars ... and Mitch was a king ... Do you know what it is to lie in the arms of a king?"

I stopped up short, horrified at my outburst. Then I spun on my heel and rushed for the door, with Finn still under my arm and the cheque fluttering in my fingers. At the door, I turned again and apologised.

"I'm sorry. I shouldn't have spoken like that. I loved him and I'll never stop loving him. I hope, Mrs. Swan, that when your times comes, you will die of a normal natural recognised disease and not of something that wafted out of a Patanga millennium."

So I failed to escape from Mrs. Swan and settled back into the miserable routine and the year ran away as slowly as treacle in the Arctic, and she was cruelty and spite and hatred and hurt to me.

Then one day we were doing the letters and the colour

brightened her face. There was one from Roger Hawkins and she opened it and read it, threw it down on the table and clapped her hands.

"He's coming to stay for Christmas. We haven't had him here at Christmas for eight years. Of course he pays flying visits, but he always makes some excuse for Christmas. This year, he'll actually be here. I can't believe it's true."

She turned into another woman, eager to be alive, with plans to make and work to be done, a life to enjoy instead of bear. Mrs. Pat was fetched and I had to take down a stream of orders. Casey would take me into Milton for the shopping, or maybe Histington, but village shopping would not be good enough for Roger. We must get on to Fortnum's and Harrod's and Jackson's of Piccadilly. It was late for Christmas orders, but I must insist that it was urgent. The stuff must be sent off today and if it didn't come in time, they'd have to take it back. The big bedroom must be turned out, a fire lit there and the bed aired properly and the furniture polished. Where was Casey? It would be his job to find a Christmas tree, and holly and ivy and mistletoe, in the wilderness that was the back garden.

"We must decorate the house between us. I feel like the Father of the Prodigal Son. 'This my son has come home again. He was lost and is found.' It's going to be like the old times, all over again."

7

ROGER HAWKINS

It was a bitterly cold day with an east wind that keened across the flat country, the day I took Mitch's Christmas wreath to the churchyard in Histington. I parked the white Alvis near the lych gate and the flagged path reminded my feet of the way to the grave. The old pain took me in the roots of my throat and the fact that the chrysanthemums I had brought the week before were dead too, was a small unnecessary additional sorrow. I knelt to tidy them away and felt something hard in the pocket of my coat. It jogged my side as I worked. I picked out a jar of capsules and put them back again, set up the holly and ivy and mistletoe and Christmas roses above his breast. I prayed that he was safe and happy, that soon I might see him again. Then the capsules were in my hand again, clinking temptation to me. I had forgotten all about them. They had lain in my pocket since the day I had come to the Manor. I had forgotten to burn them, forgotten that I had a path to Mitch, yet God would never let me go to heaven, if I committed the sin of taking my own life. I might never meet him in the whole of eternity and there were eminent men, who believed that, not only myself. There was no escape by that route now or ever. I bowed my head and wept and my tears splashed through my fingers into the green of the wreath. I did not see the bearded man till he spoke. He had come along the grass edging of the path and he stood there looking down at me.

"It can't be as bad as all that," he said in a pleasant voice and I spun about and saw Roger Hawkins for the first time. He helped me up and wiped my tears with a silk handkerchief from his breast pocket, pushed back my hair from my face with a cool hand, lifted my hand to scrutinise the wedding ring.

"Father? Brother? Husband?"

I pulled myself from the arm he put round me and tried to get the capsules back into the secrecy of my pocket, but he was too quick for me. He took them and jinked them round with the old familiar sound and he walked round the grave to read the headstone.

"Mitchell Summerfield Allington? So you're *that* Mrs. Allington? You're the pretty Mrs. Copperfield and you're all wrong for Milton Manor and you needn't look surprised for I know all about you, except how you got these capsules."

My hand was in his and he was leading me down the path and into the church. The door creaked and the smell of damp and mouldering years came out to meet us. He put me into a pew half way up the aisle and set himself down on the front of the pew with his feet on the seat near me. His handkerchief landed in my lap and I dried my eyes and tried to pull myself together, but could think of nothing to say.

"You don't belong in Milton Manor. You're a honey-coloured faun. Imagine my aunt finding herself a honey coloured faun for a secretary and that secretary business was a confidence trick, if ever there was one. She wanted a lady-help, but God help you! You can't like it there. No wonder you're miserable."

I wondered where he had been to get such sun-tan and dimly remembered that he hired out a yacht somewhere. His eyes were like agates and his beard was black in a Spanish line along his jaw. He had a gold ring in the lobe of one ear and there was swash-buckling, piratical, devil-may-care, foreign air, to him.

"You're not supposed to come till the six o'clock train to Histington," I whispered. "Pat Casey is to meet you with the Rolls."

"I hitched a lift from town with a teenager, but she pitched me out at the Red Lion and told me to walk the rest of the way. She was very accommodating, but I got tired of her. She took me so far but no farther."

His laugh was alien in the dim, damp sanctity of the nave,

but he was jinking the capsules round, as if they mesmerised him. Then he unscrewed the top, emptied some into his hand, looked at them, replaced them, screwed the lid closed again, raised a brow in question.

"They were from when Mitch ... died. I was supposed to burn them, but I put them in this pocket and forgot them. The coat's not been worn since I went to Milton. It's been hanging in the hall."

"You were thinking just now that they were the way out. It was written all over you. If I hadn't been delivered at the church by the accommodating teenager, you'd have done it, Mrs. Allington."

I shook my head and he agreed with me, threw the capsules back to me, said I'd have gone to hell and it would have served me right and what was my name? His aunt called me Elizabeth, but that wasn't right for me.

"Beth? Liz? Lily-bet? Never Elizabeth."

"He called me Liz-Jane."

"Very well then, Liz-Jane. Isn't it like my aunt to insist on Elizabeth, but anyhow these capsules are no answer to your problems. Your heart isn't in the grave yonder. You're only a kid. Your whole life is to come."

He jerked my head up roughly with a finger under my chin and studied my face without mercy.

"Have you forgotten what it's like to be kissed ... properly. Your man was ill for a long time. He was a dry-as-dust archaeologist. He was older than you or so they tell me. Have you forgotten the art of long, languorous, lingering kissing? Maybe you never even learnt it."

I jumped up and tried to escape him, but he barred my exit from the pew with one foot and grinned down at me, before he grabbed me by the shoulders.

"You're quite something, even with your hair in a mess and your face a-wash. Don't be afraid of me. I know my reputation will have gone before me ... that I'm a sea-faring man from the Med. and they're the worst. I know I have a wife in every port but each one of them is happy. For God's sake, stop keening the dead and look forrard. Let's get back to the venerable decayed pile and break out the booze. I could use a drink and I'm sure you could too."

He made no attempt to kiss me, though for a moment I knew he considered it, just took my hand and led me down the aisle.

"Transport?" he said and I told him that the Alvis was at the lych gate.

"That Alvis yours? Another pretty rich girl? My luck seems to be in today. Why on earth do you play lady companion at the Manor, if you've got money?"

I made him no answer. He would learn soon enough that the Inland Revenue had taken care of Mitch's fortune, that and an attitude about money that cared nothing for insurance and deposit accounts and counting the cost of things, nothing for looking to the future and making provision for the rain, when it came and it had come, in torrents and sweeping everything before it.

He pushed me over when I tried to get in the driver's seat and took the wheel himself, drove with a reckless speed and that surprised me, but I did not care. He could drive me to the devil if he wished.

"She's all the family I have, the old girl. I have to show up now and again to keep her sweet. If she knew I was on the way already, she would have been at the door waiting for me, a mug's liking for a old woman to have about a man."

Then he was tearing up the gravel of the drive and skidding to a halt, making a fanfare on the horn that must have startled the whole household. I knew that Mrs. Swan was resting on her bed and I was well aware that the Alvis belonged round the back, but it was useless to attempt any guidance. He was out of the car and up the steps, beating a tattoo on the front door, that made him one of the canoe-Indians of Patanga sending out a message on the war drums.

I climbed out of the car and watched, fascinated by his impact on the old house. Miss Mannion opened the door to him and was swept up into his arms and twirled round and round in a circle that must have scattered her brains. Then Casey was there and with a firm handclasp and a clapping of fist on chest. Casey came to take the Alvis round to the back yard to unload the luggage, a sailor's duffle bag and a zip-along case. I stood at the door and saw Mrs. Swan come running, like a girl, down the front staircase to greet him. She had thrown a shawl about her shoulders, but apart from that, she was still in her slip, her hair captive in its boudoir cap. He caught her up as if she were a child and cradled her in his arms, kissed her, till she begged him to stop. When he put her down, she was so dishevelled that he kept her in his arm, the boudoir cap gone and her hair loose round her shoulders.

"You should think shame arriving early with nothing ready."

He let her go and stretched his hands out to enclose the hall, the twenty-foot tree, the holly bunched everywhere it could go, the ivy trailing round the pictures, the mistletoe under the central lamp. The light winked red against the holly berries and caught the yellow of the bunches of celandines, that I had found in a sheltered part of the garden. Mrs. Casey had turned on the blink lamps of the tree and it was a glory in its tinsel and Jack frost, with the crackers from Fortnum's thrown down at its feet, like white and red and blue treasure.

"Nothing ready for me?"

His laughter took all the unhappiness from the house and tore it to shreds and made nothing of it and I stood there, not knowing what to do. Mrs. Swan's eye lit on me and there was a silence. I moved across to the kitchen door and knew myself to be no part of the happiness, that had arrived at Milton Manor. I felt like any poor relation, not knowing my place, but Mrs. Swan put me into it sharply.

"Go to the kitchen and help Mannion with the tea. Get that car of yours stabled. You know it's not allowed in the front drive."

I took off my camel coat and hung it on its accustomed hook and I forgot the capsules and left them in the pocket and there was no excuse for me to do that. In the glass I saw my face, my hair falling on my shoulders, the pink in my cheeks, my mouth sulky and I knew that I was sulky. I would have passed as a sixteen-year-old teenager with as much knowledge of the world as any sixteen-year-old teenager.

If ever I learned humility, I learned it that Christmas, for in my years with Mitch, I had been fêted and spoilt with kindness. I was on a sea-saw. Sometimes, Mrs. Swan wanted me present. Sometimes she dismissed me with a wave of her hand. I would have been far happier in the kitchen as a permanency with Miss Mannion or better still banished to the Caseys' wing. Roger mostly paid no attention to me. I thought he studied my relationship with Mrs. Swan in the first hour of his arrival. I even heard Mrs. Swan's words to him, as I passed them on my way to the kitchen, and it was unimportant to her whether I overheard it or not.

"Don't get any ideas there, Roger. Sex, yes, but no money. Why do you think she's working here? It's gone with him to the grave, after the treasures he found for the nation. That's the thanks they give you, the tax people ... and mind you imprint that in your head. Glory doesn't bring in the cash, the way muck brings brass, and don't you count on anything after death. It's a great leveller is death."

I dined with Mrs. Swan and Roger on Christmas Day, but he took care not to pay much attention to me. They talked about people and places I had never known. I might have been Roger's young sister, no, not even that. We pulled Harrod's crackers and read out mottoes and exclaimed at the luxury of such charms to be found in a bon-bon. He put on a Robin Hood hat, turned up at the side with a gay feather in it for decoration. Then he found a witch's hat from somewhere and put it on her, did not let her see it till she looked in the mirror and then she scolded him, and he took her to the mistletoe, that hung in the hall and kissed her and was forgiven.

Then she had gone upstairs and we were alone and I saw the other side of him. He stood at the fire, picked up a cigarette, lit it from a paper spill from the mantlepiece and there were twin fires in his eyes.

"Are you a woman? Are you grown up yet or are you a waif from fairy lands forlorn?"

He had kept a diamanté coronet from the crackers and he put it on me.

"That witch-hat suited her and this suits you. You're a

woman, very desirable. Maybe that's what you are, mystery girl, but perhaps you're just an unobtrusive honey-coloured doe-eyed dolly bird."

I took off the coronet and threw it into the fire and Mrs. Swan was back downstairs, all suspicion. I ran for the kitchen door and heard her voice loud and imperious.

"Enough of this tom-foolery! I've always told you that one day the English will be feasting at their Christmas turkey and plum pudding, the whole of them too full to surfeit and well-being to care and the lean hungry men will come in with long knives and then, the English nation will be brought to their knees, and the paper hats still on their chopped-off heads."

I ran through the baize door to the kitchen, but I paused and heard the end of it.

"Now, Roger, the time has come to talk business. Can you tell me where all this money goes? I'm not made of it, though you think I am. It's cupboard-love brings you home, like your compass. I'm not the north pole star. I've warned you. What excuses have you got this time?"

I heard her scream as he lifted her up. He saw that he had not kept her stoked up with enough alcohol. It was unkind to think that, but I knew it was the truth. Finn barked at them, excited by all the festivities, and I wanted to go in and pick him up and take him out of some evil that was forming there. instead I played eavesdropper and kept my ear against the baize.

"One of these days, you'll find out, Roger. You'll be sorry when I'm dead and gone and there's no Manor House to come creeping back to with a pile of unpaid bills to put on my desk."

I crept to the kitchen and found Miss Mannion and together we tackled the washing up. Presently the Caseys came in and we made what joy we could with the left-overs from the feasting. There were crystallised fruits and some almonds and raisins and stuffed dates and I knew that I should have been grateful for the rich crumbs from Mrs. Swan's table. Then after a long time, Roger came into the kitchen and the place lit up in fun, for he had the effect of bringing cardboard figures to life and resurrecting the dead spirit of a feast.

"I want a kettle of hot water. This is Xmas or have you all overlooked the fact? I'm going to make grog. This house is as cold as charity and I've been frozen in that parlour more ways than one. The damn fire's nearly out, for a start ... or maybe a finish."

He opened the flue on the boiler and the flames flickered against the formica window. He had brought in cut glass tumblers from the dining room. There was a bottle of rum in his pocket and he set it in the middle of the kitchen table, splashed a good tot of rum into five tumblers and presently doused it with boiling water. He passed a drink to each of us with a tea cloth over his arm and pretended he was a waiter and he cheered us along with a toast.

"A happy Christmas to you all ... happiness to the ship and to the people who dwell aboard it ... and prosperity. We mustn't forget prosperity. We must never forget prosperity."

He was high with some private excitement. He kissed Miss Mannion's cheek, hugged Mrs. Casey, clapped Casey's shoulder and lifted an eyebrow at me.

"I've got news for you We've been talking finance in the parlour, my aunt and I, but the old lady will never open her mouth about it to you. It's as well I tell you, for you deserve to know that there's a Christmas present for you all."

He took his drink and sipped it, smacked his lips, drained it at a gulp, and the gold ring gleamed in his ear and the smell of rum grog pervaded the room.

"We talked about the will. We always have the will out for an airing, but I've never spoken of it to you. She's not forgotten any one of you, not even pretty little Mrs. Allington. Mr. Rickaby's drawn up a new draft of the document and my aunt's signed it. She's left you money, not that a thousand's much money these days, but it ain't chicken feed. If you're still in her service on the day she dies, you each stand to gain a thousand."

He poured himself another drink and drank it down with the same speed and he was more than a little tipsy.

"She's a great old warrior and she's got a rough side to

her, still there's a good heart hidden in there somewhere. She'll not forget those that stood by her."

The drawing room bell clanged and he went off to answer it and I knew him for a puppet on a string, like every one of us. I did not trust him and thought he might have been joking cruelly with us, but what did it matter when I remembered the Quicken Tree and how it had been with the fire burning brightly and how the stone mantlepiece had looked with the holly wreath above it and all the Christmas cards on ribbons round the room?

"He's always the same," Casey said. "Don't put too much faith in what he says, Mrs. Allington. He'll hang round here for a while and then he'll be off to sea again. Don't get mixed up with him, lady, and turn the key in your door at night. Don't ever leave your bedroom door unlocked ... not while he's in the house."

I never did leave my door unlocked, not since I had heard or imagined that I heard the footsteps on the landing and the steps along the corridor, not since I had seen the handle turn. Besides, Roger was a charmer and perhaps he thought he did me a favour, when he waylaid me behind Mrs. Swan's back and tried to feed my hunger for what he called proper kissing, "long, languorous, lingering kissing". He fancied himself at dalliance and the mistletoe in the hall had been a trap. After a peck at my cheek, he had moved in for proper kissing. The tiger grip on my arms and the assault of his tongue in my mouth, trying to force surrender had recalled the grave at Histington and his words still spoke in my mind. "Have you forgotten? Maybe you never even learnt it? He was older than you."

I had broken away from him with all my strength and had struck him with every ounce of force I had in my arm, yet that had not avenged me. Even a back-hander across the other side of his face had not settled my debt, though it had convinced him and he had taken a step back and laughed.

"Not a honey-coloured fawn then? There's a lioness in there, but isn't it time you forgot the dead lion?"

Mrs. Swan had appeared and I had been glad to see her. She looked as us suspiciously for a moment as well she might, but then her mind switched and she gave me some news that she should have delivered days before.

"We're going to a sherry party at the Rickabys' on Boxing Day, Elizabeth. You do know you're invited, but I may have forgotten to tell you. Mr. Rickaby was over on business on Tuesday and he told me that Anthony and his mother are home from Canada. Apparently, you know him quite well and the Rickabys insist that you come with Roger and myself. It slipped my mind ..."

On Christmas night, I lay in my bed and remembered Anthony Rickaby, the Forensic Pathologist from Histington, who had never failed to stop in the High Street to pass the time of day with my schoolday self. I remembered the washed out blue jeans and the scarlet ribbons in my hair and how I had been asked to his people's house to tennis parties. I looked back into that other world at the Girton college girl and her short frilly pants and how she had let him down time after time in mixed doubles, till eventually I had smashed her in a singles, six love, six love, six love and how Anthony Rickaby, whom I loved more than all the world, had laughed at me.

"I didn't know that a honey coloured faun could play match tennis."

They had both called me "honey-coloured faun". It was strange over so many years, but I moved on to the Camford General Hospital and the typists' pool and the days, when I achieved the position of pathologist's secretary. Miss Bunn! That was the old secretary's name and she had died suddenly and Dr. Rickaby had been very grieved, yet he had stopped to talk to me, alien on level two or was it three ... windows all along the side so that it was like a track of light.

"You can be loneliest of all in a crowd," he had said. The smell of the autopsy room came clearly across the years, and I remembered from the other life what it had been like to sit on a stool and take down dictation, to type it out later, with my carbon scribes and lay the heap of typescript on his desk, a faithful-spaniel retrieving a shot hare. I remembered the court-rooms and the evidence, the "expert evidence". There had been a visit to Histington now and again, to Mr.

Rickaby's house in the High Street and Mr. Rickaby was the solicitor, who had just delivered a verbal message to Mrs. Swan. I thrust Milton Manor back and called up the past, the dark lonely common, where a girl might be done to death. Then a bulldozer had dug up bones at the castle Site and Mitchell Allington had taken Camford like an emperor, and myself watching his eyes, green in the glass over the staff-room mantlepiece, and myself trying to evict "a Mr. Mitchell, commercial traveller in osteological products", who wanted to sell bones to Dr. Anthony Rickaby.

Mitch and Anthony and I had dined out in the Garden House and I had seen crêpes suzettes for the first time and Mitch had called it food fit for the Pharoes of Egypt, but it was only because of the long jade ear-rings he had given me ... and his love for me had burnt me up like a torch and my infatuation for Anthony had dwindled and died, only for the look in his eyes, as he watched us walk along the tarmac to the jet to Cairo, Professor and Mrs. Mitchell Allington, with the whole world at our feet.

I could never forget the pain and emptiness in Anthony's eyes.

He had gone to Canada.

His letters to me had started with that first one after Mitch's death and I had it still, full of love and tenderness, so that I knew he had loved me, as my friend Kit had told me, standing on her head and waggling her feet in the air, and with the thought of Kit, I smiled and fell asleep and there was no moving of the handle of the door, no whispering in the landing, no steps along the corridor only a small voice that sang in my dreams, but there was no reality in it.

> "Taffy was a Welshman. Taffy was a thief.
> Taffy came to my house and stole a joint of beef.
> I went to Taffy's house. Taffy wasn't in
> I put a red-hot poker under Taffy's chin ..."

Then I was asleep and darkness covered the earth and Christmas day was over and it was the Feast of Stephen, and time to get up and dress and take up the burden that living had become.

8

THE WHITE KNIGHT

Yet I was looking forward to the sherry party that Boxing Day evening. Mrs. Swan and Roger had some secret disagreement on between them and were like two spitting cats. I kept away from them as much as I could and was glad when the time came to change. I had a black dress, well cut, very plain, that I thought should be suitable for my station in the Manor. What jewellery I still possessed was locked in a safe at the bank and what Mitch had called "my purple and gold regalia" was packed and put away and would never be worn again. What use had I for a sable coat, for an evening cloak of white mink that touched the floor? I would never sell them, for that would be a betrayal. Besides, there was a seller's market, that made such things profitless. Far better to put them away and remember the way Mitch had looked at me, the evening I came down the long staircase, with the mink falling softly from my shoulders and the jade ear-rings, matching the dress.

The black dress would never be out of place. It would not disgrace me in the society of Milton and the white Royal Stuart tartan stole with the fringed ends lifted it a degree of fashion. I took out the sage green ear-rings and held them in my hand and put them away again. There were many memories, that would be taken out tonight and put away again, but just for now, Mrs. Swan was almost ready and it was time for me to go to her room. She was very splendid indeed in a long black dress, dazzled with sequins and she surveyed me through the lorgnette as usual and told me I was dull and dowdy.

"You look like a crow in that black. Roger likes his women to be smart."

He was sitting on the bed going through the contents of her jewel case, as if he was making an inventory and he winked at me, as he took out an emerald ring and put it on her finger. Then he had found the necklace that matched it and was fastening it round her stringy neck, while she watched him in the mirror.

"Those glitter-stones will have the boys after you tonight. I can see you getting yourself wed again one of these days ... and that's enough gems. No more. You're perfection."

He made a game of her and she was fool enough to be taken in by him. He opened the wardrobe and found her mink coat and wrapped her up in it, hugging it round her as if he loved her, but it was quite clear to me that they had been nagging each other all day and there was more hate than love in him.

He spun round on his heels and laughed and made a great joke about the fact that he would see what he could do about me. The jewel box was rifled again and there was a diamond clip pinned to the shoulder of my stole, Scots fashion. Then he shook his head and unpinned it again, took the stole and threw it on a chair, picked out her sable stole from the wardrobe drawer, where it was kept. He draped it on my shoulders and clipped her diamonds on the fur and he had an eye for style. Back at the jewel box, he helped himself again and he knew his way around it.

"She's the pearl necklace and twin set type, Aunt Swan," he said. "Let her borrow some of your fine plumage for the evening like poor little Cinders."

I was angry, but I refused to let them see it. Mrs. Swan was angry too, but for once, she could think of nothing nasty to say. She had to hide the fact that she was jealous of what he had done, angry at my being given the use of her valuables, angry at the way the whole day had gone and how could I know how it had gone?

"You must have had lovely things once, before you were widowed, dear. You'll know how to look after the jewels and the furs and let me have them back safely when we get home tonight."

"It's bad enough to be bereaved, but to lose everything as well ..."

She looked sharply at Roger and it was written in her face that she was silently implying the same thing she had said before. "Don't get any ideas there. Sex, yes, but no money. Why do you think she's working here?"

It was quite clear to me all at once. He had been haggling all day with her for money and maybe I had been discussed as a prospective match and turned down. I was not penniless of course, but the house mortgage had not been cleared and there was interest and rates and soon the valuables would have to go. Mr. Rickaby would never have told her my business but he knew how precariously I lived, and how glad I had been of a roof over my head while things were brought to order and my assets balanced against my debts.

Casey drove us in the Rolls and I had got my anger under control. The strange scene of dressing for the ball had quite put the thought of Anthony out of my head, but as we reached the house, I thought of him again and my heart started to beat fast. I knew the house of old. I took Mrs. Swan's coat from her and put it on the stand in the hall, and she glittered into the sitting room and left me. Nellie Pluck must be somewhere about. She was an old retainer and I knew she still worked there. I had not met her for ages, but she knew me at once, appeared at my side, not a day older than when we had last met. Her smile turned on the sun for me. I felt I had come home from school. Almost I expected she might be carrying the loaded tea tray out to the garden for a tennis party, though outside, there was sharp down-beat of frost. The branches rattled together with a brittle noise like the clicking of celluloid capsules. There would be no leaves on the big mulberry and the goldfish would be gelid under the ice in the pool. Through the open door of the sitting room came the "rhubarb-rhubarb" of the company of players, like a buzz-buzzing of bees.

"My, you're a fashion plate and no mistake. No more little quiet mouse in a patched blazer. It's smashing to see you."

Nellie launched me into the sitting room with a proclamation of "Mrs. Professor Mitchell Allinton," as if I were royalty. The faces turned towards me like sunflowers seeking the sun and I was shaking hands with Mr. Rickaby. Mrs. Rickaby engulfed me in her arms and held me tightly. There were tears of joy in her eyes and she brushed at them with no patience in the world.

"I thought you'd never come. I've rung you a dozen times, but you've always been out, or working. They keep you prisoner in the Manor House. Short of calling at the front door with a pistol, I couldn't think of any way to rescue you, and Anthony had no more luck than I."

She looked about her and said he was somewhere about.

"If he doesn't soon get a chance to see you, he'll burst!"

Old Rickaby had a tray in his hands and he offered it to me, saw me established with a sherry and worried whether it was dry enough for me. Then I was swept away by somebody whose name I could not recall and we plunged into a conversation about nothing. Then an elderly man stopped by to ask me if I would give a talk to the Rotary Club and he would be in touch. I seemed to twirl round and round in a slow waltzing progression through the massed people, first one way and then another and making no sense of anything anybody said, only giving automatic answers, sipping at the sherry now and again, with my eyes anxious for a glimpse of Anthony, but with a strange shyness too. I saw him at last at the far side of the room, over in the bow window, with a big jug, that sparkled like Mrs. Swan's diamonds. I put up a finger and felt the clip safe at my throat and moved on to talk to Dr. Jones. He was exhausted with the work of the practice—winter of course. Imperceptibly Anthony was coming nearer and nearer and I wondered when he would see me. The noise in the room made a jumble in my head. It was too stuffy. I would have given much to make for the garden, but I had positioned myself in the wrong square. I was like a piece on a chess board. there were moves that could be made and moves that were out of order and a pawn must only go one square up or across or diagonally to take. Then suddenly I knew he saw me. I was looking at him at the time and I took my sherry in one gulp. He was six feet away and two across. I thought, in a ridiculous fashion, still mixed up with chess. He was in front of me in two strides, maybe three, his cut glass jug pouring some red concoction into my sherry glass with no thought of what I had already been drinking.

"I thought you hadn't come. Mrs. Swan's been here for ages and Hawkins too. I thought that perhaps you'd changed so much, I wouldn't know you, or I'd changed so much, you wouldn't know me. There are so many people here. It's like a Rugby scrum."

"Dr. Anthony Rickaby," I said. "Professor of Forensic Medicine now, 'the Expert'. It's so good to see you again."

I did not need Kit to tell me he loved me. It was written in his eyes for anybody to read. It was written in the way he put the jug into a stranger's surprised grasp and took both my hands in his. It was in the kiss that brushed my cheek and the way my hands were released and his moved up to cradle my face for a second.

Kit might have been there standing on her head, with her feet flapping in the air, but she could only tell me what I knew for myself and there was something stirring in me. It had never gone out, the old fire I had felt for him. It had been like turf ashes in a Connemara cottage, when the night has gone over and the dawn has come up the sky. All that was needed was a gentle breath to fan the grate and a spark would come and then the tiny flame and at last the warm glow of friendship, perhaps.

It was all there. It was not the time or the place to ask if a woman can love two men at the one time, really love them, year after year after year. Let it rest tranquil. Tomorrow was another day and I knew peace such as I had not known for a very long time.

I did not know, that the game had just started ... the beginning game. I was on the chess board already and there were more pieces coming into play. How could I know that the white knight had just taken his first move and the the game would be played to the finish, to be lost perhaps or to be won? There was nothing to tell me it was happening. How could I know about it? How could I judge what importance I had, when I thought I had none?

We stood there and talked, Anthony and I, and there were

no company of players, mouthing nothingness all about us, just he and I and the old memories that came to take the place of the ritual of a sherry party. He was back to take the chair of Forensic Medicine at the University at Camford, and he would be attached to the Camford General Hospital. Could I give him any valid excuse not to accept my old position as his secretary?

"You know, you must know, Kit is back. Her father married again at seventy plus and cast her off like one of her old tennis shoes?"

Then the magic was gone and I was indeed secretary to Milton Manor, kneeling in front of the fire in the sitting-room there, with the old dog jumping from the tartan blanket, eating up the biscuit he had saved till our return and presently settling down in my lap with a sigh, breathless from his exertions. I worried a little because he did not seem well after dinner. He scratched at the hearth rug and rumpled his blanket up in a ball, turned round and round and round, looking for snakes in his basket I told him, and rubbed his tummy. Mrs. Swan wanted to call the Vet, but Roger suggested we try one of her stomach powders. She agreed with that, for "the Vet never did anything but say it was something Finn had eaten." Roger already had one of the powders out of the box and he passed it across to me and made a great joke about it, but I was against the idea. Surely it would be too strong for a small dog? Roger went off and rang the Vet and came back presently with the instructions. Half a powder would be just fine and I was to administer it to him. I was used to giving them to Mrs. Swan. It seemed obvious that the Vet and Roger had laughed about the whole fuss and flurry about an old dog.

I split half the packet into the fire and took poor Finn on my lap, opened his mouth and tilted the powder on his tongue, held his muzzle and stroked his throat, told him to be a good boy. He behaved like a gentleman, God help him! He always did, and soon he was better and we all went to bed.

I switched out the light at once for I was very tired after the day. It seemed no time at all, that I had a most vivid dream, for somebody came to sit on my bed and took my hand in his, leaned up to switch on the light and it was Mitch. There was no mistaking the green of his eyes, though they say that dreams have no colour. He was alive again and had come to me and I was happy. I looked at the fair hair and the lines at the angles of his eyes that came from laughter ... at the crisp hair, so fair it seemed an aura about his head. In the dream I knew he was dead, but somehow he had come back. The window was open and the curtains billowing into the room. "Though he were dead, yet shall he live," I murmureed to myself and recognised it as one of the happy dreams, that came so often and left me desolate, so that desolation pursued me into life, when I woke up, and on through the day.

In the way dreams have, he was not sitting on the bed any more, but looking at the stole Mrs. Swan had lent me, picking up the diamond clip. I worried that I had not given them back. I had even forgotten to take the capsules out of my coat pocket in the hall, but Mitch told me it was no matter. He opened the locked drawer that held the green jade ear-rings and held them in his hand for a long minute. Then he smiled at them and laid them gently on the dressing table.

"Were they not good enough for Milton Manor?" he asked me softly and I told him I would not insult them by wearing them when I went out with Mrs. Swan and he laughed at that in just the old way and the room was lit by glitter-dust.

"Have you forgotten it all ... the feast fit for Isis and Osiris and with crêpe suzettes as well ... the dryness of old bones, the wonder of holding a shard in your hand, that had been held just so five thousand years before ... the thing you called the 'big beastie', that ruled the world for so many millions of years, an overlord, that makes a puny thing of no account?"

I shook my head and felt my love for him a warm safety that enclosed me. I wanted to lie in his arms. I wanted him to be the king of creation again and well I knew, he was in his grave, though he sat there and took my hand in his, his face serious.

"Do you remember Patanga and the chiefs in bark

canoes—the way they watched us, maybe warned us and we paid no heed to them? Listen to me. You're in danger, just as great as we were in that burial mound. I've sent a knight to help you and he'll carry your favour. There's a game to be played out there. My God! There's nothing I can do about it, and I love you. I will love you for the whole of eternity and try to shield you with my love, for love is stronger than death ... but there is such evil—such evil that you could never imagine. Now it begins. Now it begins."

It had been a happy dream, but the happiness had vanished and the room was full of icy draught that blew the curtains into the sails of a wind-jammer. There was wild urgency in the jangle of the bell, that woke me. Mrs. Swan had pressed it to summon me in the night, but urgently, urgently. The room was dark and I groped for the light switch and shrugged on my dressing gown and slippers. I knew that Mitch had been a dream, yet my eye looked for him and did not find him. I stood in Mrs. Swan's room and felt horror engulf me, for she was out of bed in her nightdress and her hair, Medusa-like, round her grey face. She was kneeling beside Finn's basket, screaming that he was dead. I knelt and put my hand on him, curled in a ball, just as I had left him and here at least was no dream. He had not even tried to get out of his basket. His going had been very peaceful. I got her back to bed and tucked the blankets round her, tidied her hair, sponged her face, tried to comfort her, but she was wild with hysteria, screaming that she wanted the doctor and I had a sharp recollection of Dr. Jones at the party, exhausted with the winter's work.

Mrs. Swan was given to hysteria. I had seen her through such attacks and Miss Mannion had heard the noise and come. She went to get Roger Hawkins and by the time he arrived, Mrs. Swan was calming and he sat down on the chair by the bed and took her hand in his, told her that he would ring the doctor first thing in the morning. Just for now, she must take a sleeping pill and try to remember that Finn was an old dog. "He had had a marvellous life and a peaceful death." There were to be no regrets.

We could not find her pills. They were not in their usual

place on the table. They might be on the floor. I searched and found only the big crack in the boards. They must have fallen through it in the struggle to get her settled back to bed. Such things always happened in an emergency, as if fate went awry. We gave her aspirins and brandy in hot milk and I sat by her bed with her hand in mine, went asleep at last, my hand against her side and did not wake, till Miss Mannion came with early morning tea.

Roger Hawkins waylaid me on the way back to my room and whispered to me that maybe we should have a post-mortem done on the dog and I remembered the grim post-mortem room with all its attendant indignity and over-ruled him firmly.

"He was an old dog. He went asleep quietly and she'll be glad he's at rest with no more breathlessness, no more of the ills of age. Casey will dig his grave under the Tree of Heaven."

Dr. Jones came to see her during the morning and agreed with what we had done.

"He's been too fat for years. Get her another dog. She'll forget this one."

Mrs. Swan was preoccupied with her own heart and Dr. Jones sighed and looked at the ceiling, doubtless thinking of all the other patients waiting to be seen.

"You've had a pain in your chest for years. Your investigations have all come back negative. There's nothing to worry about, only the sadness of losing poor old Finn and he's under the Tree of Heaven, where he always sat. Casey put him there and Liz Jane saw to it that he was wrapped up in his own Scots blanket and had his ball and his lead with him. It's the influence of Egyptology, I suppose. As Professor Allington's wife, she must have seen how the Egyptians looked after their dead."

On the way downstairs, he told Roger that there was no cause for concern about his aunt. She had mild failure, but it was consistent with her years. There was no limitation of life-expectancy and the chest pain was "wolf-wolf". She was to stay in bed for the day and he would call again.

I saw him to his car and went to look at Finn's grave. It

was quiet in the shrubbery and the whole garden was held in the silence of the frost. A dog barked down in the village and the sound carried clearly to my ears. Then I strolled towards the yew hedge and heard another sound from the barred window of the Caseys' quarters, indescribably slobbering, hiccoughing misery, that prickled the hairs on the nape of my neck. I thought of the ghost lady, who walked the corridor with the wailing baby in her arms. I thought of my dream about Mitch and how the curtains had billowed out ... and the atmosphere of cold. In my room, the jade ear-rings were lying on the dressing table and I had not left them there. I had seen Mitch take them from the locked drawer with no key to turn the lock. I had seen him put them down on the dressing table. They could not be there, but they were. In the glass, my face was like wax with shock. I felt sick and faint at the implications, that overwhelmed me. Yet I could have walked in my sleep and taken out the ear-rings and left them.

My thoughts were disturbed by Miss Mannion, who burst in upon me, with no permission. I was astonished to see her open my wardrobe and grab the sable stole, scramble the contents of the drawer in the tall-boy and find the pearl necklace and the diamond clip. Without a word, she grenadiered out of the room and across the landing to Mrs. Swan's room, where presently I followed her. Miss Mannion glared at me as I came in, told me that she had been obeying Mrs. Swan's orders and I stood at the foot of the bed and looked down at Mrs. Swan, helplessly, knowing that this sort of scene was the worst thing in the world for her and completely wihtout reason.

"When I lend a person something, I want it returned. I made that clear, but you hoped I'd forget. You're crazy!"

There was a hideous scene and I tried to remember that she was a sick old woman, who had just lost her favourite dog. I sat down, because my legs gave under me. I explained that Finn had been ill and I had forgotten.

"And you refused to send for the doctor. You think you rule the house. You wanted me to die and you'd have got yourself a sable stole and a diamond clip and a pearl necklace. Don't you know you had thousands of pounds worth of my property and it was all very convenient for you?"

She kept on and on and on and every word she said was unforgivable and my temper was out of control and away and I was on my feet by the door, my hands deep in my pockets. Somewhere was the thought of the jade ear-rings, that had been left on the dressing-table. Somewhere was Mitch's voice warning of danger, like the danger of Patanga. "Now it begins," he had said, and the words threw petrol on the fire and I cared not that she was sick and old, cared not that she had lost her dog, only mourned for Finn.

"I'll have no more to do with you till you give me an apology," I said and God help me I managed to get some of Mitch's imperiousness into the words. "I'll leave anyway, but I will not communicate in any way with you till you've taken back every word you've just said. Send Mannion to fetch me and say you apologise. I'll be in the sittingroom for half an hour and then I'll pack my bags and get out. You can contact me through Mr. Rickaby. You've laid yourself open to an action for slander. You know well I had no intention of stealing your property."

"You're sweet on Anthony Rickaby. You and he stood there in the middle of the party and his hands on your face and he kissed you. You got a slut-name for yourself, 'Mrs. Professor Allington', announced at the door and asked to speak at the Rotary Club. Who do you think you are?"

I stood on the landing with the door shut at my back and Father Gillson was coming up the stairs with a tread as soft as Miss Mannion's, asking me how was our Sister-in-God?

He threw a last smidgeon of petrol on the flames, that were flagging, so I went on with it.

"Poor Sister-in-the-Devil! She's a wicked old woman and it'll take more than the solace of the church to get her into heaven."

He had come to give her communion at her own request and I must have been quite a surprise to him.

"I've had enough of her. Thanks be to God I've got some will left. She'll not break me. If I'm not broken by what life has done to me already, Mrs. Swan will never break me.

She'll not conquer me. She's nothing but a witch, who trades on unhappiness, in poor devils who haven't the means to stand up to her ... and in case I don't see you again, I'll bid you good-bye. I might have played chess with you, for I like chess and you'd have made a good bishop. I won't be in Milton Manor after today, but you were kind to me and I thank you."

His arm was round my shoulder, but I made no sense of what he said to me.

"My dear child. What has upset you? She thinks highly of you. She's provided for you after her death. I'll let you into a secret. She's left you a substantial sum in her latest will. Try to see her as somebody who wants help."

I stamped down the stairs and found Casey, told him all that had happened and ranted and raved and said it was a pity it was Finn that had died.

"Finn was more of a loss to the world," and there was Roger Hawkins over by the door looking at me and I scowled at him, but he was all conciliation, offering his aunt's apologies, saying it was a woman's storm in a teacup.

"She'll apologise. Go up to her after she's been shriven. She's taking the holy waters now."

He might have been the devil for the look in his face.

I took the poker and thrust it through the bars of the kitchen range and the fire was no hotter than my rage. Then I remembered the capsules. They were in my pocket in the camel-hair coat in the hall. It was time they were burnt and here was a fire. I went past Roger and found the coat, tried first one pocket and then the other and there was nothing. A trickle of ice water ran down my spine and I was filled with the foreboding of what Mitch had meant in the dream. There was a black rising cloud on the horizon to walk up my sky. I turned back to the kitchen to ask Roger if he had taken the capsules and stopped up short. There had been enough hysteria for one day. Slowly I walked up the stairs one step at a time and sat for a long time with the jade ear-rings in my hands. Had Mitch found the power to come back to me? Surely enough, danger had threatened the house today. I must call a halt. I must make what peace I could with Mrs.

Swan. Then I must get out. The thought of working again at Camford General was a vision of paradise. Anthony Rickaby would want no reference from Mrs. Swan, relict of Swan, the Iron-monger.

I would sit on the stool and take dictation. I would go out with him on police cases, with the siren splitting the traffic before the urgency of disaster. I would put my typescript down on his desk and wait for the slow smile and the kindness ... the understanding of how lonely one could be in a crowd ... and Kit ... Kit with the too short jeans and the knitted socks and the old tennis shoes.

Mrs. Swan had her jewel case out on her bed and an aquamarine clip in her hands.

"It matches your eyes, Elizabeth. It's a peace offering. Go to the mirror and pin it on your dress. Anthony Rickaby phoned just now and he wants you to lunch with him tomorrow. Mannion has the details. I said yes, and of course, I apologise for all that nonsense. It was just the upset about Finn, and I didn't think you meant to keep the things. It was all nonsense and that's Dr. Jones at the door. He's coming to look me over this afternoon and he says I mustn't be upset, so we'll think no more of your leaving Milton Manor. I couldn't do without you."

I kept out of her way all the afternoon, but there was no escaping dinner in her bedroom with Roger Hawkins too, "to cheer the old party up." He flirted with her, teased her, jollied her along in a way that was sexual and ridiculous between aunt and nephew. She was so much better that she decided that she did not need her after-dinner powder, but he picked up the box and insisted on it, handed me the little white packet, and the glass and all the equipment. I stirred the mixture round the glass.

"If you really don't want it, I'll tip it down the basin, Mrs. Swan," I said. She took it from me and swallowed it, wiped her lips on her table napkin, said the powder tasted bitter and I was to be sure to complain to the chemist. Then I washed out the glass at the basin and put it back on the tray and we played cards, but she could not concentrate and neither could I. In an hour, she was nodding off and wanting her sleeping

pills and I remembered that I had not been able to find them.
I had forgotten to get a fresh prescription from Dr. Jones. I
searched the floor again and Roger helped me, but Mrs.
Swan had dropped off to sleep and was snoring softly. I took
the tray down to the kitchen and Roger mixed me a rum
punch with sugar and lemon. Miss Mannion and Pat Casey
had one too and we all decided that it was time to call it a
day.

I thought the rum strong and peculiar tasting, but Roger
said it was some stuff that "had travelled the Med." I washed
out the glasses at his bidding. They were Waterford treasures
and must be preserved for posterity, he explained. The night
was late and peace was coming down. I could hardly find the
energy to go up the stairs to bed. In three minutes, I had
fallen into sleep. It seemed a lifetime, till I heard the knock at
the door, but I was too drowsy to care. For a moment, I was
back in the Quicken Tree and it was P.C. Causer who
knocked. Then I opened the door and it was Miss Mannion,
with two plaits on the shoulders of her dressing-gown and
her face livid.

"For God's sake, pull yourself together, Mrs. Allington. I
found her. I went in there and found her, on her side in bed
as if she was asleep, but her mouth hung open. I think she's
gone."

I knelt by the bed and felt Mrs. Swan, cold as any stone. In
school, I had held a stone in my hand and thought about
Falstaff. Mrs. Swan was more terrible than any stone could
be. I pulled the sheet up over her face and Roger Hawkins
came into the room after a while, his face sallow under the
tan. Dr. Jones was on his way. Roger had sent for Father
Gillson too."

It was becoming mist-patchy as time does on such
occasions.

"You were right this morning, Jones," Roger said in the
hall. You told us to be prepared for anything. You knew her
heart was failing and she didn't stand the strain of last
night."

There was a tear running down Roger's cheek and I

thought that he had cared for his aunt more than I had judged.

"She didn't last long after her faithful friend. You know Uncle James gave Finn to Aunt Swan one Easter Day, a puppy in a big cardboard Easter Egg. Finn was the last link between them."

"Burial, not cremation? I'll give the certificate, of course. I only saw her this afternoon."

I was having pangs of conscience. He said the nurse from the undertakers would lay her out and I said that would not be necessary. I would do it myself. I knew she would prefer it."

It surprised Dr. Jones, but he agreed that it was the best thing and then Miss Mannion was in the room with a blue and white shroud in her hands.

It's from the Convent. The nuns sent it over. They will come to watch and pray soon."

They came to set up a vigil. There was a table at the foot of the bed with an altar ... holy candles. Monseigneur Gillson was intoning the prayers for the dead, Miss Mannion was on her knees and there was a smell of incense and the incantation of prayer and response like the drowsy humming of bees. Even in the night, the prayers went on and the nuns replaced each other in pairs, pleading for the soul of Mrs. Swan to be happily received at the gates of heaven. The next night, I still heard their soft voices across the landing, when I opened the door of my bedroom. I had been in the room of prayer myself a dozen times, but now I just stood on the landing. I thought I heard a scratching at the way to the corridor and I saw that the knob of the door was moving. I caught it and it turned in my hand.

"Is there anybody there?"

The whisper echoed against the high ceiling and came back to me.

. Then a voice started to sing, a soft ghost voice that had nothing to do with the living or the dead.

"Hush a bye, baby, on the tree top.
When the wind blows, the cradle will rock.

When the bough breaks, the baby will fall.
Down comes the baby, cradle and all."

It went over and over and over, like a stuck disc needle.
Then "Come away to sleep again. Come away ...
away ... away."

Then again I heard the inhuman choking, bubbling,
hiccoughing sound that I had heard from the side wing and a
shuffling, and a silence that cut off all sound.

"Is there anybody there?"

There was no answer and I was filled with a great terror. I
ran for my room like a hare chased by the harriers, tore off
my dressing gown and jumped into bed, pulled the blankets
over my head. After a long while, I slept, but I went from one
nightmare to another and each was worse than the one
before. I woke in inexpressible horror and my door was ajar,
although I had slammed it shut. There was a smell of incense
and candles still, hot wax, charred wick. I went to the door
and looked at my watch in the light reflected from Mrs.
Swan's room. It was four o'clock and I was afraid to go back
to my dreams. My black dress was on a chair and I dressed.
The clasp of aquamarines was in the lapel and I took it out
and it had no blue fire in the darkness, her peace offering. I
pinned it inside the pocket, for it was unsuitable in a house of
death. In a moment, I must go into Mrs. Swan's room again
and pray.

The slam of a car door surprised me. I went through to my
sitting room and looked down on the drive. The sitting room
should have been dark, for there was no moon in the sky and
I had not turned on the light, yet there was brightness and
the light came from head lamps. In the drive was an
ambulance, no, not an ambulance proper, a kind of utilicon.
The open door at the back held a nun in a bright spot, her
draperies fluttering in the breeze. Another nun got down
from the driver's seat, clasped her hands as if she prayed,
then shivered and looked back over her shoulder at the house.
Her face was a white mask and she was no real creature, but
a ghost that inhabited nightmares. There was no reality
about her in the world. She was waiting for something. I

must be dreaming again. They were bringing a figure out to
the utilicon, hunched up, shambling along between two
people. I recognised the shining peak of Casey's cap and his
wife's silver grey hair. The sound came again, the gurgling
strangled hiccough. It was a nightmare of the worst kind.
The sweat stood on my forehead, ran down between my
breasts, for the figure was resisting. It pulled back, like a
beast led to the shambles, bent head swinging, whining in
pain and distress. Then it was inside the van. I opened the
window and leaned out, but before the doors slammed shut, I
heard it again, the same soft voice of the corridor.

> Taffy was a Welshman. Taffy was a thief.
> Taffy came to my house and stole a joint of beef.
> I went to Taffy's house. Taffy wasn't in.
> I put a red-hot poker under Taffy's chin.

I slammed the window down and ran back across the
room, tripped, fell full length and that woke me up. I was in
darkness for there was no light and I was creeping back to
my bedroom. I must have been walking in my sleep. Outside
in the drive, there was no utilicon, no nuns, only the Tree of
Heaven, bending its branches to the wind, whispering a song
to my dreaming ears. Yet I was dressed. I must have dressed
and walked in my sleep and seen something, that had never
happened. I opened the door to the landing and prayer was
comforting sound. The nun by the bedside moved over to
make room for me to kneel by her. Mrs. Swan lay with her
rosary clasped in cold hands, her nose pinched and sharp, her
eyes closed in serenity, young again. I bent my head and went
asleep and was awakened hours later by two other nuns.
There was breakfast to be prepared and the house seemed
cold and dank. The stove in the kitchen had gone out and I
re-set it and lit it, and the flames at the mica window
comforted my mixed-up, frightened mind. The clock had
increased its speed and time was whirring away ... white
cloth on the kitchen table, for it was warm in there ...
cornflakes, good strong tea, bacon and eggs. The nuns were
like children let out of school. Clasping their hands in delight,
young and fresh in their faith. Death was only a step from

life to God and Mrs. Swan had been a good woman. She had arranged for a stained glass window in their chapel at the Convent and she had left all the gorgeous silver and glass. The Reverend Mother and she were like sisters.

They talked softly about Mitch and in the earliness of morning, the room took on another dimension, as if heaven was as real an ante-chamber, as the hall outside the kitchen door. Mitch was in heaven, they told me, as if they had just passed him by and seen him. He would not want me to be grieving after him. I would see him again one day, as sure as the sun would soon come up the sky.

They went back to the Convent at last, driven by Casey in the Rolls and I wondered where Miss Mannion was and Roger Hawkins or Mrs. Casey. The door to the Caseys' wing from the kitchen was locked and except for the two fresh nuns by the bed upstairs, I seemed to be alone in the house. I had cleared and tidied the breakfast things and the kitchen was warm, no hint of the icy weather outside, no cold that pressed down on the house. I shut the door to the hall and sat down at the table, and my eye-lids were heavy with sleep. Today, they would move Mrs. Swan's coffin to lie in the Convent Chapel and next day would be the funeral. Between now and then, the prayers would go up in a never-ending skein to heaven for her soul's redemption. I would have to leave. My cases were packed and ready, but I had nowhere to go, except home to the closed-up desolation of the Quicken Tree. I seemed to be trapped in a desolate land, where I had walked before, but the stove hummed to me. I was sleepy and sleepier and my folded arms on the table were pillow enough, and somebody had said I was to go to the Rickabys' house ... I could not remember ...

I woke with a hand on my hair and for one happy moment, thought it was Mitch. I stayed mouse-quiet and hoped that he would not go away and his fingers came down to lift the curtain of hair from my face. Yet he went away as he always went away and I was back to the lonely awakening of all my mornings.

"I've come to take you to Wellington House, Liz-Jane. It's nearly noon ..."

I looked up and saw that it was Anthony Rickaby, my camel coat over his arm. He held it out for me and I put it on, told him that the nuns were upstairs and I did not know where the Caseys were, or Roger Hawkins. He buttoned the coat for me, pulled the collar up round my ears, pushed the hair back from my face again, yet I was still fashioned with the fears of the night.

"Are you sure I'm to go home with you?"

"Father was to invite you. I expect he forgot."

I must go upstairs and see Mrs. Swan before I left the house. Anthony read the dread in my face and took my hand in his, brought me through the hall.

"We go out the front door and we bang it shut behind us. You've slept late, Liz-Jane. The lady is in the Convent Chapel by now. Casey and his wife and Miss Mannion and Roger Hawkins are there, for they followed the coffin. I found your cases upstairs and they're in the boot of your car in the drive. Casey drove me here. You were fast alseep and you've had a dreadful time. You don't have to come back here ever again. You don't have to go to the funeral tomorrow. The last you'll hear of Mrs. Swan will be at the reading of her will, for she's made you a beneficiary, but the reading of a will is no Assizes matter, and it will be in Wellington House and my father will be her solicitor and yours."

"But I don't believe she left me anything. She didn't like me. The nuns thought she was kind and generous. Have I done her a fearful injustice?"

"You've done her no injustice. She was everything nasty and wicked I can think about her. Let's get out of here, for God's sake!"

Then we were in the car and away down the drive, flashing across the flat fen till we came to Histington, and a great weight had shifted off my soul. I drew a deep breath down into my lungs and smiled at Anthony, as he turned the Alvis round the side of Wellington House into the back courtyard. Presently we were in the hall and he brushed my cheek with his lips again, as he had done the night of the sherry party and said "Welcome home."

9

THE LAST WILL AND TESTAMENT
OF AGNES AMELIA SWAN

It was like stepping from midnight to high noon, from hell to heaven. There was no mourning in Wellington House, only the normality of a happy household and a welcome fit for the return of the prodigal son. They had even seen to it that Kit would be there to welcome me, dressed in the black skirt and white blouse that she wore in the secretary's pool and not as I remembered her in the too-faded shrunk-short jeans and the hand-knitted football socks and the old tennis shoes. Mrs. Rickaby took me into an embrace and then Kit's arms were strangling my neck and the edge of the medical dictionary dug into my shoulder. It was a coming-home present from her. It was all over the hospital that I was coming to work there again—with Professor Rickaby and I would surely want the dictionary I opened it and looked through the pages at the "Saint-like" drawings in the margins.

"Maybe I've taken it for granted that you and I will be a team again, Liz-Jane," Anthony said. "I think I asked you at the sherry party. I know I told you Kit was back, but it has all been so hectic that I forget what you said."

"I didn't say anything that night. I had a position and maybe I owed loyalty. There's no debt of loyalty left. You've put me on top of a mountain, haven't you —shown me all the kingdoms of the earth? The answer is yes and I thank you."

The next twenty four hours passed in a jumble. Kit and I had a back-log of talk to make up and we chattered for hours. Then there was an argument over dinner with the Rickabys and they ruled that on no account must I attend Mrs. Swan's funeral. Mr. Rickaby and Anthony would go and they would represent me and the morning would be spent looking at the Quicken Tree. Mrs. Rickaby and Kit and Nellie Pluck had spring-cleaned it, opened it up and it was ready for my residence.

"But I could never afford ..."

It seemed that Anthony had arranged the salary I must get, both for my work at the Camford General and now at the University. Had I forgotten he had been given the Chair of Forensic Medicine? His father, my solicitor, had assured them that living at the Quicken Tree would be well within my means ... all that and the Alvis too ...

I could say no word as we carried out our inspection of what they had done to the Quicken Tree. All it had had for months had been dust-sheeted furniture and a visit when I could get time off to open the windows and air out the rooms, light the fires—run the Hoover over the carpets. Now it was obvious that experts had been at work. The carpets had been out to be cleaned, the dust-covers were gone, there was a shine on the woodwork, that smiled at the coal fire in the study. The central heating had brought life back to the house. The daffodils must have come from some greenhouse, The Christmas roses, the celandines told us that winter still had us fast, but there was an orchid in a tall vase by my chair, that could only have been sent by Mitch. How could I speak? How could I thank these people for what they had done? And the orchid?

I found myself alone in the bedroom and they had the kindness to leave me alone. I knelt by the bed and put my face into the soft quilt and presently Anthony found me there. I buried my face deeper into the softness, as his hand stroked my hair.

"That orchid, Anthony. It was the sort of thing Mitch would have thought of."

"I imagine he did think of it. Who am I to buy orchids? Yet I bought that one. My mother flew out to Canada and fetched me home ... insisted on the most extraordinary route back. I was in some exotic place the other day, Marakesch or Athens or Rome itself. We were brought in to refuel and there was an old woman selling orchids and that one was dew-starred, straight from paradise, and I stretched out my hand and bought it, had it packed for transportation, yet well

I knew that I was just a catalyst, Liz-Jane. 'There are stranger things in heaven and earth.' Mitch was capable of strange things in life. Why should he be any different in death?"

"But you, Anthony, every word you've spoken, everything you've done ... ?"

"Tomorrow is another day. This is a odd old world. I love you and I'll always love you, but this is not the time nor the place. This is the day for you to view the Quicken Tree and for us all to wish you happiness again."

His hand came down to mine and he helped me to my feet and together we went down the stairs and they watched us arrive in the hall and their joy was bright in their faces, but just before we reached them, Anthony's whisper was at my ear.

"The old woman with the flowers. She had her pitch in a different place that night. Seven days out of seven for fifty two weeks a year, she sets up her stand at the steps of the Hotel Imperial, but that night, they had an excavation. It was no geological dig and archaeology didn't come into it in the least. It was possibly a burst water main or a leaking from gas, but it was a dig. My God! It was a dig."

It was such a lovely day, but the next day was haunted by the Manor House, for first there was the funeral and Mr. Rickaby and Anthony in dark suits and black ties, leaving the house for the ceremony. Then by six o'clock, the office was ready for the reading of the will and they were all there. Mr. Rickaby looked at me over the tops of his glasses and smiled encouragement. He picked up an envelope from the desk in front of him and broke the seal and red chips and dust fell to the blotter. Nellie Pluck, in a fresh crisp white apron, was getting ready to pass round the silver tray of sherry. Mrs. Rickaby had shaken hands with each of them as they arrived and worried that Monseigneur Gillson had caught a chill at the grave-side. I guided him to the chair by the radiator and he rested one hand on it gratefully for its warmth. The Reverend Mother from the convent was sitting by another nun and both of them, stiff-backed with their hands folded in their laps. The Caseys were humble behind Miss Mannion's chair, but Roger had taken the Chippendale chair by the desk, the most important person present, teeth very white, beard very black, the gold ear-ring glittering in the light from the desk lamp. Then Mrs. Rickaby was gone. Mr. Rickaby cleared his throat and started proceedings and before he started, I had no idea of what was to follow, only the story that Hawkins had told us in the kitchen that night in another world, that, and what Father Gillson had said to me, when I decided to leave Milton Manor.

"Mrs. Swan's will may come as a surprise to you, and I'd like to say something, before I read it ... explain the small size of the estate in relationship to the establishment, she maintained ... When James Swan died, he left a sum in advance of four hundred thousand pounds. Well invested, it would have brought her enough to live on comfortably, but she had commitments, which some of you may know. She thought it wiser to buy an annuity. She wished me to explain to you in particular, Mr. Hawkins, that you have shared the benefit of this annuity for many years. 'You've eaten your cake and you can't afford to have it.' The annuity was taken out in the first place to see that you had a substantial allowance every year."

Roger finished his sherry in one gulp and Nellie refilled his glass, as the question came out like a shot.

"The annuity dies with her?" Roger asked and Mr. Rickaby answered him with a nod and the dry-as-dust voice went on.

"There was another claimant, a person some of you may know, a close relative of the deceased. His name is not to be disclosed in the will, but she set aside a large sum of money, so that the interest could be used for the support of the claimant to the day of this person's death. The sum of money will then revert to the money left to the Convent."

The envelope was open and parchment papers crackled in his hand.

"I will omit at Mrs. Swan's request any mention whatever of the special beneficiary."

The familiar lawyer-jargon put a picture together piece by piece like a jig-saw, yet I knew that Mr. Rickaby wanted it finished and done with as soon as might be with dignity and respect. There was five thousand pounds for the Convent, for a floor of mosaic, also a memorial window to James and Agners Swan, of special design was all set out ... and also to the Convent, calf-bound missals, altar furnishings, and so on and so on. The Superior nodded her head and was moved visibly at such generosity.

"She loved our little chapel."

"Also to the Chapel, her entire collection of silver and glass, her personal jewellery, to be used in whatever manner the Community think best."

So it went on.

"To Monseigneur Ignatius Gillson, of Milton Presbytery in the village of Milton, Lincolnshire, in some part payment for years of spiritual comfort, the residence known as Milton Manor, all the outbuildings thereof and the land thereof, the furniture and all indoor and outdoor effects, perhaps to found the Home for Elderly Catholic Clergy, that has always been his dearest ambition."

The priest had been sitting with a hand cupped to his ear, leaning forward a little, to catch the low voice. He got up and went to the window, his palms pressed together in front of his chest, said she was a good woman, and that she would receive her reward in the life after death.

Item followed item. Mr. Rickaby glanced at the ceiling and paused sometimes and the whole thing seemed to stretch out to an intolerable length and the parchment sounded like dead autumn leaves.

Patrick Joseph Casey was to have the sum of one thousand pounds and the Rolls-Royce car, the "laundulette", which would be used for hire to provide an income. Mrs. Casey was to have a thousand pounds. Miss Alice Mannion was to have one thousand pounds. They must all three be in Mrs. Swan's employment at the time of her death, in the manner of such bequests.

"To Mrs. Elizabeth Jane Allington, if she be still in my employment on the day of my death, the sum of one thousand pounds on the understanding that she cherish my dog, Finn, if he is still living and keep him in comfortable circumstances, so that he can end his days in peace."

There was also a small sum of money in trust for Finn's care, but it was negligible and the dog was unhappily dead. The small sum of money would revert to the estate and we had come almost to the end and the most important beneficiary and I dared not look at him, knowing what an annuity can do to the residual estate.

"To my nephew, Roger Makepeace Hawkins, the residue of my estate."

"And how much is that?" Roger demanded in a stranger's voice.

"A thousand pounds, maybe a little more or less."

The stem of the sherry glass snapped in Roger's hand and he put the glass down gently in the ash tray and got to his feet as stiff-legged as an old man.

"There's nothing to keep me here any longer," he said and went off through the door as if he walked in a fugue and presently we heard the engine of the Rolls come to life and fade along the street outside. Mr. Rickaby covered the awkwardness in his gentle way, saying that Mr. Hawkins had been very upset by his aunt's death.

"The reading of a will is an ordeal for the relatives and friends. He forgot that if he took the car, he'd leave the company without transport, but of course, my son will run the sisters and everybody else home."

I went up to my bedroom at last, knelt at the cretonne-covered window seat and my thoughts turned into an account that would not be balanced, no matter how I added the figures and re-added them. Perhaps I had been completely wrong about Mrs. Swan. She had been so generous in death—the Rolls to Casey, the bequests to him and his wife, to Miss Mannion, to me ... the Rest Home for tired old priests, the beneficience to the Convent. Roger was the one piece of the puzzle, that did not fit it. I thought that he had known nothing about the annuity. I had been looking at his face when the glass snapped in his hand. Certainly, he must have got large sums from her during life. Was she inhuman enough to act out the fable of the goose that laid the golden egg? If she was as spiteful as I had found her, she would would have got satisfaction every time, she paid money out to him, knowing what was to come. It had not worked out, the fable, for he had not killed the goose. It had died of natural causes. Who was the unnamed close relative? There had been mystery at the Manor, with its grey lady and the whispering Tree of Heaven, the gurgling, strangling, hiccoughing noise and the child rhymes. Had I really seen that ambulance drawn up in the front drive? Had I seen somebody struggling to get away and if it had not all been a sleep-walking dream, was that person the close relative, being taken from the Manor wing to a place of safety? Why had she left money to me ... all that money to look after a sick dog? She had known that she could trust me. Finn would have been very happy at the Quicken Tree, but he might have missed her sorely. He could have been the nucleus of a new home, where he and I lived. I could not have gone to work of course, unless he came with me. Now I planned a full-time position at the Camford General and at the University as secretary to Anthony Rickaby. Yet I mourned the little dog, for he has been a champion, when I had wanted a champion. It was time to put the past behind me, not the past that included Mitch, for that would never die, but all the days I had spent at Milton Manor. They were written on a page that was turned over and must be forgotten. I had a new life to lead. I found myself singing a little song as I made my way downstairs again. I was beginning to be happy again, I who had thought never to be happy again. Yet somewhere in my head, I recalled the voice of the woman, who had sung in the night.

"Hushabye baby on the tree top.
When the wind blows the cradle will rock ..."

POISON PEN

The next days passed in such pleasant business, that they were over before they started. There was much straightening out of affairs at the Quicken Tree, much organisation at my department at the Camford General. I had to be assimilated into the University as Anthony Rickaby's secretary.

The Quicken Tree was pleasant pain, but I thanked God that it was possible to live there again, even if loneliness lived there too. I would have welcomed Finn to snap at the heels of visitors, for he had carried life with him for all his age and a house can be very silent. I welcomed visitors with open arms and they came in numbers, determined to keep me too occupied for thoughts of what had been lost. They banded together to make sure that I was not too much on my own ... Mrs. Rickaby, Anthony, Kit, who was a constant factor, Dr. Jones, P.C. Causer, the Queen Sec. from the Hospital. Dr. Alex Brown came through Camford on his way to join a ship as doctor at Southampton. He stayed the night and we talked the hours away about the old days. His son had made a perfect recovery and his responsibilities were at an end. He had taken to the life of ship's doctor, back again with loss of his wife, which had sent him to Patanga.

We talked for hour after hour and very confidentially. Mitch was not lost, I told him. I could feel him around me sometimes, as close to me as if he still lived in the house and would live there for ever. Alex Brown had the same comforting sense that his wife was not finally lost, that she stayed near by and could stand behind his shoulder, in the bad moments and send small rays of happiness from some happy place she inhabited, though there was no understanding how it could happen, but happen it did.

The Hospital and the University were not so haunted as the house by Mitch for me, nor the Regional Headquarters nor yet the Courts. I had started off on the routine work with Anthony and we worked well together. I found it engrossing and filled with interest. Soon, I became known in the Division and an odd time, the constable on point duty would salute the Alvis as I drove by and fill me a sense of pride, that might go before a fall.

The autopsy room at the Hospital was the same vast place in the basement, straight out of a horror magazine, but it became familiar and lost its terror. It began to get the air of a country club about it, with the camaradie between the doctors and the students, the police, the nurses, all the ancillaries, who made up such a splendid team. The Assize Court lost all its high mightiness, with Anthony at my side and my only job to feed him with neatly typed statements and nag at the Clerk of the Court to take his evidence early so that he could be released.

Yet there were still the awful hours, the sort of cases as that first one had been, when Anthony had said to me.

"But it's a sobering thought you know. 'All the King's horses and all the King's men couldn't put Humpty Dumpty together again' ... and little girls still were done to death."

I was working in my room at the hospital, the day Inspector Franklyn called and he came with no telephone call in advance to advise me of his arrival. Anthony Rickaby was with him and it was such an ordinary happening nowadays, that I was not surprised by it. There was something they wanted for referral, no doubt, and it would soon be dealt with.

"Something has come up, Liz-Jane. I think we can deal with it, but it's not pleasant." Anthony said and perched himself on my desk. I stayed sitting at the typewriter and knew that tea would come in automatically by courtesy of the tea-lady.

Inspector Fanklyn told me that he was sure I could help in the case. "You were in on it yourself. We'll get information from the horse's mouth."

I could not believe what he was saying, but he was quite

unconcerned about it. It was the sort of thing he must deal with every day. They had received an anonymous letter at H.Q. It was about the death of Mrs. Swan.

"That's why we should crack it in no time. You were a witness of all that went on in that blasted place. The letter's anonymous, of course, and it alleges that the late Mrs. Swan did not die of natural causes, says she was poisoned."

That brought me to my feet at once as I protested that it was absurd.

"It's from some crazy person. Mrs. Swan had a heart attack. Finn's death was a shock to her. She was old."

"The letter says the dog was poisoned too," Anthony put in joke, for macabre jokes flourished in the pathology department. It was no joke nor ever would be.

"Of course, he wasn't poisoned and neither was she. I prepared his meals and he was never out of my sight. I saw to some of her meals too. It's just some crackpot ... "

Sergeant Bacon came into the office in time to hear my words and he and I were old friends. I had known him since my child days, when he and I had scrumped apples together in the village orchards.

"Who was named as having been the poisoner?" I asked and poured him a cup of tea at the same time and Anthony's hand was on my shoulder.

"It's best you don't know. It might bias your evidence and you're invaluable as you have an open mind on what went on in the house."

Franklyn's face was urbane, his moustache a toothbrush pencilled on a long upper lip, his hair receding from a lofty brow, his whole appearance, professional, yet jaunty too.

He told me he had been to the Manor House to interview Mr. Hawkins, who was still there. He had interviewed Miss Mannion, ditto. He had seen the Holy Father and the Holy Sisters and the Staceys. He had seen the lot ...

"And you left me till last. I must be very unimportant."

"Maybe," he said, "or maybe you're our spy in the camp," and took the pipe from between his teeth, asked my permission to smoke, opened the tobacco pouch and went through the routine as usual. "The talk is off the cuff. If we

get too official, you'll have to call in your solicitor," he said
and it was a great joke, but Anthony had no laughter for it. It
seemed there was something more—an item of jewellery,
missing from 'the effects.' The nuns had noticed it gone.
They checked it out. It was a small aquamarine clip."

"It's not missing," I told them and had to laugh at the
storm in the tea cup. "I have it on me this minute, as a matter
of fact. We had a quarrel. Mrs. Swan gave it to me as a peace
offering. I didn't wear it after she died, for it didn't seem
right to wear jewellery. It doesn't matter these days, but the
Manor was old-fashioned. See, I've pinned it inside this
pocket. I haven't had the dress on since then, till today."

He took it into his hand and pursed his mouth up,
examined it carefully and slid it back to me across the desk.

"So Mrs. Swan gave it to you?"

I nodded my head and he asked me if I had any proof and
of course, I had none.

"But no doubt you believe me?" I said lightly.

"I believe you." Then he went off at a tangent.

"Is Alice Mannion trustworthy?"

"You could trust her with your life's blood."

"And Pat and Mrs. Casey?" he pursued.

"They were the salt of the earth."

"And Roger Hawkins?"

"I hardly knew him, but he'd not harm Mrs. Swan. They
got on well together. She lived for his visits."

He was off at a tangent again.

"You had a jar with a number of dorminal capsules in
your possession, white capsules, about so long."

He indicated the length with his finger and thumb.

"Powder in tough plastic case in a brown glass jar with a
screw-on-lid. Where are they?"

I whispered to ask him how he knew about them, but he
reiterated the question and the friendliness seemed to be
leaking out of him and I could not meet the brown eyes, but
stood looking down at the blotter, feeling as guilty as I could
possibly have been about something I knew nothing about.

It came out in a whisper, how I had neglected to burn
them, how they had been Mitch's capsules and I had left

them in the coat in the hall of the Manor. Somebody had taken them. They had been in my hand in the churchyard at Histington and then they had disappeared into thin air. The pocket was deep. They could never have fallen out.

"How did you get rid of them?"

There was a new menace within myself that tempted me to lie to him, but I refused to give into the temptation to say I had burned them.

"It sounds very silly, but I think somebody took them out of my pocket. I had them in the graveyard and I put them back in the pocket in the church. I hung the coat in the hall again. When I looked for them, they were gone."

Again, he swung away from the point.

"The terrier at the Manor died. Who gave him the powder?"

I told him all that had happened, how Roger had rung the vet and I had given Finn half the powder. "I put the first half into the fire."

"Into the fire?" said Anthony at my back. "Why on earth did you do that?"

"I just did it. Why not?" I said and he smiled at me and told me that he would have done the same himself and I was not to be considering myself as a murderer, because I happened to be one of the forensic team and that I was to take no notice of the police, because they always relied too much on circumstantial evidence. Then Sergeant Bacon and I had some more talk about the stealing of apples in country orchards and what a pleasant pastime it was and we all parted good friends, but there was an unease in my mind. They refused to tell me who was the accused.

"It would prejudice further questions," Franklyn said and I wailed that I hoped there would be no further questions.

"Nobody would want to kill an old lady like that," I protested and Anthony made fun of me. "You're your father's daughter, and he the king of detective fiction. You make a statement like that. Nobody would want to kill her! Your father would have found a motive for every person living in the Manor House the night she died."

I knew unhappiness again. I thought of nothing else for

the next two weeks, but the exhumation of Mrs. Swan, the exhumation of the little dog too. My mind conjured up pictures, that were familiar enough by now, but I was closed out. I was involved. I could no longer stroll into the P.M. room. I could no longer telephone the doctor, who did the autopsy. Anthony attended, but not I. Another secretary sat in and she must not divulge or discuss. Mr. Rickaby himself warned me against any conversation about the matter with anybody, and fear rose in me like fevered mercury.

Then one day I was out for a walk in Histington and the Raspberry Ripple drew up beside me with Bacon at the wheel and Franklyn in the back, his brown trilby an inch off his head.

"Good-morning, Mrs. Allington and how are you today?"

He fire-crackered off on his usual statements.

"The result of the P.M.'s back. I had it at H.Q. half an hour ago. I rang Mr. Rickaby, senior, your solicitor, and he told me you were out walking."

I gripped the window edge and his voice went on, clipping the words out like tram conductors used to clip the fare tickets.

"Mrs. Swan died of an overdose of barbitone, the dog too."

It can't be true. I was there all the time. I ate what she ate. She had nothing different except her powder."

"The powder killed her ... almost for sure."

"But I gave it to her. Nobody else ever did. It can't have poisoned her."

"Something poisoned her."

He offered me a lift to the Quicken Tree or back to Wellington House, but I shook my head, begged him to tell me whom the letter had accused of being a poisoner, and he watched me, watched every shadow of expression on my face and was all policeman.

I told him that nobody would have wanted to harm her. If Miss Mannion had wanted to murder anybody, it would have been me. "Would it indeed?" he asked coldly and the joke died a small death."

"Please let me see the letter?"

"Your solicitor advises not. His son, the Professor of

Forensic medicine advises not. Do you know that the Professor plays chess. I play it myself. He thinks we can solve murder mysteries the same way we play chess. The Professor has it in his mind to play a game like the Ancient Mariner ... to dice for lives on a chess board ... "

He closed the window and Bacon took the car off down the road and that night, I learned what third degree interrogation was like.

I was alone in the Quicken Tree, hoping that Kit might come for a visit. There was a bright fire in the sitting room and a peace that filled the whole house, as if Mitch had come back again, alive and well, to spend the rest of eternity with me. The knock on the door startled me and it was Anthony Rickaby. He was unlike his usual self, as he stood looking down at me, where he had positioned me in the centre of the sofa. It was clear that he knew the result of the autopsy. It was clear that he was in league with Franklyn and Bacon. I knew it by his gambit words, calm against the disorganisation of my own mind.

"I like to set up pieces on a board. Will you help me?"

So Franklyn had been talking to him?

He made up the fire and I protested at that, for it would last all night. Coolly he told me that we might need all night and at that I begged him to stop shutting me out.

"Tell me the name of the accused."

"When we've finished, I'll tell you. It might prejudice you and we can't allow that. Try to help us. Start with Mitch's death. I'm sorry about asking this, but it's all connected with the other affair. I want you to tell me every little thing that happened, what you did, how you felt, what you said to this person or that, every last bitter little thing."

He was tearing himself to pieces, just as much as he was tearing me and he went round the room turning off all the lights except the standard lamp behind me. It might look as if he set the stage for a love scene, but nothing was further from his mind.

"Just because of what you say to me tonight, Liz-Jane, an innocent person may go to prison for life. That's on my oath, so leave nothing out, even if it seems unimportant to you. I

may understand it. Don't think of me as being here. Make
me background, nothing more or less. Talk to yourself, not to
me, but for the love of God, tell me the whole of it."

He sat down in one of the armchairs by the fire and took
out pipe and tobacco pouch and I watched him miserably
from across the room, thought his voice bleak and unfriendly,
when maybe it was nothing of the sort.

The night Mitch died, I sat by his bed and prayed that his
breathing would stop ..." I began haltingly. "Now and
again, the log would send out a shower of sparks ..."

I told it very much the same way as it's been told here. It
went on for a long time. The clock struck eleven and then
mid-night. Sometimes, I stopped talking for five minutes ...
hid my face in my hands. Now and then I got to my feet to
pace the room. Twice he fixed me a drink and put it in my
hands, but. he was a disembodied spirit. There was no
softness about him and no sympathy. His face was in truth as
expressionless as if he played chess with great concentration,
even when my account ran into disjointed passages. I turned
my head into the cushions and wept at one stage, but he made
no effort to comfort me, just waited for me to compose myself,
as a high court judge might have done. The events moved on
slowly from dreams and nightmares to reality and sometimes,
I could not separate one from the other.

"I must have walked in my sleep, have dressed and gone to
the window. I had even changed the aquamarine clip. I told
you I pricked my finger, but the drive was empty and the
utilicon gone and there was no light then."

"You pricked your finger? he shot at me and heard my
account of the scratch on my hand, that was there the next
day.

My voice was hoarse when I came to the end of it and he
put another drink in my hands and stood with his back to me
watching the flames.

"So that's how it happened?" he said softly and my mouth
was dry even with the drink—and my throat ached and I was
not far from tears.

"Who was accused in the letter?" I croaked. "You
promised to tell me."

He turned round and looked at me, as calmly as if it were his turn to call at bridge.

"You were."

I jumped to my feet and sloshed my drink all over the floor.

"Oh, no, Anthony. Not I! You can't be telling me the truth."

"You were alleged to have opened up the capsules of dorminal and to have given the contents to Mrs. Swan, in lieu of her stomach powder, on the night she died. You were accused first of all, of trying out the powder on the dog. That's what the letter said 'to make sure the powder was lethal'."

The ague in my hand chattered the empty glass against the mahogany of the table. I clasped my temples, shivered with fright, cried out to him that he could not be serious.

"I was never more serious."

"You can't think I did it, Anthony?"

He stayed by the fire and made no motion to approach me. I thought it obvious that his feelings for me were changed.

"I know who did it," he said after a long time. "It's a different matter to prove it. I'm setting out a chess game ... top level. I told you."

He watched me in the mirror as a cat watches a bird.

"Who did it?" I whispered.

He did not make any answer to that, only said that the Inspector had agreed to play it his way and I looked at the floor where the drink had splashed and the words mumbled out of my lips.

"I should have known I was the one. She gave me a bad time of it. She insulted me, called me a thief and that was the day before she died. I knew about the legacy. Somebody told us ..."

"Roger Hawkins," he said coolly. "Before three witnesses in the kitchen."

"Of course," I cried in despair. "I told you that just now and forgot it again. I don't know what I'm saying. You must think I'm crazy."

Still he watched me in the glass over the fire.

"Mitch was a lucky man to have your love," he said. "Thank you for the full confidence you've given me tonight. You had high courage to turn back the clock the way you've done. I think you're the finest person I ever met ..."

My eyes blinked open like a Dutch doll's, but now it was his turn to be different. His phrases came out slowly and haltingly and in little uncertain runs, and he had turned to look directly at me.

"Can a person love twice, as you loved him? He was lucky. I've said that, haven't I? Maybe, you'll find love in your heart again. If a miracle did happen for me ... I've loved you for a long time. Before you married Mitch, I loved you. I'd be proud, if you loved me ... and that's said. Let it lie between us. I trust you implicitly. Nothing can change that, nor alter my love for you. The times may get rough. They will get rough. Try to think of it as a game ... of chess. We've got a full board ... the tattling little pawns, the Bishop, the Monseigneur himself—Franklyn and Bacon for two rooks. We've got opposing knights and one of them with a gold ring in his ear. Yet it's not all set up yet. Which is black and which is white? ... We know only the White Queen. She's in hazard."

He put a hand on either side of my face and I thought he meant to kiss me, but he only said I looked very tired.

"Go to bed, White Queen. One of these days, I'll tell you all you mean to me, but not yet. It's not time, but one day, one day ... one day ..."

It might have been better if Anthony had told me the full story of the Manor House, as he knew it, or if Mr. Rickaby had. They left me in ignorance of some issues I could have known, but professional confidences might be broken and that was all against the rules of solicitors and forensic specialists. They did not realise that I was a fly caught in a spider's web, struggling to escape. My confidante as usual was Kit and she with no more wisdom than I ...

The next day was Sunday and she and I were discussing some of the things I had told Anthony. She was engrossed in the west wing as usual, for I had just told her about it.

"Are you sure you *didn't actually see* a utilicon? You

pricked your finger with the clip and you must have been
awake after that, not sleep-walking. Of course, there was
somebody kept prisoner there all that time. They had to get
him out when Mrs. Swan was dead and he's the relative
unnamed in the will. Go over there one night and have a look
at what's in the wing. I'll come with you. We can slip in and
out, if we pick a really black night."

"But Roger Hawkins and Miss Mannion are still living
there."

She passed that off lightly, said that I could say I had
forgotten something.

She had not been serious, for she confessed before she took
herself off to Camford that wild horses wouldn't drag her
into the Manor, but Anthony would go with me.

"I'm only joking, honey. Anthony obviously knows all
about it and he'll tell you when it's time for you to be told.
Now I must be on my way for the fog's coming up."

I took her into Camford in the Alvis and indeed the fog
was thickening to soup. I was glad to get back to the Quicken
Tree, but sorry that Kit had told me a fact that I might have
been better not to know.

"The fog won't stop Roger Hawkins taking Miss
Mannion to Benediction at the Convent tonight. They go
every Sunday, come rain, hail or snow. Maybe they both have
something on their consciences—I should think that the ghost
lady waits till they're both out and walks up and down the
corridor and sings to her baby."

I had pleaded work to be done, so as not to go to
Wellington House. I parked the car in the garage and went
up to the bedroom in the Quicken tree, for I wanted to think
things out by myself. There was one of the strange uneasy
moods on me, when I could feel what I called the glitter-dust.
It was thickly foggy outside the window, yet there was an
aura of Mitch in the room and the same brightness, like
reflected dust motes all about me, that I had taken to calling
the glitter-dust. I threw down my handbag on the bed and it
opened and discharged its contents and there in the centre of
the jumbled heap was the key of the Manor. I had forgotten I
had it. I had intended to leave it on the hall table in the

Manor the day I left. The colours of the quilt melted and blended and ran together under my eyes and the key was highlighted, above all the paraphanalia of a lady's handbag, this modern yale key that must have replaced the ancient solid instrument, that had been wont to open Mr. Swan's mortice Victoriana.

Words ran across my eyes like a teletape. I had the key. Roger and Miss Mannion would be out at benediction at six o'clock. It was foggy, foggy, foggier and the white Alvis would be camouflaged and almost without sound. There was a parking place at the side boundary. The Caseys lived in the Convent grounds. I had a torch. I was not afraid and that was a lie. I was terrified, but without excuse. There was a wild excitement about putting on the black slacks and sweater, the dark anorak, the dark scarf that hid the bright of my hair, the silent discreet crêpe-soled shoes. If I could not find the courage to play detective, I knew, I could never live with myself again.

Mr. and Mrs. Rickaby had gone out to supper with friends. Kit was tied up safely with some activity at the hospital. The way was clear and the glitter-dust held the fear at bay and I was in the Alvis and creeping along the road at a snail's pace, finding the park-space, that was never used, at the side, stopping the car with no sound, slipping along without trace, the fog reaching trailing hands to clutch me. There was a car coming down the main avenue and I cowered back into the bushes and put up a hand to pull the scarf down. Roger Hawkins was at the wheel, bending forward, to try to see the road ahead and presently there was nothing except the dripping of the trees and the dying thrumming of the car engine to silence. I slipped through the gateway like swathe gauze, knowing that it was not too late to turn back, acknowledging myself a coward.

The avenue snake twisted as usual and I wondered if there were ghostly people that watched me. Here were the steps and the flash of the torch for a second and the yale in the lock and the lock turning smoothly. The door groaned in protest, but tonight it was louder than usual. It might awaken the dead. I hesitated for ten seconds and then I was inside and the door shut. I was as quiet as I could, yet the traitor door might have been closing me in my tomb with the sepulchral noise it gave, I was committed now. I had too much pride to let myself out on the front step and run for the car, as fast as my legs would carry me.

TAFFY

The hall was immense, far bigger than I remembered it. If I opened the drawing room door, would Mrs. Swan be sitting there with Finn in his basket at her feet, I wondered. The lorgnette might come up to survey me. Then I sent such thoughts out of mind, switched on the torch and swung through the baize door into the kitchen. It was a huge chamber of echoes, with a shadow crouching in every corner and a ceiling as high as the sky ... an atmosphere still of damp and decay, but missing all the familiar smells, bread and hot toast, pceled oranges, Casey's cigarette, shoe polish, silver polish. The mica window of the stove had the look of a wall-eyed dog. Miss Mannion had settled for electricity for cooking, on a small stove and there was an electric fire for her to turn on when she came home.

I scuttled across the tiles to the back hall, to a door I had never used, stopped with a hand on the latch and then clicked through into a flagged corridor. It was like Alice in Wonderland. There were doors to choose from and the first was the obvious choice. It gave on an apartment as big as the kitchen, tiled floor too and the same smell of disuse. There was a strong kitchen table covered with an oil cloth square, a child's pink-edged tablecloth, with figures in garish colours. I switched on the torch. I saw pictures crude, shocking, Grimm's fairytale pictures, garish ... a man running past houses, red twisted nose, jester's hat, sirloin of beef under his arm. "Taffy was a Welshman, Taffy was a thief. Taffy came to my house and stole a joint of beef. I went to Taffy's house, Taffy wasn't in ..."

I left it as it had been, grabbed the torch and switched it round the room. There was a schoolroom fireplace, with a fire-guard about it, brass-edged on top, shabby, old, battered. The mantlepiece was immensely tall and there was a picture over it, yellow, browned with the years, yet unmistakably Mrs. Swan as a girl—the high aristocratic nose, the proud lift to the head, but there was a softness, that had been lost with time.

The picture frame was edged with old Christmas decorations, a red paper-chain from Christmas long gone—faded, drooping, tattered at the edges, all awry in the hanging—a balloon, but most of the air gone leaking away. It moved in a draught, where no draught should be and I wondered if somebody had opened a door in the house. There were rustlings and squeakings in the shrubbery and a distant sigh from the Tree of Heaven. Within, were all the noises of an old house, a step where no step was, the slamming of a door, a scratch at the wainscoting. The scratch-scratch swung me round and there was a person in black, who confronted me at arm's length. My heart stopped, then pounded in my chest. There was a drumming in my ears and then I saw the wisp of fair hair under my scarf and knew my own image in a looking glass on the wall, patchy-silvering, black-spotted in the torch light, no different looking to what I would be in death, with the terror that possessed me. I stepped back and tripped over a clog-shoe, such as a man might wear. It had no daintiness or gentility about it, but an air of cripple shoes, heavy thick-soled, the upper crude, ill-shaped. Here was the creature that had clumped along between the Caseys, with "the Hunchback of Notre-Dame" appearance. The rhyme went over and over in my head. Here was the dream world and the nightmare world, surely, and my search not half done? The dresser was empty, no, not quite! There was a tin plate, a bone-handled spoon, battered, as if they had been stamped on.

"Hush a bye baby on the tree top."

These were the trappings of Taffy. This was no baby. The hackles rose on the nape of my neck and I was out of the room and into the room next door, with not much care about silence. It was quite empty. The last room had a barred window. I knew that already and there was an air about it as

if somebody had just gone and would soon be back. A heavy
oak chair lay on its side. The windows had the monk-cassock
curtains that all the room had. There was a stain like blood,
three feet across the floor boards like a giant ink blot. The
chair was meant to imprison a grown man and there was a
medieval air to it as if it boded torture—a medieval torture
instrument in tough hewn oak. There were shoulder loops
and a belt for the waist and the buckles were turned so that a
prisoner might not easily come at them ... and the marks of
teeth on leather, where somebody had tried to bite their way
out of captivity. I could think of no other explanation for
what I had seen—I got out of the room quickly and remembered the barred windows and the strange cry. There were
stairs to be faced, upright, utility—carpet gone now, if there
had been one. Even the top corridor was no romantic place,
where a grey lady walked. The smell of damp and decay had
crept along it, but in the first room, lingered a wisp of
lavender and a silvered hair clip and the trace of Mrs. Casey
and her spotless motherliness. In the middle room was a
hospital bed with shuttered sides for "patient control", straps
too, but of webbing. There was a deal Jack-in-the-beanstalk
cupboard in the room and somebody had painted it in with
flowers a foot across, bright flowers that grew in no garden,
poppies that chased each other and spilt over and went
running across the walls of the room. It was Walt-Disney
insane, flowers and animals and children, all together
higgledepiggledy ... a nightmare of a room, a room for a
child, but here had been no child. I picked up a bib from the
mattress, an outsize bib, of rubber-backed towelling, a
frilled-edged bib, but this bib had no gaiety, even if the edge
was frilled. This was a grim utilitarian bib, that could have
been used on age-dissolution, not early childhood, but with
the user adult in years. I stood by the cot bed and something
entangled my toes, seemed to run spider-like across my instep
and here was Joseph's coat of many colours, knitted of wool
in a scarf that had no beginning or ending and was
unravelled and unravelled, red, orange, yellow, green, blue,
indigo, violet ... grey strands down like wires, kinked,

ripped, torn, twisted and turned, by a crazy mind, while the long hours ground slowly away.

Here was a manic room. Across the walls in scarlet was written TAFFY in letters six feet high, letters that jiggled this way and that. It was not the work of child's slap-dash hands. It had been slapped on carelessly but cunningly executed by a steady hand. The childish hand had unravelled the wool, but this had been painted, this Walt Disney manic sequence with love, to please somebody who was simple to please.

I walked along to the end of the corridor and knew that Mrs. Swan's room lay opposite the back hall. The answer should be there before me and I grasped at trailing end of clues that escaped me. The person that had been led out to the utilicon that night had been Taffy. He had used the cot bed and the torture chair, that had only been a grown-up high chair, that had been essential for his control. I had heard Taffy trying the locked door on which my hand now rested and somebody had spirited him away, with her "Hush a bye baby on the tree top". He was no baby ... not any longer, but there might have been a time, when he came there first, when he was a child in arms—a toddler, a growing-up little boy, with the stigma of mental or physical abnormality and of a serious nature too. There was only one person he could be and that was the unnamed claimant and Mrs. Swan had provided for him, till his death.

I was out on the back hall when I heard the car coming up the drive and it sounded like the Rolls purring home from Benediction. Here was I, caught red-handed. My brain ceased to work and I stood there at the head of the stairs and wondered why I had thought that the draped figure was funny. Then the door of Mrs. Swan's room opened but it can only have been the draught from the door, that Roger Hawkins opened to let Miss Mannion enter the hall below. I dropped the torch in my fright and it rolled, flash-signalled across the landing and came to rest against the banisters with its bulb mercifully out. I blessed the sepulchral hall door which drowned the noise.

"God! What a night!" said Roger's voice and Miss

Mannion was telling him she would set out his supper in the sitting room.

He came steadily up the stairs and in a moment I was in Mrs. Swan's room and Miss Mannion was going past into her room. I was a ghost mouse with my cheek against the panel of the door.

"I'll finish the packing later on, Master Roger. I'll just slip off my coat and into my apron. Supper won't be long."

"God! I'll be glad to be out of this morgue tomorrow."

I got out of it in half an hour, but I failed to collect the torch, where it lay against the banisters. I was through the front door and away like a hare along the avenue and the fog closed me about with anonymity. I drove the Alvis home quite recklessly and garaged it out of the discomfort of the weather. Then I went into the kitchen and toasted myself for a long time before the boiler stove, drank half a tumblerful of sherry and then another, but all that did was to scramble what brains I had in my head and make me sleep like a dead log all night, but there were strange dreams came and Mitch moved through every one of them and he told me what a brave girl I was and through the whole night ran a signature tune, that went round and round against a carousel of gallopers at a fair, of "Taffy was a Welshman, Taffy was a thief" ... till I wondered if I had sent myself crazy with fright in the night and the fog.

I was not given much time to gather my wits together. I could have done with a day in bed, after I had awakened from my sherry-induced sleep of that Sunday night, but there was a phone call from Mr. Rickaby before I had time to leave for the Hospital in the morning. He would be obliged if I would call at Wellington House on the way past. With my permission, Anthony would sit in on the discussion and perhaps we might go into the Hospital together afterwards when it was over. Inspector Franklyn had some new points to discuss in the Swan case and Mr. Rickaby thought, as my solicitor, it might be as well for himself to be present.

It was a cold damp windy day, but Wellington House refused to acknowledge it. Mrs. Rickaby kissed me and brought me through into the office, said that every body had arrived but me. Nellie Pluck was through presently with some excellent coffee. Anthony came over and touched my cheek. The Police stood up at my entry but I got an impression that there was offialdom about—and no camaredie. The window panes were rattling with the gusts and there was a lion roaring in the chimney. The fog was quite blown away and I was glad of it, even if my brain was as foggy as ever. You could hear the high-pitched shrilling of the gale in the spinney and we drank our coffee and made a little conversation and then we were all police case again with the Inspector's opening.

"We're progressing with our case, but I wanted to put some facts to you, Mrs. Allington. I'd like your comments on some factors-explanations perhaps, if that's not too strong a word."

Now was the time to tell them all that I had broken and entered the Manor last night and I wanted explanations too. Guilt delayed me and the chance was gone. I knew about breaking and entering and my torch still lay on the top landing.

"Your own solicitor will be here to guide you. He insists upon it. He'll stop you answering any of my queries if he thinks you may prejudice yourself. This is in no way intended as an accusation. We want your help. We're grateful to you."

He wanted to know exactly how many people knew that I had had "dorminal" in my possession and I sighed with relief that that was all it was, told him that Kit had known and Roger Hawkins, my daily woman, Mrs. Flower—anybody who might have looked in my pocket in the hall of the Manor House—and everybody went past the hall stand.

"It was careless of you to leave a lethal dose of drugs kicking about like that," he remarked. " 'Sweet, sweet poison for the aged tooth'. That's what Shakespeare said."

He veered off in his disconcering manner.

"When did you first hear that you were a beneficiary under Mrs. Swan's will?"

I knew we had been through that and argued with him,

said it was at Christmas sometime, when Roger had come
into the kitchen.

"A lot happened at Christmas. I want this pin-pointed
exactly."

"Christmas day after dinner, I think."

"And you gave the dog the powder on Boxing day?"

I told him that Roger had telephoned the Vet first, but
surely he knew that and now he shot the floor out from under
me by asking me if I was interested in the fact that Roger
Hawkins had categorically denied that he had ever done any
such thing ... the Vet too."

"He went out to the hall. I heard the bell ring ... "

"It looks bad for you if they both deny it."

Mr. Rickaby put his hands together and looked at the
Inspector over the horn rims of his glasses and told him that
he could infer no such fact, scolded him that he was trying to
intimidate me and Franklyn took no more notice of him than
he might have taken of a fly zooming past.

"You and your daily help, had some discussion on or about
the day you left for the Manor House. There was some talk
between you about using the dorminal capsules to 'put paid
to the old duck if she got past bearing' and you meant Mrs.
Swan. I quote."

Had she said such a thing? I had no memory of it, but it
might be true. I knew I wouldn't have said it or thought it!

"I don't remember. It was a silly joke, if we did."

"A joke in such circumstances, on such a sad day?"

"I don't know. I forgot to burn the capsules. The boiler
fire was out. I was in a dreadful state of mind."

"Yet not so very dreadful that you could not indulge in bad
taste jokes, Mrs. Allington? 'Put some of the bombs in her
soup'. I quote again."

Anthony was sitting on the edge of the desk and his hand
touched my arm for a moment and was gone again. He
frowned at Franklyn and there was no friendliness between
them.

"If this bullying doesn't stop, Inspector, the interview is at
an end."

Franklyn asked him if he had his father's authorisation for

such a statement and Anthony got more angry than I had
even seen him.

"I have my own authorisation," he said shortly. "For
God's sake, be civilised. This isn't an inquisition. Stuff the
thumb screw and the rack. This is a colleague who has fought
at your side and mine."

The wind blew down the chimney like a lion and Franklyn
turned to ask me why I had burned half the powder I gave
the dog and again I was caught up in the tumbler drier of my
own fear, for surely I had answered all these things before?

"I don't know. Mrs. Swan would need a whole powder."

"But Finn might have needed another half dose."

"The Vet said a half dose would be enough—"

He raised an eyebrow in scorn at me and asked me if I had
forgotten that the Vet denied having given any advice at all. It
seemed that the powder was harmless and it might have done
the dog good.

"It was bismuth and bicarb, and there was nothing wrong
in the first place with Mrs. Swan's stomach. That powder
was what's called a 'placebo', which means 'I please'. It
wasn't the powder that killed Mrs. Swan and it wasn't the
powder that killed the dog."

"Finn was given a noxious substance, so was Mrs. Swan.
You have no jot or tittle of evidence that my client gave either
of them anything remotely harmful and well you know it. I'd
be glad if you'd watch your words, Inspector," exclaimed old
Rickaby.

The Inspector was not done with me yet.

"You're careless with lethal drugs, lady. Your solicitor
can't deny that."

He turned off to another tack, his voice louder and more
frightening than ever, how Miss Mannion had made a
statement to say that I had refused to send for the doctor the
night the dog died.

I protested that it was not necessary and he laughed me to
scorn. I might say she was hysterical and not ill, but she died
the next night. I might say that Roger Hawkins thought that
we should not call the doctor out, but he had a different

statement from Hawkins, that said that he, Hawkins had tried to persuade me to send.

Anthony laughed at that and went to fetch his pipe from the mantlepiece.

"The obvious answer to that is that Hawkins and Miss Mannion are telling lies. For God's sake, Franklyn, don't be so highly-sprung. You're like Solomon, but you're cutting the damned baby in two."

The Inspector raised an eyebrow and asked him if he recalled that I had said Mannion was an honest woman.

"There was trouble between Mrs. Allington and Miss Mannion and Mrs. Allington left Mrs. Swan's room and refused to go back. She demanded an apology. She called you a thief and you wouldn't wear it and then there was all that business of the aquamarine clip. You met Father Gillson on the stairs. He's made a sworn statement that he told you about Mrs. Swan's will and he's no liar. You didn't tell us about the priest telling you you had been left a legacy."

"So I'm threatened by the Black Bishop?" I muttered.

"I said Mrs. Swan wouldn't break my will, but perhaps she did."

Anthony's voice was a lance en guard above my head.

"Gillson is as deaf as a post, Franklyn, and if Mrs. Allington was weeping, he'd not have heard one damned word she said. I've had a full account from her about all that happened and I'm quite ready to stake my soul on it, that she's telling the truth."

It was strange to see the White Knight move across the board to protect me from the Black Bishop. It was a chess game, just as they said and I stood in my square on the board with my head bent, knowing I looked like no queen that ever was. Franklyn might have been my executioner, as he brought the sword down on my bent neck.

"One of my constables was at your house the morning your husband died. This is most unpleasant, but it has to be said. He told me that you thought of putting a pillow over your husband's face ... thought of a mercy killing. He didn't think anything about it. People say daft things, but then you didn't have the body removed to the Chapel of Rest and after

you went to the Manor, there's been all this killing. I'm
sorry ... truly sorry" ...

I was back in Wellington House, my mind empty.
Somewhere in the room, I could hear Mr. Rickaby speaking
to the Inspector as rarely he must have been spoken to before.
Why had he, as my solicitor not been informed that such a
statement was to be put in. In good faith, he had permitted
the interview and the Inspector had behaved in an ignorant,
bullying, ungentlemanly manner. He was nothing but a
boorish lout and he would be glad if the police would leave
his house at once.

Anthony's hand was on my shoulder and his voice was
almost a whisper. If they wanted the whole story, he was in
my full confidence. He had been told by me everything that
happened the night of Mitch's death. I was being crucified at
his feet, loving him and having to watch him die. Mitch had
not the knowledge that death was inevitable. I had known I
was to lose the one person I loved. I had hung there with no
benison of drugs. I was sentenced to remain conscious to the
last second of Mitch's death, without tranquillisers, without
euphoria, sentenced to suffer the last bit of his suffering.

He released my shoulder and confronted the Inspector and
now it was Knight to Rook.

"Put yourself in her place, Franklyn. Look at her now.
You've shone your bull's eye lantern on one trap after
another, under her feet, in pitch black. If her head bends in
shame, it's because she may have misjudged a sick old
woman, who was nothing but a cantakerous old bitch."

He paced the floor for a while and then challenged
Franklyn to put himself into my place, to find himself with
no assets and have to seek employment with an employer
who, more or less, blackmailed him to stay, who humiliated
and thwarted him at every turn. I had been broken in heart
and spirit, yet I had come out of it all with honour.

"You're a bloody great bully, Franklyn and I'd thought
you a good policeman. You even put yourself up to be a
Sherlock Holmes and a chess player. You couldn't find out
who killed Cock Robin, but I'll do it for you. It's time we

stopped short with third degree and started to invoke forensic medicine. Just give me carte blanche."

Franklyn had found his cap and was making for the door and I was surprised that he was smiling and we were still colleagues.

"I'm off to the Manor House," he said. "Like Pontius Pilate, I find no fault in you, Mrs. Allington. There's not enough evidence against you. I'll tell them that at the Convent and at the Presbytery and at the Manor House, that there's a smear campaign against you and I want to know why."

Anthony took me off to the sitting room and we had coffee with Mrs. Rickaby, but he had decided not to go to the Hospital. He would meet me there in the afternoon, but now he had urgent work. He left me at the Quicken Tree and I waited till he was out of sight and drove to the Church. I bought chrysanthemums at the greengrocer's and then walked along through the lych gate and replaced the sad flowers on the grave. I prayed to Mitch, as often I did, asked him to save me, to come to me, for sorely I needed his help. There was the glitter-dust feeling after a while and the day seemed bright and sunny, where no sun shone. There was the same feeling that all was right in the world, the same sensation as if I floated above the ground and walked on the seven hills. Even the church had lost its coldness and dampness. It was so quiet that it was impossible to guess that we were near to the High Street, impossible to think that this was any Lincolnshire Church with God high above the altar in the East window.

"Please let them find out who killed Mrs. Swan."

It was to Mitch I prayed. "Show them I'm not the one."

In my heart I prayed with all the depth I had in me. I loved Mitch and I would never stop loving him. If it was possible for a woman to love two men, I loved Anthony Rickaby too. I had loved him before and I had forgotten it for a while and Mitch had swept me up into a great maelstrom that overwhelmed me. I did not know if it were possible to split love in two. Time was long and went on for ever. I talked silently, knowing it a sin not to talk to God direct. The glitter-dust was dying out as if twilight had come and then the door of the church opened and I spun round. There was a man at the end of the nave and the last mote of the glitter-dust caught the gold of the ring in the lobe of his ear, as he came sauntering up towards the Rickaby's pew where I knelt. His teeth were just as white as his beard just as black and there was an excitement that hung about him, that I had noticed on the night of Mrs. Swan's death. I stood up and tried to come out of the pew, but he barred my way.

"Good morning, Liz-Jane," he smiled, but I had no friendliness for him, just blurted out at him like a naïve schoolgirl.

"Why did you tell lies about me to the police?"

"Oh, come on!" he laughed and I stuttered out about what they had said about not ringing the Vet, about wanting to send for Dr. Jones the night of Finn's death, about the things he had said that must be lies, if I were not crazy.

He took it all coolly.

"If you're throwing accusations about, can you tell me why you broke and entered the Manor House last night? Did you know you left your torch and it had your name on it? Have you told the police you're a burglar as well as a poisoner?"

I went back into the pew and sat down, for my legs would hold me no longer. Then I found the key in my pocket and gave it back to him.

"You left the sackcloth curtains pulled across here and there. You left a trail of your scent five feet high. You left open those doors, that ought to be shut and you shut those doors that ought to be opened and there is no truth in you."

His laugh echoed from the roof of the church and I thought of the sound of "dead priests, that were laughing in their stalls." I sat six feet away from him at the far end of the pew and he asked me what I made of the west wing, as casually as if he asked me if I would take coffee with him in Fuller's.

I whispered that there might have been something in there connected with the murder, but I could make very little of it.

"You probably knew about it, but I didn't know. I heard strange noises in the nights and there were barred windows

and the strangest things. The Caseys must have kept a
prisoner there. There was a picture too, an old one of Mrs.
Swan over one of the fireplaces."

I had no right to be talking to him in the first place, but I
must find out and I did find out, for he seemed friendly
enough to tell me.

"They had a person in there. It was complete 'hush-hush'.
It was Mrs. Swan's sister's child though, not Mrs. Swan's. I
had two aunts. You made a mystery out of nothing. Mrs.
Swan's sister had a spastic kid and that was a disgrace in
those days. Then she died and Taffy came to live at the
Manor. The Caseys have seen after him for years. For God's
sake, why didn't you ask me? Why did you go to all the
trouble of going into that place last night and frightening the
wits out of yourself? It's all above board. They pretend
nobody knows, but they're all in it—the Convent and the
Monseigneur, Miss Mannion. Old Rickaby knows all about
it, but he plays his cards damn close to his chest. You'd never
have been told—no maids were, not that you're a maid. The
maids all left because they thought the place was haunted.
Friend Taffy was O.K. Nobody ever hurt him. That's not his
right name of course, but he was never called anything else.
He's a handful to manage and he's a bit miserable if he's too
confined—gets out now and again and wanders around. The
Caseys love him. Aunt Swan wasn't too keen, but she signed
the cheques for twenty four years and she saw to him in her
will."

"He's the un-named claimant," I whispered.

"He's the un-named claimant and now you knows the
family secret, will you tell me why you lied about what I
did?" he demanded and sat himself on the front of the pew
and looked at me with candour.

"Come now, Liz-Jane, we have no witnesses except the
God in the stained glass window and he's not able to give
evidence. "Tell me why you killed the old girl, for just a
thousand pounds? Were you so hard up?"

"I didn't kill her."

"I think you did. You're making it up that I rang the Vet,
about Finn having the powder. You know well that I wanted

Jones sent for that night for Mrs. Swan. I was scared witless. You knew Jones would issue a certificate and he did. You knew he'd only be too glad to issue the certificate, for he'd missed the diagnosis. You knew nothing of drugs. You gave the stuff the trial run and curled Finn round his basket with very little of it and the old woman was weak and had a dud heart, or maybe she thought she had. It nearly worked. Just satisfy me by a confession. The old gent in the white night-shirt won't split."

He went to stand with his back to the chancel and the east window threw a coat of many colours all about him and I remembered Taffy's unravelled wool and felt the glitter-dust feeling again and knew the power of extra-sensory perception and the air was full of dust motes, all a-dazzle with the coloured sun.

"That's not the whole explanation of Taffy," I said, but he took no notice of that.

"You'll not get away with it. Franklyn'll have you like a terrier jumps a rat. He'll hatchet you and all the Professor of Forensic Medicine can do, won't stop him."

I knew it had all happened before. I thought I saw how it happened, but there was no reality about the scene now. It was the same as it had been in the ancient ruins of the dig in Suffolk. There was a fishpond and the place the grave had been ... and the motes dancing in all the colours of the spectrum like Taffy's wool.

"You killed her," I said. "You poisoned her."

"Why should I kill the goose that laid the golden egg? I knew the annuity would be all that was left, I had lived high on the hog on that same annuity, but you killed it too. I'm as poor as you are now. I had no motive to kill her in the world. Of all the people in the house, I had no reason to do it."

I turned from him and went stumbling away down the nave and his laughter followed me.

"Don't tell the police about Taffy. He's no help at all. The police don't believe a word you say. I've only to tell them about your escapade at the Manor last night. They'll see what you are, not a helpless little widow, but a determined little dolly-bird, out for every half-penny she can get, with her sights cocked at the Forensic gent now that the King is dead. It's just "the King is dead. God save the King" That's it and young Rickaby out of his head about you, too pixilated to diagnose a case of poisoning as classical as any he'll find in his text-books."

I ran out of the church and jumped into the car, drove it for miles along fen roads and the east wind whistled coldly across the grey land. There was no glitter-dust left anywhere in my world. There was nothing for me for the rest of my days, but a small prison cell and the dreadful institutional atmosphere, which could never know the way a spirit can be lifted up and the way things strange and impossible can be encountered ... where nobody could ever come to believe that a girl might love one man and then another, yet with her whole heart ... how a woman might lose her King and then after a time of sorrow, she might come to find another ... how again in a million years, she might find her King and know him for who he was, know how he had loved her for all time, and how he had watched over her and shielded her. There was knight and there was king and I could in no way solve the puzzle of my woman's heart.

I could in no way solve the full truth of Taffy. In some impossible way, Mitch had shown me that Roger Hawkins had told me half truths. I waited till night came and with it came Anthony, worried because I had not appeared at the Hospital. I had done the work at home and I had it ready for him, but he told me that it was not typescript, he was worried about.

"Will you never understand?" he demanded of me and I cast back to the night when I had uncovered all my emotions to him. I was quite unable to keep secret what I knew about the west wing, though I imagined Anthony knew it all, for his father must have known the legal side.

Anthony listened in silence as I gave him the minutest details of the west wing, told him about what had happened between Roger Hawkins and myself in the chapel.

When I had finished he took me in his arms and kissed me.

"And that *was* the way of it?" he said and I felt the flames kindle and burn brightly ... hoped I knew they would continue to burn.

"There was a bit of the jig-saw missing. I didn't know about Taffy and of course, there's more to that part of it."

He laughed and said it was a pity that my father was not with us. He was going up the skies of the United States like a rocket and he was likely to keep going. I had written to him, but for the last few months he had not bothered to reply and so I told Anthony.

"You'll have to make do with me then," he smiled. "I've always fancied myself at detective fiction."

THE END GAME

It was strange how Anthony and I lived our lives in much the same way as we had done before the day I had walked into the staff room and tried to tell Mitchell Allington that my chief was not available for an interview about the sale of bones. I still attended post mortems. I still marshalled the scribes for a top copy and six carbons. We spoke very little about the tragedy that hung over us, but Inspector Franklyn and the police in general showed no coolness towards me. It was all the more surprising then when Mr. Rickaby, my solicitor, arrived at the Quicken Tree just after breakfast about a week later and said something had come up.

"Good or bad?" I asked, and he told me it was a bit of both.

"There's been an item found in a safe deposit of your late husband's. We did not know of its existence. It will make an enormous difference to your estate, for it will come to you." He took out a sealed white envelope and broke the seal into the usual chips and dust of blood-red sealing wax. He emptied out the tobacco pouch and the bone must be inside it, the very bone that Mitch had placed with respect on the staff room table. There was glitter-dust over-flowing the room and my eyes dazzled with tears and a voice was in my ears, low as the voice of the Tree of Heaven.

"It's mine to sell, but the Complex would never be able to afford it. It's very old indeed matched against the two million years of human man ... impossible to set a value on it. It certainly made me such as I am. It's yours to do with as you please ... even to keeping it as a good luck charm in a tobacco pouch, for that is what your late husband did."

I could not speak, could only feel the dazzle of the

brightness and the knowledge that there was eternity all about me and I was not the White Queen perhaps but a very small pawn in eternity. Then a long time after or so it seemed, Mr. Richaby was speaking about the bad part of his news, his eye on the clock over the mantelpiece.

"Anthony's gone off early to Police H.Q. Franklyn and he are setting up the plan for the end game. They've fixed a confrontation. I'm to produce you at the Manor in Milton this morning. You're to bring the camel-hair coat, the one that held the capsules in the pocket. He gave me a most vital message for you, terse and precise. I can't make anything out of it, but he said you'd know."

I argued that I had no intention of ever setting foot inside Milton Manor again. I had been helping the police. I had been grilled. I was sick of being lectured about carelessness with drugs. I was sick of false accusations. I could take no more ...

His face was more serious than ever I had seen it, as he implored me to treat the whole matter as of the utmost importance.

"Anthony told me to tell you it's the end game. There's to be a reconstruction of the crime and it will end in check mate ... end finally and for ever. Disregard the rook attack. That's vital. *Disregard the rook attack.*"

He bent towards me, his hand on mind and told me that poverty was a thing of the past for me. There was nothing but happiness before my feet.

"Play it Anthony's way. He values your happiness above heaven."

I put on the camel coat, that now contained no capsules. Instead it held a tobacco pouch and an item that made me rich above princes, but I valued it as a good luck token, for it seemed to enclose me with glitter-dust and set my feet above the ground. It seemed to offer me immortality and eternal happiness, yet I shuddered at the familiar gates of Milton Manor.

"Don't forget. You're to write off the strong attack of the rooks," said a voice in my ear and I wondered if it was the Tree of Heaven, or only old Mr. Rickaby.

I was glad of the warmth of the coat against the chill day. I was horrified when I went up the steps and into the Manor, for I had had little idea of what a reconstruction meant. There were police cars, a patrol, a Panda, a Raspberry Ripple. There was the Casey Rolls. There was the utilicon. There was a motor bike, with a police helmet dangling from its bars, and a tinny microphone voice.

"We're to go straight through to the sitting room. You're the last arrival. Miss Mannion had opened the front door, the original Miss Mannion in black dress and white apron. Sergeant Bacon stood at the door to the sitting room, his back square to it. In the hall, each door was guarded by a constable. I was no chess player, but it looked as if indeed we were moving to check-mate.

Bacon opened the drawing-room door and I was astonished by the number of people present, grouped in the circular mirror, the black of two nuns, Monseigneur Gillson, Roger Hawkins over by the window, Miss Mannion now, who went to stand beside him. Casey was awkward in the centre of the room, turning his uniform cap round and round in his hands, his wife tucked as close to him as she could get, her silver hair a-gleam. Anthony came across the carpet to greet me, put his arm through mine and led me to the fire. It had only been lit half an hour or so and there was nothing to take the chill from the great room ... dank, dim, miserable, musty.

Then Inspector Franklyn was standing opposite me and in no time, Bacon was at my right side and I remembered the traditional rook attack and the door was shut to keep me on the board. Soon, Mrs. Swan might come in, leaning on the ebony stick, with Finn waddling-panting behind her. I could almost see the assessment lorgnette, but Anthony sent her on her way, his lips against my ear.

"Franklyn fancies himself a member of the French Sûreté. We're to have a complete reconstruction."

I gasped out "Oh, no!" and two police heads swivelled sharply to look at me.

"May I have the coat Mrs. Allington?"

Franklyn was across the room and into the hall in a flash

with Bacon marshalling the rest of us behind him. Father
Gillson was muttering that we would catch our deaths of cold
and that it was all most inconvenient. Anthony's jacket was
draped round my shoulders. Then in the hall, stood the
Inspector with the coat held out to me.

"Hang it where it was on Christmas Eve, when you came
back from the Church."

I did as he said, and he handed me a bottle of capsules.

"Put them in the pocket, exactly as they were."

I felt relief that flooded over me like a giant wave, but it
ebbed at his clipped voice.

"They're not the original capsules. They're duplicate and
made up by Phipps, the chemist. The original jar's still
missing and not to be found."

I could have wept at my disappointment and I stood there
and listened as he started off about carelessness with drugs
again. Then even he had had enough of it. He swung about
on Roger and pointed out to him the fact that he had had
equal opportunity of obtaining the lethal drug. The coat had
hung in the hall. They stood there like sheep before a
shearer, as he tackled them one after another. There was a
shocked horror as he pointed out that not only one of them,
but each one, had passed the coat several times and they had
only to stretch out a hand. Then he was back to me.

"Reconstruct for me, Mrs. Allington. That night after the
sherry party at Wellington House, on Boxing Day."

He steered me into it and I told it haltingly, as best I could.
The old argument started about whether Roger had
telephoned the Vet or whether he had not. Then came the sin
I had committed in burning the first half of the powder and a
deal of futile remarks from all sides. My words turned
themselves about and came out looking-glass fashion. When I
actually described the administration of the powder to Finn, I
put my face in my hands and shuddered and Monseigneur
Gillson came walking diagonally across the room, the black
Bishop come to life.

"Tell the truth, Mrs. Allington," he said and I knew he
thought me a liar.

"I carried Finn upstairs. He had been asleep on my lap. I curled him round in his basket in Mrs. Swan's room."

"So we went upstairs and put the old lady to bed?"

Franklyn's voice was sharp and no-nonsense-precise. He moved fast and straight, as the rook moves. Sergeant Bacon blocked my escape from the rear and there I was in danger from the rooks, where I must remember no danger lay, if Anthony were to be trusted.

"Upstairs, first floor."

He did not have to tell any of us the way. I stopped at the stair foot beside the marble lady and whispered to Anthony that I could not go up there ever again, but Anthony had my arm in his hand and Bacon blocked my flight and Franklyn waited like an avenging god on the landing. I went stiffly up the stairs and Anthony murmured to me that I was the White Queen. I could move to any square I choose ... left, right, forward, back, across. "Play it my way, my darling."

In the bedroom, I looked at the bed and expected to see her there again, eyes closed, mouth open, face blotched. Miss Mannion was jumpy too. She started at Franklyn's hand on her arm.

"It's later on, Miss Mannion. The dog's dead. He's there curled in his basket."

The basket, the rug, or one like it, they had spared no trouble in the reconstruction.

"The dog's dead, Miss Mannion. Madame is having hysterics. You come into the room. Go on from there."

The account came out again all Alice-through-the-Looking Glass. They were seeking the bottle of pills that Mrs. Swan always took to sleep at night.

"They were gone," Miss Mannion said. "It was a full bottle, fresh the day before. Mrs. Allington looked for it and she pretended to be surprised, but she didn't look far ... said it had fallen through the crack in the floor."

Dr. Jones saw the crack the next day. He agreed with me," I put it in self defence. "He said not to worry and he wrote out a fresh prescription."

"Evidence corrobortated," Franklyn said. "Let's have the floor up."

I could not believe that they were going to rip the floor up, yet it was happening before my eyes, Bacon produced a bag of tools and Casey stepping forward to help him. Monseigneur Gillson darted across, black Bishop again, and objected strenuously. They had no right to interfere with the structure of the house. They had no legal authority and the house was his responsibility.

"I have my own authority," said Franklyn and snuffed him out, but Bacon was kinder and tried to calm him, said that the boards would be replaced as good as new.

Now there was a square hole that gaped in the dust beside the head of the bed and Franklyn curled a finger to bid me to make a search for the bottle of sleeping tablets. A torch appeared in his hand as if he had rubbed some magic lamp and there was the plaster of the ceiling below, the fluff and dust of years, the spiders' webs, the smell of must.

"A small bottle like that might have rolled," I muttered and that meant more boards sacrificed.

"Come and look again, Mrs. Allington. You know what they were like."

Casey's finger nail chipped at the boards and he exclaimed that there was dry rot in the joists and that the place would soon be down about our ears and then there was a long delay, while the priest threatened to ring the Chief Constable, creaked down on his knees and examined the damage, the police had done. Then the rooks were finished with the search.

"We'd better get this hangman's drop, covered, Bacon. Get it done soon and by an expert. Casey's right about the dry rot. I daresay it's all over the house. You can smell it."

He swung about on me and asked me where the tablets were and I looked at him in surprise.

"They were in your charge, Mrs. Allington."

"Presumably they were in Mrs. Swan's charge," pointed out Rickaby mildly. "I must ask my client at this point to give the Inspector an assurance that she did not take the tablets from the old lady with intent to poison either her or her dog or anybody else."

I had only time to nod my head, when Franklyn was after me again, to ask why I had not wanted a P.M. on Finn.

"I didn't want to upset Mrs. Swan. She was upset enough."

"Yet you were against sending for the doctor for her that night."

."She'd have hated to have him cut about. He was an old dog. His heart was bad. It was so obvious, what he'd died of."

"Was it?" he shot off at me and I knew I was puerile, as I stood there muttering about the place Casey had laid him under the Tree of Heaven, that he had always moved back into its shade on a hot summer's day.

"Do you regret now that you refused an autopsy?"

I said I did not know and he almost shouted at me that it might have saved my employer's life. There was no trace in him of the friendly Inspector, whom I knew well from Forensic cases.

"The person that poisoned the dog, certainly did not want an autopsy carried out on his body."

It went on and on and my mind turned to a void.

"When you gave Mrs. Swan her powder the next night, you washed the glass at the basin. Why?"

Again I shook my head.

"Was it because you had given her poison too and you didn't want it traced?"

Mr. Rickaby was protesting loudly, but Anthony said that it was presumably because the powder had been given in her bedroom. If it was in the dining room where it was usually given, there would not have been a basin handy ...

So it went on, and on and on and over and over and over.

"Why did you say to Casey that it would have been better if Mrs. Swan had died and not the dog?"

And Casey's protest.

"Glory be to God, Mrs. Allington. I never told him. Mr. Roger done that. You said it the night in the kitchen but you never meant it. There was rage in you, because she was trying to make you a thief. Why are they twisting and turning every word you said to make a noose for your neck?"

A thought consumed me with the ice of terror. Surely they

did not hang people any more, or were poisoners hanged by the neck till they were dead? I knew this must be a frightful nightmare and that I must soon awake. Bacon had taken over from his chief and he was the kind one, or so I had thought.

"The night Mrs. Swan died, but before she died, did you give Mr. Hawkins some noxious substance in his drink to make him sleep—not to poison him, just to keep him from prowling the house?"

That was when we had had the rum with the strange taste. Roger had given it to us in the kitchen and he had said it had "travelled the Med." I had washed the glasses out and Miss Mannion should have done it, or so Bacon said, and I stuttered out some description of the scene, but nobody remembered the strange tasting rum, that had "travelled the Med.", and surely they could not all have forgotten it?

Slowly we went through the awful details of the actual death and I found myself out on the landing, with the bunch of them grouped about me, talking about the nuns and the prayers and the smell of the candles and the noise of the bees, that the prayers made. I was beside the door to the corridor and I reached out a finger and touched the handle.

I whispered how I had caught it and how it turned in my hand, how I didn't know if I slept and dreamed it all, how I had heard noises at night and as I spoke, my voice was a thin whisper of terror and I was far more frightened, than I had been that night and the handle was turning again, turning slowly, slowly, and the door opening. I tried to scream, but no sound came, that could come from human throat, only a hoarse, cracked, witch screech, for he stood there, toe to toe with me, the hunched up caricature of a monstrous, adult child. His face was placid, the eyes blue, almost serene.

"You didn't dream it, Mrs. Allington," said the Inspector and I knew that here stood Taffy. Mrs. Casey was beside him in a moment, gathering him into her arms, soothing him, backing him along towards the corridor.

"Come away to sleep again, my dotie. Come away ... away ... away."

He was handsone, yet his Creator had miscast him. His body was twisted and gnarled, his limbs awry. He might have been a marionette with the way his limbs jerked on joints, that angled obtusely. Grimaces broke the perfection of his face, like a stone through glass. The rainbowed wool was in his hands and he tore at it and tore at it and his clogs were garlanded with it, as it hung about his feet.

"Taffy! Christ Almighty, Franklyn! Why the hell have you produced Taffy?"

Roger's face was a photo-flash of horror and I think that mine matched it. I was shaking with shock and Taffy was coming towards me, breaking away from Mrs. Casey. "He's only trying to say you're a pretty lady, Mrs. Allington," said Mrs. Casey. Then she had taken him away. The door to the corridor was shut and Franklyn had turned to me.

"Then it wasn't a nightmare, no more than the utilicon was? They took him to the Convent that night and he's still in their care. You'll confirm that, Sister Paul?"

"Of course, I will. He lives in a cottage with the Caseys and he's far happier than any of us. He has those that will love him and care for him till the end of his days. There's the money to see to it too, thanks to Mrs. Swan, God rest her! She was a saint."

The sallow of Roger's face was suffused with anger against Taffy, against the nuns, against us all.

"She wasn't a saint," he cried. "Don't let the nuns fool you about that. They don't know that she was trying to redeem her soul with all that stained window and mosaic floor for the little Chapel, the cut glass goblets and all the china, the silver and what-have-you legacy. It was gold to stuff up their small prim mouths, but they never wondered why she took such care of Taffy. 'Taffy was a Welshman. Taffy was a thief.' Who do you think he was, for he must have been somebody's child? There's a cygnet for a girl to have and he belonged to Mrs. Swan's sister, illegitimate too. What you don't know is why he was spastic. It wasn't done in those days to have a baby without a man to father it. Legal abortion wasn't in fashion yet. Mrs. Swan herself was barren and I've always thought that her husband was Taffy's father. At any rate, she wasn't going to see it all come out, so she tried to abort the pregnancy herself and she botched it—left it too late. She'd

have done better today, when even schoolgirls have sex
education. As it was, she was left with a dead sister and a
baby who grew up to be a Frankenstein's monster. It's funny
when you think it out. She went to Taffy's house and she
stole, not a roast of beef, with her crude surgery. She turned
Taffy into a thing instead of a person and she stole his soul
and lost her own. Who can ever pay the price of what she
did? It explains all that stuff in the will. She wanted to buy
herself out of hell."

The nuns were clasping their hands over their ears in
disgust and disbelief. Then little Sister Paul came softly
across the room to me, not believing a word of what Roger
had said.

"He's making it up. She *was* a saint and we all loved her.
Yon shouldn't have done harm to her, Mrs. Allington. For
pity's sake, admit what you did and let's get the whole thing
done with."

Quite suddenly, I was sick of it. I wanted no more. I
looked round the cirle of faces and saw that they all believed
that I was the guilty one. I wanted open air and freedom. I
would have faced Patanga again, to get away from the Manor
House in Milton, faced the canoes that lay off the shore
watching us and Mitch at the start of it all. Mitch! Mitch!
Where was he now?

"Very well. I did it, Inspector," I said and I was on a
runaway horse and nobody could stop me, nothing, not even
the grinding pain from Anthony's fingers in my shoulders.

"She wasn't a saint. She was wicked enough for what
Roger Hawkins says to be true. I belive him. She nagged me
and nagged me and not only me. She was cruel to every
person in the house, in small mean ways. She seemed to love
Roger, but she fought with him too. There was hypocrisy
between them and a deal of falseness and arguments. This
house is damned, but what's been said and seen just now
explains a deal of it, the ghosts that walked in the night, the
whisperings ..."

Anthony cut in on me, explained that if I was set on
making a confession, I must do it in the right way. I must
come down to the Station, but we might as well fill in some of

the detail here. Surely I had had enough training in crime by this?

He was the only one that had not moved back from me. The others had edged off, but still he held me fast and I went on with it.

"Do you think I killed Mitch too? If you think that, Anthony I'll confess to it? I don't remember much, except that I wanted it to be over and there was no hope left. I couldn't bear the way it went on and all the happiness ran away, only that I had to pretend that he was getting better and it was a lie."

I was back in the staff room in the Camford General Hospital with Mitch, imperious, opening the tobacco pouch and setting the bone on the table. Then I was borrowing plumes to go to dinner with him. Almost I could see the blaze of the crêpes suzettes, feel the glory that moved with Mitch always. I must try to explain motives, but I was high with mania and riding the gallopers on the Fair and not an atom of sanity in anything I could think.

"There was so much laughter in the glitter-dust world. I looked back down eternity and forward along eternity and I knew that it's true what they sing. There's nothing important but love. It goes on for millions of years, but maybe death conquers it ..."

My voice was cut off short, as he shook me like a rag doll. My head went back and forth and the hair fell over my face. I pushed it back and looked at Anthony, stern, implacable, but setting me free, as he judged that my hysteria was done.

"I'll confess to anything you like, Anthony. Can I go now?"

"I've told you, you must reconstruct the actual murder of Amelia Swan. Weren't you even listening to me?"

I was past understanding why we were in Mrs. Swan's bedroom and why Miss Mannion was there, dressed in black dress and white apron, with the tray in her hand—the glass, the box of powders, the milk and the spoon, brought back out of time and space. They had even provided writing paper in the desk. I noticed it for the first time. They still edged away from me, for I was a fearful power—a self-confessed

poisoner. Even the jar of dorminal capsules was in my hand
and Miss Mannion had put the tray down on the desk and
scuttled away.

"These were what you used or capsules of a similar
nature? You didn't use Mrs. Swan's sleeping tablets?"

Anthony might have been giving evidence in court and
presently he might put out a hand for a typed copy of his
statement and ask the permission of the judge to consult it.

"They were lethal too. Did you know that?"

Here was the Professor of Forensic Medicine with another
fallen Humpty Dumpty. I was smashed and could never be
put together again and well I realised it. God knows where
Mitch was with the glitter-dust and the way he had watched
over me, even since his death. Here was the White Knight, he
had sent me, but it had only been a dream, gone with the
dawn.

"I used the capsules."

"Show me."

He laid a sheet of white notepaper down for me and told
me to get on with it and somebody had told me in another
world that the capsules pulled apart. Dr. Jones, it had been,
in the kitchen of the Quicken Tree ... I was too clumsy
about doing it and Anthony's voice was high with
exasperation.

"Get it over with. It's all there as it was that night.
Dorminal was what you used?"

I nodded my head. I could only think that he didn't love
me any more. There was no doubt that I loved him. If it were
possible to love two men in one span of life, I loved him and
Mitch had sent him to me, my White Knight, but that was
gone, gone, gone. Then the capsule parted in my fingers and
the powder spilled down in a miniscule stream to make a
small yellow heap against the white notepaper.

"It's yellow powder, but it can't be yellow. The capsules
are white." I said dully. "It's the celluloid, that's white."

The yellow powder had sprinkled across the polished
brown of the mahogany and I opened another capsule and
still the powder was yellow and Anthony left me standing
there, my eyes wide with surprise, as if I had turned

magician. He had taken two paces down and three across to confront Roger and my hazy mind was back on the chess board with the knights, white against black.

"Can you explain why the powder is yellow, Mr. Hawkins?"

Roger stood at the head of the bed, his face sallow, his eyes seeking and indeed Anthony's voice was a lance thrust, if ever a knight had come at full gallop with aimed shaft.

"The powder from white dorminal capsules is yellow. It's pento-barb. and pento-barb. is yellow. There was no trace of it in Mrs. Swan's body and Mrs. Allington couldn't have committed the crimes she's confessed to. The yellow powder would never have mixed with the white stomach powders. It would have shown up."

He shook his head slowly from side to side and his eyes held Hawkins' eyes in arrest.

"We found Sodium pheno-barb. in the body ... in the dog too. Pheno-barb. is a white powder and it came from Mrs. Swan's sleeping tablets. You ground them down, Hawkins, and you mixed them with the stomach powder, maybe you administered the pheno-barb. neat. She said it was bitter, the powder that night. It worked with Finn and you knew that that particular chemical is far more lethal with alcohol. You gave them rum, the members of the household, and they slept deep. No doubt the rum was spiked with some of the powder, but not too much. You went back to Mrs. Swan, when they were all in bed and you administered alcohol to her. You pretended it was a booze up. My God! I was there at the autopsy and the stomach reeked with alcohol, enough to turn that lethal powder into a deadly killer."

Roger moved along the bottom of the bed and sidled towards the hole in the floor.

"You're out of your head. Yellow powder, white powder? What do I know of chemistry? Your dolly-bird's confessed to murder and why the hell should I want my aunt dead? I had no motive."

"You didn't know about the annuity, that made hay of the capital. You didn't know the extent of the bequests. You thought you were heir to a tremendous fortune and you killed the goose. Ah, yes! You killed the goose, but did you write the poison pen letter? I think that was someone else."

Miss Mannion came creeping out of her corner like an old dormouse, her eyes running tears, her head down.

"I wrote the letter," she mumbled. "I knew the Mistress hadn't died naturally. The doctor told me she was well that same day. Mrs. Allington had poison in her pocket in the hall and it was gone and the tablets were gone from beside the bed."

It was almost impossible to hear what she was saying ... that she could not believe it was Mr. Roger had done it, but he was clever. He had had words with the mistress about owing some big deal of money he owed, the boat would have to be sold, and the mistress had refused to listen to him. There had been an awful quarrel. She wasn't going to keep paying out. She knew she should never have listened at the door ...

Anthony took very little notice of her. He still kept Roger in the control of his eyes. I saw him square up, saw his hand go to his pocket. He threw something down on the coverlet of the bed and I saw it was the lost phial of Mrs. Swan's tablets, empty and open, but there was no chance of not recognising it, the label the same, the instructions in Phipp's precise hand.

"There's the missing bottle, Hawkins. I found it, where you hid it."

Roger was hypnotised by the empty bottle, as I was, as we all were. His words came out between one thought and the next.

"You couldn't have found it. I threw it into the river and you'd have had to drag the whole reach. I took the cork out and it floated a while and then it sank. The water would have washed the label off."

His words ran down like a wound-up child's train. He crept back a pace.

"It was her own fault. She did tell me there was to be a new will and Taffy was to have her money for his life-time. That daft cretin could live forty years, but I might have fixed him. It's the annuity, that's sunk my ship. I never knew about it."

He smiled at old Mr. Rickaby and remarked that it was good thing to have a reliable solicitor.

"You kept your mouth shut, Mr. Rickaby, and you opened yours too wide, Miss Mannion. Why the hell had you to write that letter? I'd have got away with it ... I'll get away with it yet."

The open trap was at his heels and he stepped back. Bacon shouted to warn him and Franklyn tackled him across the bed and again they were rooks on the attack, but there was nobody there now, only the gaping hole and a dull thud on the floor of the room below, a cloud of white plaster dust, that drifted up to settle on uniform blue and clerical black.

They were gone from the room and Anthony and I were alone. He stood at the edge of the drop and looked down at the activity below him, presently turned and told me that it was all over and that Roger was dead.

I was standing by the bed with the bottle in my hands and he smiled at me, told me that it was not the original.

"Phipps made it up for me. It did its work. All we had was circumstantial evidence and it pointed to you. The trick of the yellow powder was all very well, but if Hawkins had had time to think, he'd have remembered that you had the easiest access to it. We planned for a breaking of nerve. That's why we produced Taffy as well. Maybe we broke the wrong nerve?"

Again came the slow gentle smile.

"So Humpty Dumpty is dead?" I said. "Maybe you don't care?"

He took my hand in his and led me across the floor.

"In my profession, you're not supposed to care. I find myself caring more and more with each case. It's a bad thing in a pathologist. I had hoped that my future partnership with yourself might harden my sentiment, but I think it will have the opposite effect."

We walked across the landing and I looked at the door knob, that had turned in the night and thought of the voice that sang, thought of the tangled wool, thought of all kinds of impossible things.

Mrs. Swan had wanted to help her sister. She had not intended to do the frightful injury she had done. She had destroyed herself and maybe she had turned herself into what she became, but not intentionally. I hoped that the prayers would wind up to heaven and right her debts, if she had any. Perhaps it had been a lie of Roger's? How could anybody know? The smell of must and decay was in my nostrils and the prickling of the white plaster dust. I wanted to get out into the open and take deep breaths of pure air. I wanted to run fast to the Quicken Tree and close the door against strangers, to sit before the fire with Anthony.

"And what Roger said about Mrs. Swan, about what she did to her sister, how she went to Taffy's house and stole his immortal soul, how she made such a will because she thought her own soul was lost ... was it true, Anthony?"

"Yes, it was true. Remember that I grew up in my father's house and like all children, I had a habit of using my long ears. I didn't understand a deal I overheard with my ear against the office door, till today, when the whole thing was as clear as a flash bulb. Roger might have got it from his aunt when she was maudlin with alcohol. He tempted her to drink too much and he may have got confidences. God help him! Maybe he got that damning fact the night he killed her."

It was an awful thought and I thrust it away from me. Here was the lady with the lamp and the linen modesty and I forced myself to wonder what the elderly clergy would make of her. The activity was intense in the hall and in the room below Mrs. Swan's bedroom, but Anthony and I were outside it. We were the only real people there. The others, the police and the nuns and the Black Biship and the Inspector and the Sergeant were cut-out cardboard figures in a child's theatre with no more reality than any child's puppet show.

His hand was warm in mine, as we stood on the top of the Manor front steps and I saw my Alvis parked, waiting for me. It must have been driven up by one of the constables at the Inspector's command for my convenience. Yet, somewhere, in the back of my mind was the half idea that Mitch himself

might have driven it and have left it there for me and gone
ahead on his way out into the world of the universe.

Anthony opened the door and put me into the passenger's
seat and there was a bearing about him as if he was taking
over my life, as indeed he was. We moved slowly and
smoothly down the drive and the gates stood open to let us go.
I had a conviction that outside might lie the glitter-dust again
and that was how it turned out to be., I give you my word on
it ...